Life should be a dream for Elizabeth Bontrager. At last, she has everything she's been longing for: less responsibility, more freedom, and a little adventure. And yet this season in her life quickly turns complicated after she finds herself the object of attention of two men, one Amish and one *Englisch*. Barbara Cameron writes a delightful, page-turning story about a young woman living out the ups and downs of *Rumschpringe* in *A Road Unknown*, the first in her new Amish Roads series.
—Suzanne Woods Fisher is the bestselling, award-winning author of the Lancaster County Secrets series

Once again, Barbara Cameron performs writing magic and delivers a heartrending, spirit-filled story that's sure to please her fans—and add many more to the list! Realistic characters, believable dialogue, picturesque settings, and a powerful story are only a few of the reasons *A Road Unknown* will end up on your "keepers" shelf!
—Loree Lough, award-winning author of 100 books

Other books by the author

A Time to Love, book one in the Quilts of Lancaster County series
A Time to Heal, book two in the Quilts of Lancaster County series
A Time for Peace, book three in the Quilts of Lancaster County series
Annie's Christmas Wish, book four in the Quilts of Lancaster County series

Her Restless Heart, book one in the Stitches in Time series
The Heart's Journey, book two in the Stitches in Time series
Heart in Hand, book three in the Stitches in Time series

Scraps of Evidence, Quilts of Love series

A ROAD UNKNOWN

Book 1 of the Amish Roads Series

Barbara Cameron

Abingdon fiction
a novel approach to faith

A Road Unknown

Copyright © 2014 Barbara Cameron

ISBN: 978-1-4267-4059-6

Published by Abingdon Press, P.O. Box 801, Nashville, TN 37202

www.abingdonpress.com

Published in association with the Books & Such Literary Agency.

The persons and events portrayed in this work of fiction are the
creations of the author, and any resemblance to persons
living or dead is purely coincidental.

Scripture taken from the New King James Version®. Copyright ©
1982 by Thomas Nelson, Inc. Used by permission. All rights reserved.

Library of Congress Cataloging-in-Publication Data has been
requested.

Printed in the United States of America

1 2 3 4 5 6 7 8 9 10 / 19 18 17 16 15 14

For
oldest children everywhere

Acknowledgments

This book begins the Amish Roads series—the third Amish series I've been asked to write for Abingdon Press.

I am so thrilled and blessed at my publisher's faith in my writing and the wonderful reception my previous series have received. When I began writing my Amish stories, I had no idea I would love creating them so much.

Writing is a solitary and sometimes lonely endeavor, but from the time a writer submits her book many people become involved—editors, proofreaders, cover artists, printers, marketing, and distributors. These people work so hard to create the final product and I want to thank all of them. I wish I could meet them in person. Maybe one day I'll take a trip to Nashville and get to do that.

I also want to thank the family and friends whose stories of their birth order gave me the idea for this book. I've heard for years about my mother's siblings and their interactions. She came from a family of nine children (she has a twin) and birth order definitely influenced their personalities and their relationships with their own families. I'm the oldest child in my family and so I was relied upon to help take care of my younger siblings. My sister has told me she sometimes felt like I was more her mother than our mother was—because mother was at work so often.

Many of my friends are the oldest in their families. I think a part of our friendships come from being able to relate to similar experiences—good and bad—from being responsible for younger siblings. Some of us grew up quickly because of this and became teachers, nurses, and so on. We grew used to taking care of others and chose occupations where we would continue this role.

As always, I want to thank Ramona Richards, my wonderful editor, who was so supportive about the content of the series and my deadline. My agent, Rachelle Gardner, also deserves thanks for providing expert advice on the business side of writing.

Thanks to Barb Sieltz for her assistance with research with Goshen, Indiana.

I hope you enjoy this book about Elizabeth, a young woman who is the eldest in her family and sometimes chafes at the responsibility, along with the rest of the series. Whatever your birth order, I hope you'll relate to a character with similar issues.

Blessings!

1

Some people say if you look at a map of Goshen, Indiana, you'd see almost all Amish Country roads lead into the town.

But as Elizabeth stood waiting for her bus all she could think about was the road leading out of the town.

The big bus lumbered into the station. Under her watchful eye, the driver put her suitcase in the storage area. She didn't have much and wanted to make sure it made it to her next home.

She winced at the word. *Home.* She was leaving everything and everybody she knew to go to a place she'd never visited in her life. It was exciting. It was terrifying.

"You getting on?" the driver asked, studying her curiously as he waited for other passengers.

Elizabeth nodded and taking a deep breath, she climbed up the steps into the bus. She walked toward the back of the half-empty bus and found a seat. She hoped she'd get a chance to sit by herself and not make conversation with a stranger. Especially an *Englisch* stranger. So many of them were curious about the Amish. She didn't want to talk about why she was walking—riding?—away from a community many of them thought was idyllic.

Oh, they liked the idea of a simpler life, but in the next breath they would shake their heads and say they couldn't imagine living without electricity or television.

She settled into her seat and tucked her small shoulder purse to her left between the seat and the window of the bus. Most of her money was pinned in a little pouch inside her dress but there were so many important things in her purse: a little address book, the resumé the job coordinator at the women's center had helped her with—everything she'd need for this new town where she'd be making her home.

Feeling a little self-conscious, she smoothed the skirt of her dark blue dress over her knees. Paula had said they could go clothes shopping at some thrift stores when she got there. Elizabeth had saved some money from her part-time job in Goshen, but things would be tight until she found a job. Paula hadn't wanted to take any money from her for her share of the rent until she got a job but she really didn't have any choice. Things were tight for her as well since she was attending college.

Paula had sent her photos of the apartment she'd be sharing. Elizabeth drew them from her purse now and looked at them. So much space just for two people. Imagine. And imagine having a bedroom of her own. She hadn't had one for . . . eight brothers and sisters. As the oldest of nine *kinner* in the family, she hadn't had a room of her own or any peace and quiet in years and years.

A baby cried at the back of the bus. It was a familiar sound to Elizabeth. Too familiar. She loved babies, but she became exhausted taking care of someone else's. She'd read once the average Amish family had seven children, but she guessed her parents hadn't heard it. Stop, she told herself. Children were a gift from God. But, oh, had He blessed her family.

Exhausted, she leaned back in her seat and closed her eyes. She'd worked extra hours at the fabric shop this week to help the owner who hadn't been happy she was leaving. Angela had said she thought she'd finally gotten someone dependable and now she was losing her. Someone else to make her feel guilty.

Lately, she'd begun to feel like everyone depended on her and it was all too much. She'd tried to talk about it with her best friend, but Lydia was getting engaged and didn't understand. With working during the day and spending so much time helping her *mamm* when she got home, Elizabeth didn't get to go to singings or other youth activities. She knew she was hardly an *old maid* at twenty but she was beginning to despair of ever being able to date and get married. And who would help her mother then? Fourteen-year-old Mary, the next oldest, didn't seem interested in helping as she should.

Now, she would have to, thought Elizabeth. She opened her eyes as a woman in the next row of seats complained loudly about the bus being a few minutes late leaving the station. Elizabeth found herself biting her thumbnail as she pondered the selfishness of leaving home now.

The driver climbed on board, closed the door, and started up the bus, but he didn't immediately pull out. The woman in the next row who had been complaining turned to Elizabeth and shook her head.

Elizabeth turned to stare out the window. Goshen was the only place she'd ever lived. She'd never left it. Never wanted to. Now she felt like the woman who complained. When were they going to leave?

A thought suddenly struck her. Maybe it was a sign. Maybe she wasn't supposed to leave. Maybe it wasn't a part of God's plan for her. Hadn't one of the ministers at church once cautioned his listeners about fighting God, swimming upstream against His plan?

Maybe He thought she was selfish, too. Maybe He thought she should stay here with her family.

The bus began moving. Relief washed over Elizabeth. Dilemma solved.

She turned away from the window. Everyone knew what had happened to Lot's wife when she looked back . . .

Instead, she glanced around at fellow passengers, feeling a little curious about them. Were they making big life changes like her? Going on vacation?

She realized the woman who'd complained about the bus not leaving the station on time was watching her. Elizabeth pulled her gaze away and glanced out her window. She had always been shy. She didn't want to talk about herself, answer questions about why she was on the bus. It might have been a good idea to change into *Englisch* clothes before she left home, but she didn't have any, and she didn't want to upset her parents more.

"So where are you going?"

Elizabeth blinked at the sudden intrusion into her thoughts and looked over. The woman across the aisle was regarding her curiously.

"Paradise."

The woman laughed and looked incredulous. "Paradise?"

"Paradise, Pennsylvania."

"Oh, right, there is a city named that there. You know people there?"

Elizabeth nodded.

"I was wondering if you were in your rum—rum—" the woman flapped one hand. "I can't remember what it's called."

"*Rumschpringe.*"

"Yeah, that's it. When you get to be like a girl gone wild."

Elizabeth wondered where the *Englisch* got their ideas about *rumschpringe*. Like the mother of a friend had once said, "You think we suddenly let our kids run wild and don't know where they are?"

In reality, *rumschpringe* was something rather tame in her community. Oh, sure, she'd heard stories occasionally about some of the boys she'd gone to school with buying beer and having wild parties. But those stories were few and far between. And most Amish youth ended up becoming baptized into the church and stayed in the community.

"I'm just going there to visit," she said.

It wasn't the total truth, because she knew she was going to stay there longer than a visit. But she wasn't sure how long she'd be there and besides, she'd been cautioned not to talk to strangers.

A big yawn overcame her. She clapped her hand over her mouth. "I'm so sorry. I was up late last night getting packed. If you don't mind, I think I'll take a nap."

The woman nodded and didn't seem offended. "We can talk later."

Elizabeth smiled and nodded. What else was there to say? She leaned back against her seat and closed her eyes.

And when anxiety rolled over her like the tiredness in her body, she told herself to stop thinking about where she'd come from and instead forced herself to focus on where she was going.

⟨⟩

Saul nodded at the driver, handing him his ticket before climbing onto the bus. He'd made the trip from Pennsylvania to Ohio and back many times and felt a little bored as he looked for a seat. Then he saw the attractive young Amish woman sitting with her eyes closed.

Indiana, he mused as he walked down the aisle. The man ahead of him stopped at the woman's row and leaned down.

"Hey, pretty lady, dreaming of me?"

Startled, she woke and stared at him. "Excuse me?"

"How about I sit next to you?" he asked.

Saul could tell from the way she recoiled from the man it was the last thing she wanted.

On impulse, he stepped closer. "*Gut,* you saved me a seat," he said loudly.

The man turned and gave him a once-over. "Oh, you two together?"

Saul looked at Elizabeth and lifted his brows.

"Yes," she said, her voice soft at first and then she said it louder: "Yes."

Shrugging, the man moved on and found a seat a few rows back.

"Did you decide I was the lesser of two evils?" he asked her as he sat down.

"Yes," she said honestly, but the shy smile she gave him took away any sting he might have felt.

He knew from a glance at her clothing, she was from Indiana. It was easy to distinguish one Amish community from another by the style of the *kapp* and the dress the women wore. The Lancaster County women wore prayer head coverings made of a thin material with a heart shape to the back of them. This woman wore a starched white *kapp* with pleats and a kind of barrel shape. The stark look of it suited her high cheekbones and delicate features.

He studied her while she looked out the window. Her skin seemed almost alabaster. Her figure was small and slender in the modest dark blue cape dress she wore. She'd looked away before he saw the color of her eyes; he wondered if her eyes were blue—sometimes women wore dresses the color of their eyes.

A baby cried at the back of the bus. Its mother tried to shush it, but it kept crying, its voice rising.

The woman turned away from the window and frowned slightly as she glanced back toward the rear of the bus. Then, when she sensed him watching her, she looked at him and he saw her eyes were indeed blue—the blue of a lake in late summer.

"Poor mother," she murmured. "The baby's been crying for hours."

"Poor us if it continues," he said, frowning at the thought of listening to a baby cry for hours. Surely, the kid was tiring and would sleep soon? "So, you're from Indiana?"

"What?"

"You're from Indiana?"

She nodded.

"I'm from Pennsylvania. Paradise, Pennsylvania."

She turned those big blue eyes on him and he saw interest in them. "Really? How long have you lived there?"

"My whole life. Is it where you're going?"

Her eyes narrowed. "How did you know that?"

"The way you perked up when I said the name." He moved in his seat so he could study her better and smiled at her. "There's no need to be suspicious. My name's Saul Miller."

When she hesitated, he smiled. "Just tell me your first name."

"Elizabeth."

"Are you called Beth? Liz? Lizzie?"

"Elizabeth."

"Ever been to Pennsylvania?"

"Once. For a cousin's wedding."

"Ah, I see. So, you were there in the fall." When she just nodded, he tried not to smile. Getting her to talk was like pulling teeth.

"Well, can't be the reason this time. Not the season for weddings."

He watched her glance out the window at the passing scenery. There was a wistfulness in her expression.

"So are you going to Pennsylvania for vacation?"

"Vacation?"

"You know, the thing people do to relax."

Her mouth quirked in a reluctant smile. She glanced around her, then whispered, "Now how many Amish do you know who go on vacation?"

He shrugged. "There are some I know who go South for the winter for a few weeks."

"*Daed* would think you were crazy if you talked about a vacation," she scoffed. "Why, when I—"

"When you what?" he prompted when she didn't go on.

She frowned and shook her head. "Nothing."

Saul fell silent for a few minutes, waiting to see if she'd say anything else. It felt a little strange to be doing it all—to be carrying the conversational ball. But he'd had no trouble attracting the opposite sex. Usually, women let him know they were attracted, and then went out of their way to engage him in conversation.

Elizabeth was being no more than polite.

"So, Elizabeth, if you're not on vacation, are you on your *rumschpringe*?"

Elizabeth was beginning to think maybe it wasn't so bad back home—even if she'd seldom gotten out. But since she had now, it seemed everyone wanted to talk, talk, talk.

Really, whether Amish or *Englisch*, people certainly were a nosy bunch. First, the *Englisch* woman had asked questions, then Saul had picked up where she left off.

She immediately chided herself for being judgmental. People who judged others often were guilty of the same thing as the person they judged. And goodness knew, Elizabeth possessed a deep curiosity about other people. Her leaving home hadn't just been because she was tired of her confining, unsatisfying life. She'd wanted to know what was out there— trapped as she'd felt being stuck at home as a caretaker of her brothers and sisters, she'd loved her time working at the fabric shop where she could interact with others.

Personal decisions were just that . . . she didn't want to discuss it with someone who was a stranger.

The bus ate up the miles and she blessed the fact Saul had fallen silent and appeared to be watching the road. The woman across the aisle now sat, nodding, a magazine unread in her hands. Even the crying baby at the back of the bus fell silent.

The weariness of body and mind, which caused her to her to drift off earlier, returned. Her eyelids felt weighted; her body seemed to melt into the comfort of the padded seat.

"Give in," Saul said softly. "You look exhausted."

She frowned at him. "How can I when you keep talking to me?" she asked and heard the tartness in her tone. When he chuckled, she glared at him. "You know, you're acting like I'm here to entertain you."

"No," he said, obviously trying not to smile. "I just find you refreshing."

Refreshing? Her? "Are you mocking me?"

His smile faded. "No, Elizabeth, I wouldn't do that. You're just not like any of the women I know back home."

"I'm different from the women of Paradise? How?"

"You're not talking a lot. You're not trying to impress me."

"So you're used to being . . . pursued?"

He had the grace to redden. "I wouldn't say that."

Now it was her turn to try to hide a smile. There was no question he was attractive with mahogany-colored hair, strong, masculine features. And those dark brown eyes looking at her so intensely. She'd seldom gotten much interest from the young men in her community. It felt exhilarating. It felt a little scary. This was a very different experience for her, this enclosed, enforced intimacy of riding in a bus, conversing with a stranger and feeling he was expressing interest in her.

Maybe she was dreaming. After all, she was so very tired. She'd been sleeping and then woken up to see him looking at her. It was entirely possible she was dreaming.

So, when Saul wasn't looking, she pinched herself and found she wasn't dreaming.

No, she wasn't dreaming, but it was certain his interest was flattering. She drew herself up. Being Amish didn't mean you didn't know what went on in the world, you were aware of bad people, and knew bad things could happen.

It was entirely possible this Saul wasn't even Amish . . .

"What?"

She blinked. "Excuse me?"

"Suddenly you're looking at me like I'm the Big Bad Wolf."

"I don't know what you're talking about." But Elizabeth had never been able to hide what she was thinking.

"*Schur,*" he drawled.

She focused on the billboards on the side of the road. They were quite entertaining to someone who mostly traveled in a buggy on roads not big and crowded like this highway. Most of the signs advertised restaurants and shopping, but there were a few to raise her eyebrows. It took her a moment to understand what an adult store was, but once she did she averted her eyes quickly at the next one they passed.

Her stomach growled. She reached for the lunch tote she'd carried on board, pulled out a sandwich and unwrapped it. She'd packed several sandwiches with her mother's grudging permission—her *daed* had been out—but she didn't know how long they would last and she had to be careful with her money.

As she did, she felt, rather than saw Saul come to attention. She glanced at him, saw he was looking at her sandwich and not at her. Well, she thought, I found a way to make him stop asking questions.

She took a bite and chewed and tried not to notice his attention then shifted to her mouth.

Manners kicked in. "Would you like half?"

"I wouldn't want to take your food."

"I have more," she said, handing him half the roast beef sandwich and a paper napkin.

She watched him take a bite and his eyes closed with pleasure as he chewed. "Terrific bread," he said. "Nothing better than Amish bread."

"It's just bread," she told him mildly. But she felt an unaccustomed bit of pride, since she'd made it.

"Almost don't need the meat," he said, his strong white teeth finishing the sandwich in several big bites.

Elizabeth ate a little faster when she noticed he was eyeing her sandwich. She popped the last bite into her mouth and wiped her fingers on her own napkin. Then she reached into the tote, pulled out a thermos and poured coffee into the plastic cap. She handed it to him, pulled a cup from her tote, and poured some coffee for herself.

When she'd tucked the cup into the tote earlier, it hadn't been because she'd anticipated offering some of the coffee to a stranger. She'd simply brought it because the cap didn't hold much coffee and could get hot.

"Coffee? You brought coffee?" He inhaled the steam rising from the cap and sighed. "Elizabeth, will you marry me?"

She laughed and sipped. "Don't be ridiculous."

"You're right. It has to be good coffee to get a proposal." He took a sip, closed his eyes as if in ecstasy, then opened them. "Well, let's set a date."

Elizabeth pressed her lips together. "Are you always this way?"

"Romantic?"

"Ridiculous."

"You have no idea how wonderful this coffee is, do you?"

"I do. But it's not worth a marriage proposal."

"Let me be the judge."

She finished her coffee and before she tucked the thermos back into the tote topped off Saul's cup.

"I'm thinking this is a blessed day," he told her.

Elizabeth thought the coffee would help her wake up, but a big yawn overcame her. She covered her mouth and felt color creep up into her cheeks.

"Sorry."

He just chuckled.

"What's so funny?"

"You," he said.

"How am I funny?"

"You're being so polite, but you're going to drop off any minute."

"I know. I was up late getting ready for the trip last night."

"Be my guest," he said. "Would you like a shoulder to rest your head on?" It was then, in that moment, he fully understood the saying, *If looks could kill* when she glared at him.

She turned farther away from him, placing her purse under her cheek for a pillow. It couldn't have been very comfortable, but in a few minutes her breathing became slow and even and she slept.

Her cool manner toward him should have served to dampen his enthusiasm for getting to know her but perversely, he found himself wanting to know her better. He knew a few people in Goshen. Pulling out his cell phone, he texted a friend of his and asked if he knew an Elizabeth.

Lamar responded he knew only one Elizabeth. "Is it Elizabeth Bontrager?" he texted. "Mary and Jacob Bontrager's oldest kind?"

"Don't know," he texted back. He thought about snapping a photo but told himself it was a bigger invasion of privacy than watching her sleep. Besides, she was turned too much away from him . . .

"Odd you should ask," Lamar texted. "Heard Elizabeth left town today. Where are you?"

"Headed home."

"How's Lavina?"

"Fine. Why?"

"Wondered if it was over since you're asking about another woman."

"Curiosity," Saul texted. "And confidential."

"Got it," Lamar wrote back.

"Talk to you soon." He put his phone back in his jacket.

Elizabeth stirred in her sleep and turned toward him. He studied her while she slept and chided himself for the invasion of privacy. But he was a man, after all, and she was an attractive woman.

She moved closer, murmuring something unintelligible, then she sighed and put her cheek on his shoulder. Saul bit back a smile and tried not to move and wake her.

But the baby cried again and she whispered, "Give him to me" and her eyes opened. Struggling to focus, she stared at Saul, then she pulled back and sat up. "What did you do? I didn't put my head on your shoulder!"

2

*E*lizabeth had never felt so mortified.

She reached for her *kapp*, straightening it, and drew back into her own seat until she was shoved into the metal of the interior bus wall.

"I didn't touch you," Saul was saying. "You just turned and put your cheek on my shoulder while you slept."

"Why didn't you wake me up?"

"I don't know what you're so upset about," he said. "It was no problem."

"No problem," she muttered. He'd probably enjoyed having a strange woman putting her head on his shoulder. A good-looking man like him probably had women finding a way to get close to him all the time.

She glanced around furtively, but none of the bus passengers was watching them. They were too busy napping, reading, or staring out their window. Elizabeth sent up silent thanks the nosy woman from earlier in the trip had gotten off the bus. She wouldn't have wanted to deal with comments from her about Saul . . .

"Honestly, no harm done," he said, spreading his hands.

She glanced out the window, but it was dark and she couldn't see anything. "How long did I sleep?"

"Only about an hour."

Gathering her sweater closer, she tried to relax.

"Cold?"

"I'm fine. It won't be much longer."

"Someone meeting you?"

She nodded. "My new roommate."

"So you're going to stay for a while?"

"Yes," she said reluctantly. "What do you do?" she asked politely, more to deflect him from asking about her.

"You mean besides ride buses and get women to rest their heads on my shoulder?" he asked, a glint of mischief in his eyes.

She frowned at him. "Yes."

"I work in a store. We sell Amish crafts."

It was so tempting to ask him about a job at the store where he worked. After all, she needed one and it wasn't such a stretch in imagination to go from selling fabric to selling things like crafts. Yes, it was so, so tempting. But how would it be to work in a place with someone who acted attracted to her?

Attracted. It was a stretch. He'd just been friendly to her, saving her from the man she didn't want sitting beside her. Maybe Saul had flirted a little. Guys did it. He might not even realize how he came off. And she was pathetic, so lonely for contact with someone her own age, because she never got out but for work.

But still, she felt some attraction and wondered if he did, too.

Well, didn't matter. They'd be in Paradise very soon. They would probably never see each other again. And maybe it was best. She needed to settle into her new home, find a job, and learn to take care of herself—when all she'd ever done was take care of others.

A list. She needed to make a list of everything she had to do. She'd been in such a rush to leave she hadn't done much planning. And if she was honest with herself, she knew it was also because she was scared—scared of finding there was so much to do to have a break, she'd frighten herself into staying. She pulled a pad of paper and a pencil from her purse.

"Folks, we'll be making an unscheduled stop for a few minutes," the bus driver came on the intercom to say. "You can get off and stretch your legs, get some coffee if you like."

He pulled into the parking lot of a fast-food restaurant.

"You're not getting off?" Saul asked her.

She shook her head.

"Want anything?"

"I'm fine."

She watched him disembark and thought about eating the last sandwich she'd packed but decided to save it since she wasn't real hungry yet. She wasn't sure of exactly when they'd arrive in Paradise and she might need to stretch her food. Then she happened to glance out the window and found herself watching several birds pecking at some crumbs from the restaurant.

His eye is on the sparrow.

She blinked. Where had the thought come from? They weren't even sparrows.

But it was an intriguing thought. She wasn't sure where it had come from—she hadn't been consciously thinking about it.

Look at the birds of the air, for they neither sow nor reap nor gather into barns; yet your heavenly Father feeds them. *Are you not of more value than they?*

The book of Matthew. She'd always found comfort in it. Sparrows didn't worry about their next meal. God provided for them. Why wouldn't He provide for her? It didn't mean she could just lie around and not work, but she didn't intend to do that. God would help His child to find a job to feed herself, wouldn't He? Everything she'd had growing up hadn't really come from her parents, but from her heavenly Father.

Feeling a little relieved, she found herself doodling on the paper. She was so busy sketching when she felt movement beside her she was startled to see Saul was sitting down, and in fact, the bus had filled again.

"I know you said you didn't want anything, but I thought you might when you saw what I got," he told her as he held out a paper sack.

She tucked the pencil behind her ear and laid the pad of paper on her lap. "You didn't have to do that."

"You gave me part of your sandwich," he said, shaking the bag.

Elizabeth opened the bag and found a Big Mac and French fries. "Oh, a favorite of mine," she breathed.

"Good. Diet Coke okay?" he asked, holding out a drink carrier. "I don't think you need to save the calories, but every woman I know drinks diet instead of regular."

She had to admit he was right.

He set the drink carrier on the floor between his feet and pulled his own Big Mac from his bag.

She felt him lean over and look at the pad of paper before she could juggle things in her hands to cover it.

"Nice," he said. "How long have you been sketching?"

She shrugged. "Couple of years. Not much time for it."

"You're good."

Elizabeth blinked. Very few people had seen her sketching, but she'd never had anyone actually compliment it. Her teacher had done so years ago, but it didn't count. Besides, Lydia had told her she had to stop sketching in class and concentrate on her lessons.

She knew she had a problem with staying focused and it hadn't gone away when she got older. Hadn't she just taken out her pad of paper to make a list and then started sketching birds? But as she munched happily on her hamburger and fries, she refused to chide herself for her inattention.

Hadn't she just been given a sign all would be all right? His eye was on the sparrow . . . He was already showing He was taking care of her by bringing her a meal she hadn't had to pay for. She smiled. He'd brought her a Big Mac just like He'd brought the sparrows—er, pigeons—their crumbs.

❧

Saul ate his Big Mac and was glad he'd bought one for Elizabeth when he saw how happy she was to get it. He got the impression she didn't go to McDonald's often.

The unexpected stop there had been welcome. Usually Lavina packed him food for his trip home on the bus, but he'd decided to leave a day early and she'd acted a little upset with him over it. Which was strange because things hadn't gone well with this last visit. He was beginning to think absence hadn't made the heart grow fonder—the physical distance between them since her parents had moved the family to Indiana had caused an emotional gulf as well.

There had been a way to fix it. He could have asked her to marry him. They'd been headed down that road for a long time now. But something had held him back.

She hadn't said anything even though the visit before this one she'd hinted so broadly he began to wonder if she'd ask him to marry her, reversing the usual role. But then she didn't.

He'd brought the subject up with his father just before he left this time. "How do you know if the woman is the one God set aside for your wife?"

His father had stopped stocking a shelf and turned to study him, stroking his beard thoughtfully, as his eyes seemed to gaze inward.

"It's just a feeling you get," he'd said finally. "You just know. And if you're not certain, well, she's probably not the right one."

His father had thumped him on the shoulder in an awkward gesture of support and urged him to make another trip north. He'd insisted he could get along without Saul.

"No one's indispensable," he'd said gruffly.

Saul felt a mixture of gratitude and consternation. "You'll miss me when I'm gone," he'd called after his father's back as the older man headed for the stockroom.

But he grinned as he turned back to the order form he'd been working on. Thank goodness his father wasn't insisting his duty lay here helping run the store. Each time Saul had left, there had been no pressure about only staying a few days.

It was likely his father would be surprised to see him when he walked into the store tomorrow.

He'd cut his visit short, making an excuse to Lavina, and returning to Paradise a day ahead of the date he'd told his parents.

Elizabeth made a noise with her straw, draining the last of the Diet Coke. She wriggled her nose and grinned when she realized what she'd done. "Sorry! It was so good. I don't drink them often."

"Glad you enjoyed it." He watched her put the empty hamburger wrapper back in the bag. "Maybe we could go get lunch there sometime after you get settled?"

She paused and stared at him. "I—guess."

"You don't have to feel like it's a date," he rushed to say as silence stretched between them. "Just friends."

Elizabeth nodded.

"How long do you think you'll be here?"

"I don't know." She looked away from him, folding down the top of the bag.

He frowned, hearing a curious mix of sadness and indecision in her voice. What was it about? he wondered. Was this really a visit or had she left her home in Indiana for some reason?

"How much longer will it be before we get to Paradise?" she asked him.

Saul glanced out the window and calculated. "About a half hour," he told her.

Elizabeth sat up straighter and her eyes sparkled. "I can't wait."

There it was again, he thought. The mix of emotions. She looked excited, sounded excited. But her hands shook as she put her pad of paper back in her purse.

As much as Saul was ready to get off the bus, inhale some good fresh air, and climb into his own bed, he wanted more time to figure this woman out. She was a mystery he wanted to solve.

"Where will you be staying?" he asked, trying to sound cool and polite since she'd been wary of him asking personal questions earlier. "I need to know where to call for you. When we go for that Big Mac."

"Maybe you could give me your number," she said.

He nodded. "Good idea." He pulled a business card from his jacket. "May I?" he asked, gesturing to the pencil behind her ear.

She looked surprised it was still there and handed it to him. He wrote his cell phone number on the back of the card with the store address and phone number on it. He gave it to her, she looked at it for a moment, and tucked it safely into her purse.

"So tomorrow you have to work?"

Startled she had initiated conversation, he nodded.

"A job's a good thing."

"True." He inclined his head and studied her. There was a wistful note in her voice. "What did you say you did in Goshen?"

She smiled. "I didn't." After a moment, she said, "I worked in a fabric store."

Too bad she was just visiting, Saul thought. They could use someone like her since Miriam was taking maternity leave soon. Then he realized what she'd just said.

"Worked? Does that mean you left your job?"

She touched her mouth with her fingers and looked chagrined. Then she nodded. "I needed a break."

"I guess so," he said gravely. "I mean, you must have been there forever."

"You're laughing at me." But she said it tentatively, as if she was unsure if he was teasing.

"No. You just make it sound like you've been doing it for so long you had to retire or something."

"I just need a break. Vacation. Whatever you call it." She frowned. "*Rumschpringe*." She paused and glanced around. "I hate to use the word. *Englischers* seem to think we turn into wild things and run around getting drunk."

He winced. "Well, some guys I was friends with did, but I know what you mean."

The bus slowed and moved into the lane to the exit ramp. Passengers who were getting off at the next stop began shifting in their seats, looking out the windows.

Saul watched Elizabeth pull on her jacket and loop the strap of her purse over her shoulder. He'd seen her tucking her purse on one side of her between her body and the bus wall, guarding it carefully. She lifted her tote bag and put it on her lap.

"Thanks again for the sandwich and the coffee."

"Thank you for the Big Mac."

They were turning into strangers again now the enforced intimacy of the bus ride was nearly over.

"Don't forget we're meeting for another once you get settled."

She nodded but her attention was riveted on the front of the bus as it came to a stop.

Saul remembered his mother once complaining his father, anxious to be on his way for a hunting trip, had already left them before he walked out the door. Now he knew what she meant; he felt the same way about Elizabeth. She was already mentally out the bus door, so eager to be at her destination.

He stood and gestured for her to precede him, and they joined passengers in the line to disembark from the bus.

"Who's meeting you?" he asked her when they were standing by the side of the bus where the driver was getting their luggage.

"My new roommate." She scanned the crowd of those waiting for bus passengers. "Oh, there she is!"

"I'll see you soon, Elizabeth No Last Name."

She smiled at him. "Yes, Saul Miller. Have a good night."

He watched her wend her way to a woman her age waiting for her and then turned to look for the driver who waited for him.

"Good trip?" Phil asked, as he loaded Saul's suitcase into the van.

"It was okay," Saul said. "What's been happening here?" he asked, knowing the man would fill the drive with chatter about the latest goings-on and he wouldn't have to contribute anything.

He didn't feel much like talking now that Elizabeth wasn't near. He wondered if he'd see her again or if she'd forget about him once she was settled.

And he wondered why he was thinking about her instead of Lavina . . .

⟅⟆

Elizabeth held onto the armrest on the passenger side of the car and prayed as she caught a glimpse of the speedometer while Paula chattered a mile a minute.

"Did you have a good trip? I got a little worried when the bus ran a half an hour late."

"I'm sorry if you had to wait—"

"Didn't! I checked before I drove to the bus station."

"Oh. That's good."

Elizabeth studied Paula. They were so different in looks and personality: Paula's chin-length blond hair curled madly all over her head, she wore bright lipstick and jeans with holes at the knee and a big blue men's chambray shirt. They'd met when Paula's family had visited Goshen earlier in the year. They'd written dozens of letters since then—Paula had once called them pen pals. Elizabeth had grown to feel safe enough to feel she could talk about her frustrations and dreams, and when she had, Paula had invited her to visit.

She'd accepted the offer immediately, hoping Paula was sincere. Paula had written back and invited her to come as soon as she wanted. Elizabeth was on a bus to Paradise a month later.

"You're sure it's not a problem to stay with you for a while?"

"I told you it isn't! My parents wanted me to get a roommate."

"I don't know how long I need to stay."

Paula reached over and patted her hand. "Don't worry about it. When you decide, I'll just advertise at the college for a roommate."

They couldn't have been more different: Elizabeth was Amish, Paula was *Englisch*. Elizabeth had dark hair. Paula's hair was a streaky blond mass that made Elizabeth think the sun had run its rays through it. Paula had laughed and said the streaks came from a bottle.

It was another way they were so different. Elizabeth was shy and quiet. Paula fairly bubbled with exuberance.

"You're being quiet."

Elizabeth smiled. "That's me. Quiet."

"The deep ones are always quiet."

A laugh escaped before Elizabeth could stop it. "I'm not deep. You're the one who's going to college."

"Yeah, well, I'm not doing so well," Paula said.

It suddenly got very quiet in the car.

"Why?"

Paula shrugged. "I'm having trouble with my English class. Math, no problem. But if I have to do any writing like I have to do in English and history, I'm in trouble. College is harder than high school. A lot harder than I thought it would be."

Elizabeth bit her lip. "English was my best subject in school. I'd love to help you, but we only go to school to the eighth grade and then we go to work."

"I appreciate the offer." Paula sighed. "I just have to buckle down and work harder. Maybe go to the tutoring center at school."

Back home, Elizabeth had often helped the teacher with the younger students. Later, she helped her brothers and sisters with their homework while their mother cooked supper. But it wasn't going to help Paula.

"It doesn't sound easy but you'll be glad you did it. There aren't many jobs for people without a college education. Not in your world and not even in mine." She smoothed her skirt. "Several people in the shop I worked in had college educations. I'd never be promoted to senior clerk or manager there no matter how long I stayed."

"But I thought most Amish women worked at home."

"After they're married."

"You're too young to get married," Paula said firmly. "Women shouldn't get married until they're at least in their middle twenties. You're only twenty, right?"

"Yes."

Paula pulled into the drive of an apartment building. "We're here. Welcome home!"

They got out of the car and Paula got Elizabeth's suitcase out of the trunk. "I've got it," she told Elizabeth. "You look tired."

"I shouldn't be. All I did was sit on the bus."

"Traveling is tiring."

Elizabeth doubted Paula had ever traveled on a bus. When she and her family had visited Goshen, they'd come in an expensive looking SUV.

"Hungry?"

"I have a sandwich left," Elizabeth said, holding up her tote.

"I'm not sure it's safe to eat anything you've been carrying around your whole trip."

"It's insulated."

Paula reached for the bag. "C'mon, I'll make us some soup and sandwiches."

"I don't want you to go to any trouble."

"No trouble. My mom brought some stuff over as a welcome present. Does a turkey sandwich and homemade vegetable soup sound okay?"

"Sounds great."

Paula warmed the soup in the microwave while she made them sandwiches. They sat at the kitchen island and ate while she peppered Elizabeth with questions.

"Who was the cute Amish guy who got off with you? Do you know him?"

Elizabeth nearly choked on her soup. She'd seen Saul?

"He was just someone who was on the bus."

"Oh, so you didn't know him? Seemed like you two knew each other when you were talking."

"We talked on the ride. He's from here."

"Are you going to see him again?"

Elizabeth felt her cheeks warming. "We might. It's not a date or anything."

"Sounds promising, though," Paula said. She spooned up some soup.

"What about you?" Elizabeth asked shyly. "Are you dating?"

"I've been going with Jason since we graduated from high school. But he wanted to serve in the military. He got shipped to Afghanistan and I have no idea if he's signing up for another stint, when he's coming home . . ."

She sighed. "Everyone tells me I should look for another guy. But *he's* the guy I love. We've been staying in touch by e-mail but it hasn't been easy with Internet connections where he is. Besides, I don't think anyone realizes there aren't many guys like Jason. This guy in my Algebra class asked me out for coffee and I thought, hey, it's just coffee. Turned out he just wanted me to let him cheat on the next test."

"Oh, my! How wrong!" Aghast, Elizabeth stared at her.

Then, just as suddenly, it occurred to her she shouldn't have said anything. What if Paula felt it was okay to let the man cheat from her test? What if she felt judged? What if she kicked her out? Would she tell her to get back on a bus and go back to Goshen? She couldn't do that, she—

"Well, of course, I told him to stuff it!" Paula said, sounding disgusted. "How dare he even ask such a thing. What kind of a person does he think I am, anyway?"

Relieved, Elizabeth spooned up more soup. Why had she been worried? she chided herself. Paula had seemed to her to be a good person and she was seldom wrong about this sort of thing. Jumping to conclusions Paula would order her out . . . well, she was just plain silly. She was letting her fears get to her.

It was a big step to leave her home, her life back in Goshen. She'd been so scared. But she'd packed her suitcase, walked on shaking legs out of the only home she'd ever known, and climbed aboard the bus to bring her here to a new life—for however long she stayed.

She could do this with some faith and confidence or she could do it in fear. Warmed by the welcome she'd received from Paula, the soup she'd reheated, and now eager for the comfort of some rest in bed after trying to catch some sleep on the moving bus, Elizabeth stood. She gathered up her empty dishes and those in front of Paula.

"This was so good," she said. "I'll wash up."

Paula got up and walked over to the kitchen counter. "Let me introduce you to my dishwasher," she said, grinning. "I think you're going to like it as much as I do."

She showed her how to load the dishes and where to pour the dishwashing powder in the receptacle in the door. Then she closed the door, pressed a button, and the machine began making a swishing sound.

"That's it?"

"That's it. Let me show you your room."

The room looked huge and even had a bathroom attached. Elizabeth set her suitcase on a padded bench and let out a sigh. The bed had a brass rail headboard and a thick, soft mattress. Elizabeth sat on the bed and bounced.

"It's beautiful!" she breathed as she glanced around the room.

"I'm glad you like it," Paula said with a grin. "Mom helped me decorate. You probably have better quilts back home. This is the one she bought me for college."

She yawned. "I better get to bed. Let me know if you need anything else."

Elizabeth looked up at her. "I don't need a thing. Thank you for making me feel welcome."

"You're welcome. I think we'll have fun, roomie. 'Night."

Elizabeth got up and wandered around the room, touching the carved wooden bedside table, the little scented soaps in a dish on the bathroom vanity sink, the crisp white pillowcase. A big yawn overcame her, but she was too excited to sleep. She opened her suitcase thinking she'd hang her few clothes in the closet—no pegs like at home!—and then she saw what lay atop her two dresses.

A worn brown teddy bear stared up at her with his one good eye.

"Oh, Brownie!" she cried, picking him up and clutching him to her chest. "Why did Sadie put you in here? She can't sleep without you!"

She felt tears slipping down her cheeks at the thought of her youngest sister—just four—slipping her favorite toy into her big sister's suitcase, so she'd have something of home with her.

Curling up on the bed, Elizabeth pushed her face into her pillow, trying to cry quietly so she didn't wake Paula. It was hours before she slept.

3

*E*lizabeth woke to sunlight streaming in through the window.

She yawned, stretched and opened her eyes and gasped. This wasn't her bedroom. Her heart pounded for a moment until she remembered where she was. And bolted upright. The sunlight was so strong. She glanced at the clock on the bedside table and winced. Eight a.m.! She hadn't ever slept so late.

Quickly she made up her bed, then she dashed into the bathroom. It took a few minutes to figure out the fancy-looking shower handles, finally producing a stream of warm water. She stood under it, thoroughly enjoying the feel of the water pouring from the showerhead.

It was so quiet here. She'd never had the bathroom to herself before. Back home there'd been just two bathrooms for the family so her sisters had wandered in and out as they needed, even occasionally climbed into the tub to take a shower while chatting with her as she brushed her teeth or her hair. Her mother would be calling up the stairs, urging everyone to get downstairs for breakfast before school. The day never started without being confronted by a lot of noise and hustle and bustle.

There was no noise from family here but it wasn't quiet outside. As she pulled on her clothes, Elizabeth could hear a garbage truck picking up trash. Someone honked a horn in the parking lot down below. She heard water trickling, checked the bathroom and realized the sound came from the apartment upstairs.

When she opened the bedroom door, she surprised Paula with her hand raised ready to knock on it.

"Good morning."

"'Morning," Paula mumbled, blinking drowsily.

She pushed a hand through her uncombed hair that fell messily to her shoulders. "Coffee," she mumbled. "Need coffee."

Elizabeth followed her into the kitchen and took a seat on a stool at the island. She watched Paula fill her coffeemaker with water, stick a little container in it, then place a coffee cup below. In what seemed like seconds, coffee began dripping into the cup.

When it was filled, she removed it and set it before Elizabeth.

"It only makes one cup?" Elizabeth asked and realized how stupid she sounded. She'd just watched the machine make one cup, so yes, it just made one cup at a time. "Here, you should have the first cup," she offered, but Paula had already turned away to repeat the process.

When the second cup finished brewing, Paula drew in a deep breath of the steam rising from it and climbed onto the stool next to Elizabeth. She dumped a packet of artificial sweetener and a spoonful of powdered creamer in her cup and blew on the coffee to cool it faster.

When it was finally cool enough to drink, she sipped and then sighed. She turned to Elizabeth. "Did I say good morning?"

Elizabeth smiled. "Yes, you did."

"I hate mornings." She sat with her elbows on the counter, her shoulders slumped. The belt on her chenille robe dangled onto the floor. "Thank goodness my mother insisted I not take early morning classes."

"Really?" Elizabeth was so used to rising early this was a surprise to her.

"Yeah, I flunked one class freshman year just because I couldn't get there for eight a.m. classes. I had a nursing instructor tell me if I didn't like mornings, maybe I shouldn't be a nurse, but there are two other shifts for goodness sakes. Anyway, I have classes four afternoons a week."

She looked at Elizabeth then and her eyes widened as if she was surprised. "You're all dressed. Are you going somewhere this morning?"

"No. But I'm used to mornings. It's often dark when I get up."

"Oh man that's crazy."

Elizabeth laughed. "There's a lot to do on a farm. Animals need to be fed, cows milked. Chores done. Brothers and sisters to get ready for breakfast and school."

Paula shoved her bangs out of her eyes and studied her. "So this morning must feel different."

"Very different." She sipped her coffee. Really wonderful coffee. "Shall I make breakfast?"

"I usually just have toast. Or a Pop-Tart."

"Pop-Tart?"

Paula slid off her stool and started another single serving cup of coffee on her way to the kitchen cupboard. When she returned to sit next to Elizabeth, she pulled a package from the box of Pop-Tarts.

"Here's what I eat for breakfast most of the time," she said, tearing open the package and showing Elizabeth a thin, pale pastry. "Sometimes I don't even put them in the toaster."

Elizabeth took the pastry, bit off a corner and tried not to make a face. It tasted like cardboard.

"You want me to put it in the toaster for you?"

"No, thanks." Elizabeth took another bite and this time tasted a kind of sickly sweet jam filling.

"You're welcome to anything in the fridge. We can sit down later and figure out how we're going to work things and the money and stuff."

"Good."

"Want another cup of coffee?"

"No, thanks."

Elizabeth looked into the refrigerator. A half a loaf of bread, a carton of eggs and a couple containers of yogurt.

"How about I make us some scrambled eggs and toast?"

"You know how to cook?"

Her lips quirked in a smile. "Of course. You don't?"

"Not much," Paula admitted. "Well, I could make the scrambled eggs but I don't think you'd want to eat them." She shoved off the stool. "I'm going to go take a quick shower."

Elizabeth nodded and studied the stove. Gas, just like the one back home. She found a skillet, started some butter melting in it and got the eggs out of the refrigerator. Paula had mentioned a toaster. It made sense it toasted the pieces of bread instead of having to put them in the oven. She found it on the counter, inserted two pieces of bread into it, and pushed down the lever on the side. The toast immediately popped back up as white as can be. She shoved down the lever harder and this time it stayed down.

The skillet was ready for the eggs. She was so used to making big quantities for the family she had to think for a minute how many eggs she should make for just two people. She settled on two eggs each, cracked them into a bowl and beat them before pouring the mixture into the skillet. She stirred them and was pleased when a few minutes later she spooned them golden and fluffy onto plates.

Something was burning. She turned her attention to the toaster and saw smoke rising from it. A loud alarm began blaring over her head.

"Hey, I set it off whenever I cook," Paula said cheerfully as she walked into the kitchen. She grabbed a broom from the pantry and used the end to push at a button on the round device on the ceiling. "Toaster, huh? I think it's possessed. It pops up some times and doesn't others."

She plucked the two blackened pieces from the toaster, threw them into the trash and started two new pieces. "The eggs look good. You'll have to show me how to make them. Mine are always runny." She glanced at the toaster, then at Elizabeth. "I'll just stand here and grab the toast before it has a chance to get extra crispy."

And so started Elizabeth's first morning away from her home.

∽≪∙≫∽

Elizabeth gathered up her purse as Paula drove into an empty parking place in front of a store. "Thank you for the ride."

"No problem. I have a study group at the college library. I'll be back at one. Then we can have lunch."

"I'll be right here," Elizabeth said as she got out of the car and shut the door.

Paula waved and then turned her head to check for traffic before pulling away from the curb.

Butterflies danced with the eggs she'd eaten for breakfast, but Elizabeth wasn't about to let Paula know she'd had trepidation about being left to herself in a strange town. She'd been complaining—silently!—about being cooped up with children at home or in the fabric store where Angela, her boss, marked it on your time card if you went into the restroom and begrudged every minute spent on a quick break or lunch. When she had some time to herself to do as she pleased and explore as she'd never been able to, well, she told herself she'd better get over this sudden anxiety about being a stranger in a new city.

She took a deep breath and glanced around. There were people bustling about on the sidewalks, mostly tourists who were looking in shop windows or taking photos. They looked curiously at her, probably noticing she was dressed differently than the Lancaster Amish women.

Elizabeth watched an Amish woman walk past and envied her. The *kapps* worn here were delicate looking and from the rear, heart-shaped. She didn't like the stiff conical shape of the Indiana *kapps* but this was what she had. Besides, she hadn't come to escape her roots, but to grow some wings, get some freedom from caretaking burdens . . .

A thought struck her, one so huge and sudden she sank into the nearby bench. She could even dress *Englisch* if she wanted to—here, so far from Indiana. For once in her twenty years, she had the freedom to do as she pleased.

"Elizabeth?"

She dragged herself up from such radical thoughts to realize Saul was standing before her, staring at her.

"Is it really you? I wasn't expecting to see you here. It took a minute to realize it was you."

Elizabeth was surprised at how warmed she felt at the pleasure and interest she saw in his eyes. Yes, they'd made a tentative plan to have lunch, but she wasn't really sure she'd see him again. And now here he was, looking happy to see her.

"My roommate dropped me off. I thought I'd explore a little bit."

"Great idea. I was just going to run an errand. Could we have some coffee?"

Coffee. She'd never been invited out to coffee by a man. Never been invited to a singing—well, once, but her mother had needed help and she'd had to stay home.

"That would be nice."

The rich scents of coffee and baked goods hit her the minute they entered the nearby café. She breathed it all in and marveled at the huge menu behind the counter. So many choices. It seemed regular coffee was just not enough.

"What are you getting?" she asked him.

"Dark roast with two sugars," he said. "I'm not into fancy coffee."

She bit her lip and studied the menu again. "A latte sounds good."

He leaned over and whispered, "Lah-tay, not 'lat'" in her ear. "It's strong coffee with steamed milk."

She blushed, feeling like country mouse come to the city.

"I made the same mistake," he murmured. "I'm hungry for a snack. Let's get a pastry, too."

More choices. She chose a blueberry muffin—no way was she asking for something called a scone. Was it pronounced *scohne* or *scon*?

It turned out to be *scohne*. She found out when Saul ordered one. Okay, so she was learning. She knew she had a lot to learn about life outside Goshen, Indiana.

And herself.

They took their coffee and pastries to a small table by the window and Elizabeth said a small, silent prayer of thanks for the opportunity to sit in the middle of the morning and chat with a handsome man and enjoy a fancy coffee and a muffin.

"So, did you get settled at your friend's place last night?"

She nodded. "I didn't have much to settle. Just the clothes in my suitcase."

"How's the latte?"

"Good. A little strong."

"Espresso is coffee that can stand by itself. How's the muffin?"

She swallowed a bite. "Very good. Your scone?"

"It's always good here. It's not something my mother ever made."

He got a smile from her. "It looks a lot like a biscuit except it has blueberries in it."

"It's sweeter." He pushed the plate toward her. "Take a taste. I think you'll like it."

She hesitated then picked up her fork and did as he suggested. It *was* a lot like a biscuit, but sweeter, just like he'd said. The blueberries were ripe and just a bit tart. "It's really good."

"Maybe you should try it next time."

"Maybe." She smiled.

"So what's your plan for today?"

She finished her muffin and took a sip of the latte. "I thought I'd look around while Paula's in classes. See what places I might apply for a job."

"You don't believe in wasting time."

She looked surprised. "I'm not here for a vacation. I like to work. And I have to support myself."

Saul looked at his watch. "I guess I need to be getting back to work myself."

"You said you worked in a fabric store," he said after a moment. "Why don't you stop in at Stitches in Time? It's a shop run by Leah King and three of her granddaughters. They sell quilts, knitting supplies, all kinds of similar stuff."

"Do you think they need anyone?"

"I have no idea. But it seems to me your experience would be better used there than some other jobs."

Elizabeth nodded. "That's true."

"Unless . . ."

"Unless?"

"Unless you're looking for a change in career, not just in where you live."

She shook her head and laughed ruefully. "I think I've had enough change, thank you."

"Are you *allrecht*?"

She nodded. "Why do you ask?"

"You looked a little sad there for a moment."

"I'm fine." She stood, putting the strap of her purse on her shoulder and disposing of her coffee cup in a trash container. "Thank you for the coffee and muffin."

"Don't forget I want to treat you to lunch. Maybe day after tomorrow?"

"I'll have to check with Paula. I haven't worked out how to get around here yet. She dropped me off today."

"You have my number."

She nodded. "Have a good day."

"You, too."

They turned in opposite directions, he to his job, she in search of one. She found herself watching him walk away, then stop and retrace his steps. He looked up, saw her and shrugged.

"Forget where you're going?" she asked, grinning.

"Just thinking about something," he said and then he went into the store.

"So what did you think of Paradise?" Paula asked Elizabeth as they sat eating a late lunch.

"I didn't get to see much yet," Elizabeth confessed. She hesitated, unused to sharing confidences with another and then plunged in. "I ran into Saul, the man you saw getting off the bus last night."

Paula raised her brows. "Well, that's interesting. You didn't tell him you were going to be in town today, did you?"

Elizabeth shook her head. "He works at a store. They sell Amish crafts. He invited me to have coffee."

"Store? Say, I don't suppose they need someone?"

"I didn't think to ask."

"Guess you were thinking about something else, huh?" Paula teased.

"Like what?"

Paula elbowed her. "A guy, silly!" She peered at Elizabeth. "Oh, my gosh, you're blushing. I haven't seen anyone blush in ages."

Elizabeth shifted uncomfortably. "I was kind of surprised to see him is all. Next time I see him I'll ask him if they're hiring at the store he works at." She took a sip of her drink. "How was college today?"

Paula laughed. "Changing the subject, eh? College was great. I love being on campus. Good thing, since I'm going after a bachelor's degree in nursing." She wiped her lips with a paper napkin and held out her hand when the waitress brought the check.

"I want to pay," Elizabeth told her. "You brought me into town."

"It was on my way. Besides, it's custom for the new roomie to be treated to a meal the first day."

"It is?"

"It is now," Paula told her with a grin. She stood, tucked a tip under a plate. "We should probably get some groceries on the way home. I'm sure you noticed how bare my cupboard was."

"I think you have a container of yogurt left in the refrigerator," Elizabeth told her dryly.

"Funny girl. I bet it's different from how it was at your house, huh? The Amish raise their own food and can it and everything, right?"

"Right." Elizabeth always loved helping tend to the vegetable garden but she was never fond of the hot, backbreaking work of canning the fruits of the harvest.

"I have some homework to do, but afterward we can sit down and figure everything out," Paula said as they drove to the grocery store. "We can split the groceries and cook one meal or each do our own thing and keep things separate."

She parked and they walked into the store. Elizabeth tugged on a shopping cart and when it wouldn't budge from the others it had become stuck with, Paula tried to help her. Of course, it suddenly came unstuck and they had to grab onto it to keep from falling.

"It's possessed," Paula said, pushing it aside and pulling out another. "Quick, let's get away before it comes after us."

Elizabeth eyed it dubiously. "Possessed?"

"Bad joke. C'mon, let's get some food."

The store was much bigger than the one her family shopped in back home. Elizabeth wasn't sure if she felt more awed by all the choices or just if she was getting to make some for the first time in her life.

"What vegetables do you like?" Paula asked.

"Most of them."

"Really? Let's see about that."

They walked along the rows of vegetables and each time Paula held up a vegetable, Elizabeth nodded, and so it went into the cart. They moved through the store, stopping at the meat counter. So much of the meat and chicken was tidily packaged—the chicken skinned and boned, packages of already prepared meatloaf ready for the oven. The deli even offered already-cooked take-home meals. Elizabeth gaped at the prices.

"People need convenience these days," Paula told her.

"I can cut up the chicken and fry it," Elizabeth said, choosing a whole fresh bird. "It's one of the things I do best. We got potatoes. Do you like mashed potatoes and gravy?"

"Who doesn't?"

"What do you cook?"

"I usually make a chicken breast and some steamed vegetables. Oh, and tacos. Do you like tacos? Do the Amish eat tacos?"

Elizabeth laughed. "We eat tacos."

So Paula found the ingredients for tacos. Eggs, bread—Elizabeth had only eaten store-bought bread once when her mother had been in the hospital and Elizabeth had been too busy with taking care of the younger children to be baking.

Back at the apartment, they quickly unloaded the groceries and put them away. Paula brought her books and laptop to the kitchen island and watched with amazement as Elizabeth cut up the chicken, coated it with flour, and started browning it in a skillet.

Elizabeth was curious about the homework but didn't want to distract Paula from it.

She didn't have to.

"Done!" Paula said, closing the laptop and setting it and the books aside. "Never did it so fast in my life. It's all your doing!"

"Mine?" Elizabeth placed the last piece of chicken on the plate she'd covered with a paper towel to drain it. The potatoes she'd peeled, cut up and put on the stove to boil were done so she drained and mashed them.

"The smells are killing me." Paula slid from the stool and got two plates from the cupboard. "I can't wait to eat."

Elizabeth stirred a little milk into the mashed potatoes and added a pat of butter to the green beans.

They fixed their plates at the stove and sat at the island to eat. Elizabeth was pleased to see how Paula enjoyed her cooking—she ate three pieces of chicken and went back for a second helping of mashed potatoes and gravy. Her family always did, but everyone was so hungry after chores she never knew if her cooking was good or if everyone just ate from hunger.

With the dishwasher humming, they worked out the details of their living arrangement. Paula had written her how much her share would be, but had insisted Elizabeth could wait until she arrived to pay the first month. Paula's eyes widened when Elizabeth handed over cash.

"You shouldn't be carrying around so much cash!" she exclaimed. "We'll get you a checking account right away."

"I've never had one."

"How did you manage your money?"

Elizabeth shrugged. "I gave my check to my mother."

Paula opened her mouth to say something and then shook her head. "Listen, I don't want to take advantage of you, but what about if I pay for groceries and you cook a few nights a week?"

"I will anyway," she said. "I like cooking."

"I think I'm going to enjoy having you as a roommate," Paula told her with a grin. Then her smile faded. "Are you going to be okay?"

"What do you mean?"

"I thought I heard you crying last night."

4

I thought it was my imagination at first," Paula said. "Then when I realized it wasn't, it stopped. But you *were* crying, weren't you?"

"You didn't need to worry," Elizabeth told her quietly. "I was crying over something silly. My youngest sister must have thought I needed her teddy bear to sleep. She put it in my suitcase when I wasn't looking."

"Oh, how sweet. So you were missing her. Maybe even a little homesick."

"Missing her," Elizabeth said firmly. "Not homesick."

"It was bad, huh?" Paula looked at her sympathetically. "You hinted at it in your letters but I didn't want to ask questions. I figured you'd tell me what you wanted to. Needed to."

She took a deep breath. "Elizabeth, I have a friend who ran away from her family years ago because her father was molesting her. If something happened and you want to talk about it—"

"No!" Elizabeth said quickly, interrupting her. "Nothing like that happened. My father wouldn't—no, it didn't happen!"

Paula's eyes widened. "You're sure? It's nothing to be ashamed of. It wouldn't be your fault—"

"Really, nothing happened."

"Okay." Paula glanced at the kitchen clock. "It's nearly time for one of my favorite shows. I don't suppose you've seen much TV."

Elizabeth smiled and shook her head.

"Well, you're welcome to join me if you want. Or there's all kinds of books as you can see." She gestured at the shelves lined with books.

"I love to read, but I didn't get much time to do it," she confessed. "But I'd like to see some of your TV."

Paula plopped onto the sofa and picked up the remote. "I watch all kinds of stuff. The parents bought me a TiVo so I can record it and watch it around my homework. I used it to tape a couple of shows I couldn't watch earlier this week because I had that big report to write. I thought we could watch *Big Bang Theory* and *Downton Abbey* tonight. I'll show you how to use it later if you want so you can record some shows. It's really easy to save the show you want. There's an instruction manual in the drawer under the TV."

Two hours later, Elizabeth didn't know what to think. They'd watched a show about very smart friends who were teased by a young blond woman about not knowing about real life and then a show about people with British accents who seemed to live in two worlds within the same house—one group acting as servants to others who lived above stairs.

It gave her a lot to think about.

"I'm heading to bed," Paula said. "You're welcome to stay up if you like. I'll show you how the remote works."

"I'm ready for bed, too."

Paula turned off the television and rose. "I don't have class tomorrow. If you'd like, we can work on looking for a job for you, if you want. Do you have a resumé?"

"Yes. The job coordinator at the women's center helped me make one before I got the job at the fabric store."

"Well, I think it'll help you. We'll update it and check job listings on the Internet."

"Wonderful. I appreciate it."

"I think you should take a few days to get acclimated but I understand you just want to get started."

"I need to find something right away," Elizabeth said. "I don't have much money saved."

"I understand. I'm lucky my parents are helping me to go to school. I have a scholarship, but they bought the apartment as an investment and don't want me to work while I attend classes. It was their idea for me to get a roommate to help with expenses."

They went to their respective bedrooms and as Elizabeth changed into a nightgown and climbed into bed thought about how different their lives were—hers and Paula's.

Her parents were obviously doing well and wanted to help their only child. Elizabeth's parents weren't poor, but they certainly didn't have the money to buy a home for their daughter. And Paula's parents were helping her attend college. The Amish didn't attend college. The way they helped their children was to teach them how to do the jobs they did, whether on a farm or in carpentry or whatever and encourage them to find apprenticeships or other ways to train for a job.

Well, mostly this happened for the young men. Elizabeth lay in her bed and stared at the ceiling and worried if she'd find a job in her new town with her limited education and experience. She'd been impulsive; she hoped she wasn't going to be sorry she'd left the job she had back in Goshen. She'd hated giving it up. Going there hadn't felt like work in spite of Angela not being the easiest to work with. As a matter of fact, her job had been the highlight of her day. But she'd had to make a break from her family, her church—even her hometown.

Saul had mentioned Stitches in Time. Maybe she'd look into it tomorrow. She reached over and turned off the lamp on the bedside table. The room was dark and she felt a momentary panic. She'd been a little afraid of the dark when she was a child. Now, as her anxiety about a job and her future threatened to overwhelm her, she remembered what her father had said to her: "There's nothing there that isn't there in the daylight."

Thinking of what he'd said made her miss him. She turned on her bedside lamp, slipped from the bed and found some notepaper and a pen in the drawer of the small desk. Climbing back in bed, she started a short note to both her parents, telling them she was sorry she'd had to leave. After a moment's hesitation, she included her new address and then slipped the note into an envelope and sealed it. She'd mail it tomorrow.

Reassured, she set it on the bedside table, turned off the light, and lay back down. The darkness didn't bother her this time. She took a long, calming breath and felt herself drifting off.

~ℰ~

Saul walked into his store feeling pretty pleased about his work that morning. The bell over the door jangled, announcing his entrance.

"Hi, Saul! Wait, let me help you with that!" Miriam, one of the store clerks, exclaimed. "Why didn't you ask for help?"

Saul bent down to let her take the top box of the two he carried. "Not heavy," he said.

They set the boxes on the counter and Saul used a pocket-knife to open them. He lifted out a quilt and handed it to her.

"I'd recognize Barbie Yoder's quilts anywhere," she said, stroking it.

"It also helps that you knew I was going to talk to her this morning."

She laughed and humor lit her austere face. "True. So she's going to be letting us sell her quilts, instead of Isaac Stoltzfus."

"I didn't have to say much about how we could do better for her," Saul said, taking out another quilt and placing it on the counter. "She came to the same conclusion he wasn't doing well for her. So, here's the first consignment. I'd like to hang the biggest one on the wall, there, to spotlight it. Then let's do the display window with some of the wall hangings and put the rest on a display table near the front of the store."

"Good plan. And while you were gone, you got a delivery from Amos Zook. I put the boxes in the storeroom."

"Guess I know what I'll be doing this afternoon. Why don't you go for your lunch break?"

"I will. Did you eat?"

"You know Barbie. She insisted I eat before I left."

"It's been a little slow this morning. Maybe it'll pick up this afternoon."

"You know it will if I start working on stocking the deliveries."

"True. See you after lunch." She glanced at the window. "You know, it's looking nice outside. I think I'll take a walk after I eat." She walked into the storeroom where they had a small kitchen setup and shut the door.

Saul couldn't wait to open one of the boxes Amos had delivered. The man did beautiful work carving small symbols of Amish life: little wooden buggies, cradles, figures of Amish adults and children.

Another box held the first of the very popular wooden toys Amos and his oldest *sohn* carved: waddling ducks and chickens on a string. Often, older *Englisch* customers said they reminded them of toys they'd played with as children. They bought them saying they'd be giving them to their children or grandchildren, and it made Saul happy to think of the toys reminding the buyers of happy childhood memories and creating new ones as they played with their grandchildren.

This was why he loved working here. People in his community didn't always see themselves as creative and seek attention for their craft. *Hochmut*—pride—wasn't encouraged. Most saw it as just something they did, they enjoyed it, and could earn some always-needed cash. Saul enjoyed searching out special products and helping ease the way by finding a market so the craftsperson could focus on work, not worrying about selling.

Selling was his second best skill. He'd learned from the best, after all—his *dat*. Samuel had been one of the first to see farming was becoming harder because of rising land prices and declining crop prices. He'd seen the increase in tourism as *Englischers* fascinated with the Amish flocked here for quiet vacations, shopping, and sometimes, a chance to learn how to take home some of tranquility they found.

If he could bottle tranquility, he'd be a rich store owner, he thought.

Katie and Rosie, part-time helpers and twin sisters in their early twenties, arrived and began helping straighten the simple wooden shelves holding the crafts. Saul listened with good-natured patience as they gossiped and settled down only when a customer came in and began looking over the handmade candles and soaps.

Katie and Rosie spoke English—sometimes they sounded more like *Englischers* than Amish *maedels*—stopped chattering when the door to the shop opened and the bell jangled.

"*Guder mariye!*" they sang out in unison.

Katie helped the customer find the handmade soap she wanted to take back home as a gift. Rosie refolded some quilts and stacked them neatly on a shelf. Her eyes lit up at the sight of the new wooden carvings by Amos. She repositioned them on the shelves—apparently Saul's display hadn't been creative enough—but it was better than his, so he nodded his approval and left her to it.

He poured himself a cup of coffee in the break room and carried it out to the counter. There, he found Katie and Rosie both ringing up sales and sending customers off happy with their purchases.

They were natural born saleswomen. Nearly a year ago they'd come to him with a proposal to sell their jams and jellies in the store. They'd not only sold him on the idea of carrying their home-canned goods but working here several afternoons a week as well. The little jars flew out of the store with the twins' clever labels and packaging—they called their line *Two Peas in a Pod* after the way they said people always referred to them—and Saul suspected that he'd lose them soon to a store of their own.

Traffic picked up in the afternoon. Miriam had returned from her break and it took the four of them to handle all the visitors to the store. Quite a number of pieces by Amos left the store and a woman who said she collected quilts raved about Barbie's and snapped up two of them.

"You know, I'd have paid more," she said, giving Saul a mischievous smile.

"Oh, how much more?" he asked casually as he wrapped them carefully and placed them in a shopping bag with the store logo.

"Twenty-five percent," she said and she picked up the bag. "No raising the price now that I've paid."

"Wouldn't dream of it," he told her and waited for her to leave the store.

Then he searched through the drawer on the counter, found several blank tags and changed the prices on Barbie's remaining quilts.

A store owner used everything he learned to price his goods for the best of the craftspeople he represented.

An hour later, a light rain began falling. As quickly as customers had swarmed into the store, it was empty again and the sidewalk outside deserted.

Saul sighed. "I guess I should get back to the inventory I started this morning."

Miriam laughed. "How you dread it. Tell you what. Before Katie and Rosie leave for the day I'll get us both a pastry from the bakery on the corner. "

"A reward?"

She laughed. "Why not? I don't like the job any more than you do." She glanced at the door, then at Saul. "Well, well, this is your lucky day. Look who's here."

"*Sohn*, how's business?" his father boomed.

His father's voice was as big as he was. Saul had inherited his height but not his big, barrel-chested frame. When Samuel Miller entered the room, he seemed to fill it. When they were out together in the community, his huge presence made people think he was Saul's brother instead of his father.

"Business was good until a few minutes ago, when the rain started," Saul told him. "We sold two of Barbie Yoder's quilts less than an hour after I unpacked them and several of Amos Zook's new pieces."

"So you got Barbie to agree to let us sell her quilts for her. *Gut, gut.* You'll do better for her than Isaac." He strode over to look at the carved wooden pieces Saul had arranged on shelves. "I like this new direction Amos is taking. This is his best work yet."

He studied Saul. "I always thought you would pursue your interest in wood carving," Samuel said, setting down the piece he'd been studying.

Saul shrugged. "I didn't have the skill others do."

"You didn't give it a chance. You're too hard on yourself." Samuel was silent for a moment and then he shook his head. "But until you're ready to believe in what you do, you won't hear what anyone else says about it."

"I believe I'm good at representing the work of those God has given the gift of talent."

"God gives us all a gift," Samuel said. "It's up to us to discover it and use it."

Something caught Saul's eye. Was that? He moved to the window to get a better look.

"I can see what I'm saying is going in one ear and out the other," his father complained.

"Sorry. I see someone—" He opened the door. "Elizabeth!"

෨෧

Elizabeth turned when she heard her name called and her eyes widened when she saw Saul standing in the doorway of a store a few feet from her.

"Saul?"

"Come in out of the rain," he invited, holding the door open.

She ducked under the roof overhang and collapsed her umbrella, then shook the water from it before entering and wiping her feet. Saul took the umbrella and set it in a holder near the door.

"What are you doing here?"

"I'm out looking for a job," she said simply. "Paula helped me update my resumé and I've been going around and dropping it off."

"Well, Saul, who's this?"

He turned and saw his father staring curiously at Elizabeth.

"Elizabeth, this is my father, Samuel."

"A job, you say?" Samuel tucked his thumbs in his suspenders and studied her. "What sort of a job are you looking for?"

"I thought I'd try for one in a store first," she said. "It's what I did back in Goshen. I worked in a fabric store."

"So, let's see this resumé you spoke of."

Elizabeth glanced at Saul and after a moment, he nodded. She withdrew one from the folder she carried, frowned when she saw one edge was damp and handed it over.

"Saul, maybe you could offer Elizabeth some coffee to warm her up on a cold, damp day while I peruse this."

She saw Saul struggle to keep from grinning as he led the way to a break room just off a storage room.

"Is there some joke?"

Saul laughed and nodded. "Don't think I've ever heard him use the word 'peruse' in my life." He poured her a cup of coffee and added a packet of sugar.

He remembered how she took her coffee.

"Have a seat. Who knows how long this perusing will take."

"It's a short resumé," she told him but she took a seat. "I don't have much experience."

Sure enough, Samuel walked in a few minutes later. He pulled out a chair and sat. "Saul has probably told you Miriam is going to be going on maternity leave soon."

She glanced at him. "No, uh, he hasn't."

Samuel raised his bushy eyebrows at Saul. "No, well maybe it was one of the very few times Saul's mind wasn't on business." He turned his attention back to her. "How long have you been in the area?"

"Just a few days."

"I see. How do the two of you know each other?"

"We met on the bus," Saul told him.

"Well, Elizabeth, we have a position coming available, but I don't know if you'd be interested in a temporary job."

Elizabeth bit her lip. Her innate honesty warred with the necessity of finding work to help her take care of herself.

"Temporary would be helpful," she said carefully. "I don't know how things are here, but jobs weren't easy to come by in Goshen."

"Bird-in-hand, eh?" he asked, chuckling at the joke he'd made.

It took Elizabeth a moment to remember it was the name of a nearby town. She smiled. *"Ya,"* she said, using the Pennsylvania *Dietsch* she'd been picking up since she'd been here.

Samuel nodded, then he looked at Saul. The two men seemed to communicate something without speaking.

"Maybe we can help each other out, then," Samuel said.

He named a salary a bit better than what she'd earned in Goshen and it was full-time. Temporary, but *full-time*. When she nodded, he thumped the table with one hand. *"Gut.* Can you start day after tomorrow?"

She nodded and he rose.

"Well then, Elizabeth Bontrager. I hope you enjoy working here. Saul, I'm going to go pick your mother up from the doctor's."

"Is she *allrecht?"* Saul frowned and his fingers tightened on his mug of coffee.

"Just a checkup. Last time they did the labs she was still in remission."

He left them and Elizabeth heard him saying good-bye to the staff as he left the store.

"Well," she said. "I have a job."

"*Ya*," he said. "You have a job. Like *Daed* said, I hope you like working here."

"I'm sure I will."

Silence stretched between them. Where did they go from here? she wondered, remembering how when she'd first met Saul she'd thought about how it would be to work with someone you were attracted to.

"I—are there some forms or something I need to fill out?"

"I'll get them."

She filled out the forms while he helped a customer then handed them to him. "Could I use your phone to call my roommate?"

"Of course." He handed her the cordless phone from a nearby counter and left the room.

Elizabeth walked out of the break room and found Saul sitting at the counter making a file for her paperwork.

"Well, I'll see you day after tomorrow."

He nodded and got up to walk her to the door. She gazed up at the gray sky and smiled. "It's a beautiful day," she told him.

"It's drizzling," he said as he opened the door for her.

"Beautiful," she insisted. She'd found a job her first day looking. She stepped outside.

"Wait!" he called and he handed her the umbrella she'd left behind. "Here," he said, opening it and handing it to her.

Elizabeth gazed up at him. "Thank you."

Still he stood there, holding the umbrella.

"What is it?" she asked him.

"You have little raindrops in your lashes," he said.

If someone hurrying past in the rain hadn't bumped into him, she didn't know how long they might have stood there as though no one else existed.

"You sure you don't want to come back and wait in the store for your ride?"

Elizabeth shook her head. "Paula said she was just a few minutes away. She was out running errands."

He handed her the umbrella. "If you change your mind . . ."

She found herself smiling. "I won't melt."

Saul chuckled. "I know. Well, see you day after tomorrow."

Paula's car splashed up to the curb and Elizabeth hurried to open the door and climb inside. After checking for traffic, Paula pulled back out onto the road.

"Well, you're looking happy. Good day?"

"The best. I have a job. It's temporary, but it's a job."

"Cool. Deets."

"Deets?"

Paula laughed. "Details."

Elizabeth filled her in on everything. Well, not everything. If she mentioned Saul, Paula was sure to think she'd gotten the job because she knew Saul. Hmm. It was part of it, but not all of it.

"I know the store. My dad helped the owner with a small legal matter years ago. He brought Mom some really pretty homemade soaps as part of the fee."

"I didn't even really have a chance to look around much," Elizabeth said.

"You'll have plenty of time to do so once you start working. And by the way, when do you start?"

"Day after tomorrow."

Paula pulled into the parking lot of a restaurant not far from the apartment.

"What are we doing here?"

"We're going to celebrate you getting a job."

"But we just went to the grocery store."

"It'll keep. I think we should celebrate. My treat."

"I got the job. Maybe I should treat."

"It'll take a while to get a paycheck," Paula said, turning off the ignition. She reached for her umbrella. "Tell you what. First one inside treats."

And she was off like a shot struggling to open her umbrella as she ran.

Laughing, Elizabeth scrambled from the car, dropping her own umbrella in a puddle, and racing after her. They collided at the front door of the restaurant, giggling, and engaging in a brief elbowing to walk in first.

Elizabeth stopped, gasping for breath. "Paula, this is not ladylike."

Paula tried to stifle her giggles. "You're right. After you."

Lifting her chin in the air, Elizabeth proceeded into the restaurant, only to turn and stare in disbelief at Paula as she prodded her forward with her umbrella.

A waitress stepped forward. "Ladies? Two for dinner?"

"Ladies zero," said Paula, trying to look angelic. "But yes, there's two of us for dinner."

5

Elizabeth couldn't help noticing the man at the next table. It wasn't just because he looked about her age and was attractive with dark hair and blue eyes—he was waving at Paula.

"I think the man at the next table is trying to get your attention."

Paula glanced over and her face lit up. "It's Bruce Armstrong, from one of my classes." She gestured at him to come over. "Bruce, how have you been? I haven't seen you since final exam cram last semester."

"Got a B from old man Smithers. You?"

"An A."

"Yeah, you were his favorite."

"You know Professor Smithers didn't have favorites. You just didn't work hard enough in his class. You thought you could pull it off at the end."

He rolled his eyes. "Big mistake. Are you going to introduce me to your friend?"

Paula made the introduction and Bruce held out his hand to Elizabeth.

"Do you want to join us?" Paula asked him.

His eyes on Elizabeth, Bruce nodded. "Don't mind if I do. So, Elizabeth, I haven't seen you around. New here?"

She nodded. "I'm staying with Paula. I just moved here. "

"Ah, roomies." He looked up when the waitress approached. "I'm joining these two ladies."

"Of course you are," she remarked dryly. She handed him a menu, took his drink order and left them.

"Come here often?" Paula asked, grinning. "She seems to know you."

He shrugged.

"I think you like being thought of as a bad boy."

"Don't listen to her," Bruce told Elizabeth. "I'm a nice guy."

Elizabeth had very little experience with guys—Amish or *Englisch*—but she knew the term "bad boy."

"What's going on?" he asked them. "You two looked pretty happy coming in."

"We're celebrating Elizabeth getting a job today," Paula told him. "I'm treating her to dinner."

"It's just temporary, but it's a start."

"Hey, congratulations," Bruce said. "Let me treat you both."

"You sure?" Paula asked him. "I thought money was tight."

"The parents came through," he said, closing his menu as the waitress approached with their drinks. "They were happy I pulled my grades up this semester. Thanks to your help, I might add."

Paula smiled. "You can thank the study group."

"True. They're not getting dinner, though. Just you and Elizabeth here."

Elizabeth watched the easy way Paula and Bruce acted, joking with each other. She'd never been able to do that with a man.

Then it hit her—not until Saul.

Elizabeth went still. She had to think about it.

"Earth to Elizabeth." Paula snapped her fingers in front of her.

She blinked. "Sorry. I was just thinking about something."

"Something or someone?" Paula asked her.

"Well, I haven't seen a girl blush in years," Bruce said slowly. "I didn't think they did anymore."

Elizabeth felt her skin grow warmer, a sure sign she was blushing even more. She sent Paula a beseeching look.

Paula got the message. She nodded and turned to Bruce. "We shouldn't tease Elizabeth. She isn't used to it. She's Amish, Bruce. She's not like *Englisch* girls you've known."

Bruce gave her an appraising look, but he didn't say anything else. Of course, it was partly because the food arrived and like most of the men she knew, he was more interested in getting served.

"So, are you going to take any classes?" he asked her after he ate a bite of his fried chicken.

It took Elizabeth a few seconds to realize he was talking to her.

She shook her head. "Maybe one day." She hadn't thought far ahead. If she stayed, she could do anything she wanted. Within reason, of course. She'd only gone to school to the eighth grade so if she wanted to go to college she'd have to get her GED or attend high school.

But she was getting ahead of herself. Right now, she just needed to concentrate on her job so she could take care of herself.

Paula dipped a forkful of her chicken salad in the little dish of dressing she'd ordered on the side. "Is your dad still pressuring you to join him in his law firm one day?"

"Yeah." Bruce stabbed some green beans with his fork. "I'm coming around to the idea."

"Uh-huh. You mean you're letting him think he's convincing you. How much is this going to cost him?"

Bruce clutched a hand to his chest and groaned. "Oh, how you wound me."

"Oh, how I have your number." Paula finished her salad.

"The thing is, I was never against becoming an attorney," he said, picking up his fork again. "But he wouldn't let me decide what specialty. It's all about specialty these days. He wasn't willing to consider me going into criminal law until he thought I wasn't going to join the firm. It's time Armstrong and Childers, P.A., diversified."

Elizabeth didn't understand some of what Bruce was saying, but he intrigued her with his boyish charm and easy confidence. And when he looked at her . . . oh, my, when he looked at her she could feel her heart beat faster and a little thrill of excitement ran up her spine. Oh, my, when he looked at her . . .

She told herself he was just intrigued because she was different from other girls he'd known. That was all. She'd probably never see him again. Or if she did, it would be because he and Paula would study at the apartment or something.

Paula excused herself from the table and Bruce turned to Elizabeth. "How about we have dinner sometime?"

❧

Saul found Elizabeth waiting at the store when he arrived to open.

"You're early," he said, secretly pleased at her promptness.

"One of the students who lives in our apartment building has an early class, so she'll be giving me a ride here."

He unlocked the door, gestured for her to proceed him inside, then relocked the door. They weren't due to open for a half hour.

"Paula said she'd bring me but I hated to ask her. She doesn't do mornings."

"I see."

"I've never been around anyone who didn't get up early," she told him as they walked to the break room. "My family always had to get up before dawn, because we had chores on the farm."

He showed her the cabinet where she could lock her purse and watched her put her brown bag lunch in the refrigerator. The blue cape dress she wore made her eyes even bluer but he noticed faint lavender shadows beneath them—as if she hadn't been sleeping well.

"Miriam's going to train you. She should be here soon." Saul filled the percolator, set it on the burner and turned up the gas flame beneath it.

"When is she planning on starting her maternity leave?"

"Couple days."

He poured them both a mug of coffee and they sat at the table to drink it.

"So how will you get home?"

"Paula said she doesn't mind picking me up, but I'm going to look into the bus schedule later. I don't want her to feel like she's a taxi."

"If she said she doesn't mind, I'm sure she doesn't."

Elizabeth took a sip of her coffee. "Sometimes people find it hard to say no."

He waited for her to go on, but she lapsed into silence and stared into her coffee.

"How did the two of you meet? I mean, you lived in Goshen and she lived here."

"Paula and her family came to visit Goshen, and she and her mother walked into the shop I worked in," Elizabeth told him. "The owner was cutting fabric for Paula's mother—she likes to sew—and Paula started talking to me."

She smiled. "Paula's the most curious person I've ever met. She had all kinds of questions about the Amish in Goshen. Since she's a nursing student and will have Amish patients she wants to understand them. Before we knew it, we were corresponding. Becoming friends."

"And you just decided to move here?"

She shrugged. "It wasn't long after that." She glanced at the clock. "When do the others get here?"

There she was, withdrawing again, he thought. She'd done the same on the bus whenever he got a little too personal with his questions.

"Miriam will be here in a few minutes. Katie and Rosie come in about noon. They work part-time. More coffee?"

"No, thanks. When I drink too much coffee, I talk too much."

"I can't imagine that," he said, and she blushed a little.

"Tell me what the biggest sellers are for the store."

Good question from a new employee. And a good way to change the subject as well. "The traditional Amish crafts are the most popular," he told her. "The hand-carved wooden items Amos and his son produce. Quilts. And the candles and soaps."

They heard someone unlocking the front door and then closing it. Footsteps approached the break room and Miriam appeared. Her face looked pale, and she sank into a chair as if she was already tired, even though the day had just started.

"*Guder mariye,*" she said.

"Miriam, this is Elizabeth Bontrager."

"It's *gut* to meet you, Elizabeth."

"Are you all right?" Saul asked her.

"I didn't have an easy night," she admitted. "But I'll be fine."

"Just let me know when you need a break. Or if you need to leave early."

"I'll be fine." She took her jacket off and hung it on a peg, then locked her purse up. Walking over to the stove, she leaned over the percolator and breathed deeply. "I can't wait until I can drink *kaffe* again."

"There's water and juice in the refrigerator."

"I know. But there's nothing like a cup of *kaffe* in the morning." She turned to Elizabeth. "So, glad you're here. How about I show you the store and get you trained."

Elizabeth rose and set her cup in the sink. She followed Miriam out of the room.

Saul stayed at the table, drumming his fingers on its top. It was good they had someone to work during Miriam's maternity leave. He wasn't sorry it was this intriguing woman he'd met on the bus. He'd hoped to see her again.

But she seemed hard to know and he wondered at her reason for being here in this town. He wondered if she'd stay after Miriam returned to work.

Miriam appeared at the door. "Shall I open?"

He looked at the clock and nodded.

"Everything okay?"

"What could be wrong? We found a replacement for you."

"There is no replacement for me," she said tartly. "But there is a temporary solution."

He glanced at the door and then at her. "See if you can find out how long she intends to stay here."

"Until I come back, right?"

"No, I mean the town."

"She didn't tell you?"

He shook his head. "Every time I ask her anything personal I see her withdrawing. I haven't pushed."

"Do you want to know for the job? Or for yourself?"

"For the job," he said.

"*Schur*," she said. "I've known you for how many years?"

"Miriam."

"I'll find out," she told him. "I can find out anything."

He rolled his eyes. "*Ya*, I know."

Elizabeth fell in love.

Oh, not with Saul, although he certainly was just as nice a man as she'd thought him to be when she met him on the bus.

No, it was the store she loved. She'd never been creative—never had the time to be. But here creativity was all around. So much love evident in the hand-carved items and the quilts and the candles and soaps and . . . well, she could go on and on.

Miriam took her on a tour of the store set up in a plain and simple way with the goods showcased on the rough-hewn shelves. Elizabeth listened to her description of the piece and the person who created it. Customers liked knowing these things, Miriam said, and Elizabeth was interested, too, so she listened avidly as they walked around. Imagine spending your days and evenings creating something as your life's work—or at least part of your day.

Some of the things she looked at were made by second-generation craftsmen—the sons of Amos Zook had followed in his footsteps and worked with him. What had begun as a way to make furniture for his growing family during the long, cold winters had turned into a growing skill and a second career as his work was sold here at the store.

Elizabeth found herself wondering what was happening back in Goshen. Her family was an ordinary one, working hard to maintain their farm. During the winter, her father often worked part-time as a carpenter making kitchen cabinets in a nearby town. His work was practical, never creative.

Customers came and went. Miriam helped some so Elizabeth could observe her and then gestured at her to take the next one. Elizabeth had been dealing with customers from the time she was just ten and she helped her *mamm* out with the roadside stand at the farm. Whether it was vegetables or fabric or Amish crafts, she knew how to help a customer and sometimes even make a subtle suggestion to increase the sale.

"You were *gut*," Miriam said, nodding as the customer, a prosperous looking *Englischer*, left with two full shopping bags.

Then she frowned and rubbed at her lower back.

"Time to take a break?" Elizabeth said.

Miriam shook her head. "Don't be expecting breaks too often. We work hard here."

Elizabeth didn't take offense. She'd seen Miriam rub her lower back with one hand several times when she thought no one was looking. She glanced around the store and saw Saul working on something at the cash register.

"I'm going to go straighten the quilts on the shelf while there are no customers," she told Miriam. "I had to pull some of them out and didn't get to fold them properly."

Miriam nodded absentmindedly, her attention clearly someplace else.

Picking up one of the quilts, Elizabeth walked over to Saul. "Pretend I'm asking you something about the quilt," she whispered, holding it out to him. "I think Miriam's in labor and doesn't want to admit it. She keeps rubbing her back. I think she's having back labor."

He went dead white. Then he blinked and his Adam's apple bobbed as he struggled to speak.

"The quilt!" she hissed.

He took the quilt and pretended to look at the price tag. "What makes you think she's in labor?"

"I told you I was one of nine children. I helped deliver two of them when the midwife didn't make it to the house on time."

"You're not—you're not saying she's going to have the baby here?!" he squeaked.

"No." She rolled her eyes. Men! They thought they were so big and brave. Manly men, her brother John would say.

Then an imp of mischief took over. "At least, I hope not."

He lost even more color. "What'll we do?"

"Have you got something—some paperwork or something—so she has to sit down to do it? Maybe once she sits for a few minutes she'll realize she's not just having back pain from being on her feet."

"An order form. I'll get her to talk to me about an order form in the break room. Will you be all right out here by yourself for a few minutes?"

"*Schur*," she said, mimicking the Pennsylvania *Dietsch* word she'd heard used here.

"You promise she won't have the baby while I'm back there with her?"

"If she tries to, just yell." She had to bite the inside of her cheek to keep from grinning. Miriam might think her back pain was just discomfort but Elizabeth suspected once she sat down for a few minutes she'd either realize she needed to leave for the hospital or the back pain would ease and not be labor.

"Count on it," he muttered.

Picking up the paperwork he'd been studying, he walked over to Miriam and said something to her. Elizabeth watched the two of them walk to the back room and then turned her attention to the front of the store when the bell over the door jangled.

A few minutes later, the customer gone, Elizabeth ducked back to the break room and found Miriam getting off the phone.

"I'm so sorry," she said when she saw Elizabeth. "I'm not going to be able to train you any more today. The doctor wants me to go to the hospital and get checked out. I just called and arranged for a ride there."

"I still think you need to go there by ambulance," Saul said.

Miriam thrust out her chin. "There's plenty of time. Doctor said first babies take a long time arriving. And if these *are* contractions they're still far apart."

"I think I'll go wait at the front of the store, sit in one of the rockers." She heaved herself up, shaking her head at Saul's offer to help her. "Don't worry, I won't get stuck in the rocker. I just sat in it yesterday."

"I would never suggest—"

Miriam patted his arm. "I know. I was just teasing you. There's no need to worry."

"I'll feel better when you're at the hospital. You're sure you don't want me to go with you?"

"No need. John should be there in an hour or two. He was working out of town today." She got her purse out of the cabinet, took her jacket from the peg, and began walking out of the room.

Elizabeth watched her and was reminded of how her own mother had waddled like that the day or two before she gave birth.

"Why don't you go sit with her until her ride comes?" he said. "I'll take care of any customers that come in."

She nodded. He looked so frazzled she didn't have the heart to tease him more.

So she took a break and sat in one of the rockers and chatted with Miriam. The chairs were obviously made for parents to sit and rock a baby. They featured wide arms to rest an elbow crooked to hold the baby safely.

"If you get anyone looking at these be sure to mention Amos makes a very special rocker for newborns. I'll show you a photo of it." She started to get up.

"Just tell me where you keep it."

"On the shelf there."

Elizabeth found the photo. The rocker had just one arm; in the place of the other a small cradle had been attached. "I've never seen anything like this."

"It's a reproduction of an antique," Miriam said, looking at the photo with her. "You'd never see one in an Amish home. Too impractical. How long would a baby be able to sleep in it? A couple of months? But every so often someone comes in, orders it, and he makes it for them. Look at the price. Can you imagine?"

Her eyes widened. "No, I can't imagine anyone spending this much money on anything."

Miriam nodded. "My *grossmudder* used to say it takes all kinds." She glanced at Elizabeth. "You know, you did just fine today. And not only with the customers."

"Oh?" Elizabeth looked at her warily. Had Saul told her they'd talked about her?

"Saul has never wanted me to talk about an order form. It only happened after you went over and had a conversation about a quilt. It was nice to be asked my advice."

"Really?"

"Really."

Silence stretched between them. Miriam looked out the window, then turned her shrewd eyes on Elizabeth.

"So, how long are you staying?"

"Until you come back from maternity leave."

"You know what I'm asking."

Elizabeth nodded. "I don't know," she said honestly. "I really don't."

Miriam sighed. "I hope you find the answers you need. I'll pray for you."

She felt tears burn behind her eyelids. Her mother had said the same thing just before she left. Here Miriam, about to become a mother, was saying it, too.

"*Danki.*"

"There's my ride," Miriam said as a vehicle pulled up in front of the store and the driver honked the horn.

"I'll say a prayer for you as well," Elizabeth said, standing and reaching down to help Miriam rise. "And come see you tomorrow after you have the *boppli.*"

"So sure I'm having it today, eh?"

"I'm never wrong," Elizabeth assured her with a smile as she walked outside with Miriam and watched her get into the van.

6

*T*wins!" Elizabeth couldn't help staring as she shook hands with Katie, then Rosie.

Katie looked at Rosie. "Saul didn't tell her. Guess he wanted to surprise her." She glanced around. "Where is he? In the back?"

"Yes." She studied the two women who appeared about her age. They looked identical: brown, center-parted hair beneath their identical *kapps* and bonnets. Both wore the same dark green cape dresses.

How would she tell them apart?

"I see you've met the twins," Saul said when he walked out of the back room a few minutes later.

"How do you tell them apart?" she whispered.

"You'll see," he told her with a grin. "Watch out, they like to confuse you at first."

They did, twice giggling when Elizabeth approached to ask Rosie something and used her name and finding out she was talking to Katie instead and then thinking she had it right the next time and finding she talked to Rosie instead.

"I figured it out," Elizabeth told Saul proudly a little later. "Katie loves to be the leader and likes to talk and Rosie's a little shy. And Katie has a dimple when she smiles."

"That was fast," he said, nodding.

Elizabeth's mother suspected she carried *zwillingboppli*—twins—once and Elizabeth felt guilty now remembering how glad that there was one *boppli,* not two. She couldn't imagine taking care of two at once. God gifted a number of families in her community with twins. Elizabeth overheard the nurse at the hospital telling her mother that the more children a woman bore and the older she was, the more chance of a multiple birth.

Elizabeth shuddered at the thought.

The shop door opened near closing time. Elizabeth glanced up from taking an order at the counter and saw another surprise: Paula!

"I'm sorry, I didn't realize you were here. You didn't have to come in."

"I wanted to. I've never been in here." Paula picked up a pale green candle with a simple carved wooden base. "This would look great on the fireplace mantel. I'll take it."

"You don't have to buy anything," Elizabeth whispered. She didn't want Saul to think she discouraged sales.

"I want to. Besides, I haven't bought anything for the apartment in ages." She handed it to Elizabeth and rummaged in her purse for her wallet. "Listen, I have a kind of surprise for you. I figured I should let you know."

"I've already had a surprise today, thanks," Elizabeth muttered, remembering Miriam changing the way the day had gone, when she left for the hospital to see if she was in labor.

"Huh? What?"

"We'll talk later." Elizabeth ran the credit card, handed Paula the slip to sign and began wrapping the candle and its holder in tissue.

Saul came out with the bank deposit bag under his arm. "*Gut-n-Owed.*"

Elizabeth handed the shopping bag to Paula and introduced her to Saul.

"She bought a candle and holder," she told him. "Did you want to add it to the day's total?"

He shook his head. "Just stick the slip in the register drawer and I'll put it on tomorrow's slip. Paula, I'm glad you can give Elizabeth a ride home."

"Me, too. Although I'll have to be careful not to come in the store each time," she said, lifting the bag. "I'll go broke."

He chuckled. "She's quite a saleswoman." He looked at Elizabeth. "Next time give her the employee discount."

They walked outside and Saul locked up the door. "Thanks again for the help with Miriam, Elizabeth. Paula, nice to meet you. Have a good evening."

Paula watched him stroll to the van waiting to drive him home. "What's he talking about?"

Elizabeth started to tell her and then saw a man getting out of Paula's car. Paula followed the direction of her look.

"That's the surprise I was going to tell you about," she said.

"A little late now," Elizabeth said under her breath. She smiled as he approached. "Hello."

"Hi. Hope you don't mind I tagged along once I found out Paula was coming to pick you up." He opened the passenger door for her with a flourish and smiled at her.

Elizabeth found herself basking in the warmth of his gaze as she slid into the front seat.

"So, who's the Amish dude who came out of the store with you two?" he asked as he climbed into the back seat.

"My boss. Why?"

"Hmm. He sure was giving us the eye as they drove off."

She looked at Paula.

"We'll talk later," Paula told her.

Puzzled, Elizabeth fastened her seat belt.

Bruce leaned forward. "What do you think about going to a movie? Maybe have a pizza after?"

"Paula?"

"I have to write a paper tonight," Paula told her.

"Oh." She turned to Bruce. "You don't have to write one?"

"I'm not taking the class. C'mon, I'll even let you choose as long as it's not too much of a chick flick."

"Chick flick?"

"Girl movie. Boy, you really have been out of the loop, haven't you? How many movies have you actually seen?"

"One. Years ago."

"Well, Elizabeth, it's time you caught up."

He tapped at the screen of his phone and began reading off movies and times and giving little mini stories to describe them. When Elizabeth looked helplessly at Paula, she nodded.

"Bruce, it's not fair to talk her into some cops and robbers chase movie or a shoot-'em-up Western."

"Chick flick, huh?"

"Chick flick," she said firmly.

Bruce rolled his eyes, but then he sent a charming grin at Elizabeth and with their faces so close together, she got the full effect.

The freedom of doing something fun after work instead of rushing home to help with babies and chores felt heady. Elizabeth relaxed in the plush seats in the movie theater and munched popcorn dripping with butter—it felt like such an indulgence to have her own bag—and stared spellbound at the action playing on the big screen. She wrinkled her nose as the fizz from her soft drink tickled it and thoroughly enjoyed herself.

Then she noticed a couple sitting a few rows down. They were teenagers and the girl kept shaking her head and resisting his attempts to get friendly with her. Elizabeth watched how he yawned and stretched and casually draped his arm along her shoulders. She gave him a look and he removed it with great reluctance. A few minutes later, he did the same thing and once again she wouldn't have any part of the intimacy. The third time he did it, he got an elbow in the ribs.

She couldn't help smiling and then she glanced at Bruce.

"You're supposed to be watching the movie," he whispered in a mock stern tone.

But she saw the twinkle in his eye. She blushed and hoped he couldn't see in the dark theater. Was he going to try what the teen boy had? Like the teen girl, she wasn't ready for that, either.

"Enjoying yourself?"

Nodding, she took a sip of her drink and replaced it in the cup holder on the arm of the seat.

"You sure you don't want a box of candy?"

She giggled. "No. Have to save room for pizza."

Actually, she didn't even care if they got pizza. She'd eaten enough popcorn for two people and didn't want the movie to end. Bruce had promised Paula he wouldn't try to persuade Elizabeth to see a "guy" movie and kept his word. This was a film of a couple falling in love while they explored Venice, Italy, a place with so much water and mystery and romance. The country was more beautiful than anything Elizabeth could have imagined.

Movies were like a world unto themselves.

When it finally ended, she sat there, transfixed, and didn't move.

"Liked it, huh?"

"Yes, very much. You?"

"It was okay." He grinned. "It was a chick flick. Tell Paula I listened to her." He stood.

"I'm ready for pizza. You?"

She'd eaten a lot of popcorn, but pizza sounded good. Maybe she could squeeze in one slice. . . . "It sounds good."

✆

Saul did a double take when he looked back and saw Elizabeth talking with a man as Paula stood nearby.

The man seemed very friendly with Elizabeth . . . had she already gotten a boyfriend?

No, it wasn't possible. She'd only been in town for a few days, he reminded himself.

Then again, he didn't really know her. She'd been very close-mouthed about why she was on the bus, alone, and living here now with a female *Englisch* friend. She didn't seem the type to have run from home to indulge in a *rumschpringe* of wild behavior. And she wore Plain dresses of unobtrusive colors and a *kapp* each day.

But who knew what she did with her nights?

He shook his head. What he had seen could be very innocent. The man could just be a friend of Paula's.

Why did he care?

"Have a good day?" Phil, his driver, asked.

Saul roused himself from his thoughts. "Yes. Did you?"

"Can't complain. Looking forward to vacation next week. I have my brother, Jake, lined up to take over for me. You remember me telling you about this?"

"I do. I hope you have a good time."

"Need to stop anywhere on the way home?"

"No, thanks." What he wanted to do was follow the car Elizabeth had gotten into with Paula and the man. . . . He shook his head to clear it. Since when did he think like that?

Saul sighed. Maybe he was thinking about her too much because he didn't have anyone to focus on anymore. But he knew it wasn't totally true. He and Lavina hadn't communicated much the last month before he went to see her. There had been an emotional distance between them—not just a physical distance. They had drifted apart so much he didn't think she'd been surprised when he called to say he thought they shouldn't see each other any more.

He checked the display on his cell phone. No word yet from Miriam. Maybe Elizabeth had been wrong about her being in labor.

"Home sweet home," Phil announced as he pulled into the driveway.

"Enjoy your evening," Saul told him.

"I'm ready to go home and do that," Phil said. "I just have to hope I won't be tortured by having to figure out math homework with my oldest."

His mother looked up with a smile when Saul walked into the kitchen.

"Did you have a *gut* day?" she asked him as she turned from the stove.

He nodded and looked over her shoulder to see what she was stirring in a pot.

She shooed him away. "You are so nosy! You know you'll eat whatever I serve. Why do you need to be seeing what it is before it goes on the table? Go wash your hands and call your father."

"No need for that, Waneta, my dear *fraa*," he said, stepping into the room. "My nose called me here."

"It usually does," she remarked dryly.

Saul grinned as he washed his hands at the sink. The two of them had been doing much the same kind of talking for more years than he could remember although when his brothers and sisters had been around the table there had been so much going on it hadn't been as obvious.

"So how did Elizabeth do today?" his father asked after asking for a blessing over the meal.

"Elizabeth? Who's Elizabeth?" In the act of handing him the bowl of buttered noodles, Waneta paused and looked at Saul.

Saul held out his hands for the bowl but she kept looking at him without giving it to him.

"Someone we hired while Miriam is out on maternity leave."

She handed him the bowl and he served himself, then set the bowl on the table.

"So, how did she do?" she asked.

"Very well. She's good with customers."

"Which Elizabeth is this?" Waneta wanted to know. "Isaac and Mary's or John B. and Naomi's?"

"Neither. This Elizabeth's from Indiana."

"Indiana? What's she doing here, then?"

Saul and Samuel exchanged a look. When his father put a big forkful of pot roast in his mouth and chewed slowly as he looked at him, Saul knew he'd been handed the conversational ball.

"She's filling in for Miriam while she's out for maternity leave."

"Where is she living? Does she have relatives in the area? How old is she?"

"With an *Englisch* friend. I don't think so. And if I remember correctly, she's twenty." He took a bite of pot roast and wondered when the questions would stop.

"Is she pretty?" she persisted.

"Yes, Saul, is she pretty?" his father asked.

Saul frowned at his father. "You have eyes. What do you say?"

"I say I'd be interested in knowing if you think she's pretty," Samuel told him, grinning as he finished his supper and leaned back in his chair.

"Saul!"

He wanted to roll his eyes at his mother, but he'd learned never to do it when he was thirteen and did it once. Just once. "Beauty's in the eyes of the beholder," he said.

She threw her hands in the air. "Ask a simple question!" She stood, walked over to the counter and picked up a plate of brownies. "There's dessert for men who clear the table." She glanced meaningfully over her shoulder.

Saul and his father cleared the table in record time.

"Ice cream?" Samuel asked.

"*Schur,*" Waneta said with a smile. She carried the plate of brownies to the table and began putting them on plates and passing them to Samuel and Saul.

"I think she just treated us like *kinner,*" Samuel said to Saul.

"*Ya,*" Saul agreed. He turned to his mother. "May I have two scoops?"

Samuel snickered.

Waneta handed him a plate with two scoops of ice cream as well.

Saul chuckled and began eating his dessert.

"So, she's pretty, eh?" said Waneta.

He nodded and looked sheepish.

"What do you know about her?" Waneta asked as she began eating her brownie.

"She's a nice *maedel,*" Saul said with a shrug.

"She's not here for *rumschpringe,*" Samuel spoke up. "She's running away from something, not running around."

Saul stared at him. His father didn't usually talk like that. But there was no question he'd hit the nail on the head about

Elizabeth. While Saul still felt Elizabeth was a mystery, even as he puzzled about her being with the *Englisch* man, he didn't think she was into wild behavior. He was a good judge of character. His *dat*, too. He wouldn't have told Saul he should hire Elizabeth—even for a temporary position—if he had any reservations.

He took another bite of the brownie topped with ice cream and thought about seconds.

"Maybe I should stop by and take a look for myself," Waneta mused.

Samuel patted her hand and reached for another brownie. "You know you decided to the minute you started asking questions tonight."

She grinned. "True."

Saul's phone vibrated. He looked at the display. "It's from Leroy. Miriam's husband," he said, reading the text. "She just had a boy who weighed nearly eight pounds." He texted his congratulations and turned back to look at the plate of brownies. "I think I'll have another of those to celebrate."

"It's as good a reason as any," his mother said with a smile and reached for his plate. "One scoop of ice cream or two?"

⤫

"Paula called while you were out on break," Saul told Elizabeth when she walked into the store the next afternoon. "She said she had to see her faculty advisor and she was going to be late."

"Oh, okay." Elizabeth started for the back room to put up her purse.

"I told her I could give you a ride," he said.

She stopped and turned to look at him. "You don't have to."

"I'd be happy to. It's on my way home."

"How did you know—oh, my address is on my resumé."

He nodded.

"If you're sure?"

"I am."

"*Danki.*" She walked back and locked up her purse. It wouldn't have been a hardship to take a bus home, but rain was predicted later in the afternoon.

She was helping a customer with a quilt when an Amish woman walked in. The woman smiled at her and walked around, browsing the shelves. Katie and Rosie approached her and they greeted each other like friends, although Elizabeth couldn't hear their conversation. They looked in her direction and Katie nodded, then walked on to the front of the store to greet a customer.

Elizabeth wondered briefly if this was one of the people whose work was sold here and if she was here to see Saul. Or maybe she was shopping. Every time she looked up, the woman was watching her curiously.

"What's this pattern called?"

She returned her attention to her customer. "It's Sunshine and Shadow. Sometimes called Diamond in the Square because of the geometric shapes."

Clearly torn, the woman hesitated and bit her lip. "It's awfully expensive."

"A good handmade Amish quilt isn't cheap," Elizabeth said. "But this is made by one of the best quilters in the area. Look how many stitches per inch. Hundreds of hours go into something like this. I like to call it practical art. It warms your heart and soul to look at its beauty but it can cover you with warmth as well."

"What a beautiful thing to say."

Elizabeth stroked a hand over it. "It'll last for a long, long time. Quilts like this get passed down in families."

"You're right," the woman said. "I'll take it. It's something I can leave my daughter. If she doesn't try to talk me out of it when I get back to Florida."

Elizabeth wrapped the quilt in tissue paper and placed it in a shopping bag. She presented the credit slip to be signed and when she gave her the receipt she included a brochure of some of the store's quilts.

"Maybe she'd like to look at this," Elizabeth told her. "There's also a website listed on the back. She can look at more quilts, if she has a computer."

"The store uses a website? I thought the Amish didn't use computers."

"An *Englisch* friend of the owner takes care of it." She handed the bag to her customer and smiled. "I hope you enjoy this for many years to come."

"I'm sure I will. Thank you, dear."

She watched her customer walk away and then sighed happily. Saul should be very happy with the sale. It was her second quilt sale today.

Elizabeth closed the cash register drawer and looked up into the face of the Amish woman who'd come into the store a few minutes earlier.

"Hello. I'm Waneta Miller. Saul's mother."

"Oh, it's *gut* to meet you. I'll go get Saul for you."

"No, I didn't come to see him," she said. "I came to see you."

"Me?"

The woman's eyes danced merrily. "Just thought I'd say *wilkumm*."

Elizabeth was touched. "Why, thank you."

"*Mamm!* I didn't know you were here."

She turned as Saul approached the counter. "I just got here."

"Had to see for yourself, eh?"

"Of course."

She said something Elizabeth didn't understand since they didn't speak Pennsylvania *Dietsch* back in Goshen. But Saul looked at his mother sternly.

"Speak English, *Mamm*."

Waneta looked at Elizabeth. "I just told him I agreed with him that you are pretty."

"I didn't say to tell her what you said," he told her with a sigh. He looked at Elizabeth. "Sorry."

"Sorry for saying you think I'm pretty?" she teased, surprising herself at her boldness.

Waneta laughed. "And she has a sense of humor," she said.

"Where's *Daed*?" he asked.

"He's picking up new glasses. He'll be coming back for me in a few minutes."

"Excuse me," Katie said. "Rosie and I are leaving now."

"*Danki*," Saul said. "We'll see you tomorrow."

The twins exchanged hugs with Waneta, winking at Elizabeth over her shoulder, then hurried out of the store, holding the door open for a customer who entered.

"Excuse me," Elizabeth said to Waneta. "I'd better see to my customer."

"*Mamm*, maybe you'd like a cup of tea while you wait for *Daed*," she heard Saul say as she walked away.

Waneta sighed. "I suppose since she's busy."

Elizabeth smiled. Something told her she'd had a narrow escape.

Samuel came in a short time later and nodded at Elizabeth. "Your *fraa* is in the back room with Saul."

"How is it you escaped her asking you questions?" he asked, his eyes twinkling behind new glasses.

Elizabeth stuck her tongue in her cheek. "She asked a few, but a customer came in."

He chuckled. "Well, let's see if she can leave without asking a few more. She *is* a curious woman, my Waneta."

Before he could get her, Waneta emerged and met them at the front of the store. She tilted her head to one side and studied him. "And look how handsome you are in your new glasses."

"Just for that I'll take you to supper at the new restaurant you've been wanting to try," he said, offering his arm to her.

She laughed. "I'll take you up on it." She looked at Elizabeth. "Maybe we can go to lunch one day when I'm in town."

"That would be nice," Elizabeth said.

"An inquisition will be on the menu," Saul murmured, as he came to stand beside her and watch his parents leave.

She laughed. "She seems like a very nice woman."

"A very strong one. It's stood her in good stead as she fought the cancer several years ago."

"That must have been rough on your family."

Saul nodded. "Especially *Daed*. He insisted on being with her for every doctor appointment. Every chemo treatment. So I took over the store so he wouldn't have to be there."

"So why didn't he come back after everything was over? After she went into remission? She *is* in remission, right?"

"*Ya. Daed* decided he wanted to make the most of the time they have left. He'd worked so hard starting, then running the store."

"And he saw you'd done a good job."

He shrugged as if embarrassed at her words. "I had a good teacher in him."

Elizabeth turned the front door sign from OPEN to CLOSED and locked the door and Saul worked on the day's deposit.

"Would you mind if we stopped for a few minutes to look in on Miriam on the way?" he asked a little while later as they waited by the front door for their ride. "She's at home."

"You don't have to give me a ride—" she began.

"You can sit in the van if you don't want to go inside," he said quickly. "I'll just be a minute."

A short time later, he glanced at her when the driver pulled up in front of Miriam's home. "I think Miriam would like you to come in," he said. "Her husband said she was glad you insisted she go see a doctor."

The last thing she wanted to do was see a *boppli* . . . but she couldn't say so to Saul.

She got out of the van.

7

*H*e's beautiful," Elizabeth told Miriam.

In truth, the baby looked like a shriveled little pink peanut like so many newborns did. But what else could she say? Miriam and her husband, Leroy, were sitting there in their living room, the new baby cradled in Miriam's arms. And both parents were beaming.

"They sent you home already?" Saul asked.

"I had a baby, not a serious illness," Miriam told him with a chuckle.

"If you say so."

Miriam turned to Elizabeth. "Thank you for insisting I go see a doctor. She said many women don't recognize back labor." She tilted her head and studied Elizabeth. "But you did and you haven't ever had a baby."

"I come from a large family," Elizabeth said briefly.

Miriam covered her yawn with her hand. "Would you like to hold Daniel?"

"No," Elizabeth said quickly. Then, when the others stared at her, she tried to smile. "He looks like he's about to fall asleep there."

"Shall I go put him in his crib?" Leroy asked.

"I . . . guess," Miriam said slowly. "Tired, too." She blinked as her husband took the baby from her arms. "I think the day is . . . catching up with me."

Elizabeth frowned. Was she imagining Miriam looked pale and her eyes seemed a little glassy?

"Leroy, show Saul where we put the crib he gave us."

Saul followed Leroy from the room.

"Miriam? Why don't you go on to bed and I'll go wait for Saul in the van?" Elizabeth suggested.

The other woman stared at her for a long moment. "I—what?"

"You need to lie down. You're tired."

She shook her head. "I'm fine."

"Do you want me to fix you a cup of tea?"

Miriam frowned. "Yes, it would be nice. I can't seem to keep my eyes open."

"Why don't you go to bed? I'll call Saul—"

"No need to rush off. I can't go to bed anyway. Leroy's parents are coming over in a little while. They haven't seen the baby yet."

"I'll be right back. Why don't you stay put and rest?"

There was a knock on the door. Elizabeth went to answer it and found Phil standing on the porch.

"I'm sorry, but I need to make an emergency run to a pharmacy for a prescription for a client," he said. "Would you see if Saul would mind if I did it first and came back for the two of you?"

"I'm sure it's fine," she told him. "See you when you get back."

When she returned to the living room, she saw Miriam had taken her advice: she was lying on the sofa. As Elizabeth bent down to put the cup of tea on the table near the sofa, she frowned. Miriam just didn't look right. If anything, her face was paler.

Something made her touch the woman's forehead. It felt cold and clammy.

She jostled Miriam's shoulder. "Miriam? Are you feeling all right? Miriam?"

But the woman didn't rouse. Alarmed, Elizabeth backed away and glanced at the doorway. What was taking the men so long to return? She hurried down the hall and found them standing over the baby's crib.

"Leroy? I'm worried about Miriam. I think something's wrong with her."

"What's wrong?"

"One minute she was talking to me and the next she was slumping back on the sofa."

"She's probably just exhausted," Leroy said.

Elizabeth turned on her heel and walked back into the living room. Miriam hadn't moved. She shook her shoulder and called her name but the woman didn't stir.

"We should leave so she can get some rest."

Leroy knelt in front of his wife. "Miriam? Come on, I'll help you to bed. Miriam?"

When she didn't rouse, he turned to them. "She must be exhausted. I'll carry her to bed."

"No," Elizabeth said. "I think this is more than exhaustion." She turned to Saul. "May I borrow your cell phone?"

When he handed it to her, she tapped in Paula's cell phone number. "Paula's studying nursing. I'm going to ask her what to do." When Paula picked up, she said quickly, "It's Elizabeth. I'm worried about a friend. We stopped by to see her on the way home. She came home from having a baby today, and we're having trouble waking her. I think we should call 911."

"I agree," Paula said tersely. "I don't need to hear more. Hang up and do it right away."

Elizabeth hit disconnect and dialed 911, then gave the phone to Leroy when the dispatcher asked her for the address.

The baby began to cry. Leroy glanced in the direction of the baby's room, but Elizabeth touched his arm and indicated she'd go see to him.

She leaned over the crib and tried patting him gently on his back, but he just cried harder. She bit her lip and then with a sigh lifted him carefully from his crib and crooned to him. Still he cried.

"I know you want your *mamm*, but she can't come right now," she whispered, rocking him gently in her arms.

"Is he okay?" Saul asked her as he walked into the room.

"I think he's just hungry. I hope Miriam has some formula." She looked at him. "Saul, what are we going to do? I'm sure Leroy is going to want to go with Miriam to the hospital."

"Leroy says his parents will be here soon."

A siren came wailing down the road toward the house and pulled into the driveway. Saul held open the door and paramedics rushed into the living room. Elizabeth slipped into the kitchen with the baby to stay out of the way. She spotted a bag with the hospital's name on it and looked inside, sighing with relief when she saw the six pack of little bottles prefilled with formula. Her mother had brought home similar tote bags the last two times she'd had a baby and delivered them in the hospital instead of at home.

"We'll get some formula in your tummy right away," she promised Daniel.

Leroy came to the doorway and looked relieved when he saw her holding his son.

"We're staying until your parents get here," she told him. "You go with Miriam."

"*Danki*," he said, and a few minutes later she watched him follow the paramedics wheeling the gurney with Miriam out the front door.

The ambulance siren started up again, the sound growing fainter as it drove away. Elizabeth sat and touched the nipple of the bottle to the baby's mouth. He took it eagerly and the sound of his suckling filled the quiet kitchen.

❧

"Guess this is different from last night," Saul said.

They were sitting at the kitchen table. Elizabeth continued feeding the baby who stared owlishly at her. Saul drank a cup of coffee and watched them.

"What do you mean?"

"I saw your roommate brought a friend to pick you up yesterday."

"And?"

He reddened. "Nothing. Just making conversation."

Elizabeth didn't know what to say so she said nothing.

"Are you settling in okay? I mean, at the apartment. Things in general."

She nodded. "Paula has made me feel very comfortable. So has everyone at the store."

"*Gut.*"

"The town seems nice. It reminds me a little of Goshen."

"I've never been there."

"I've never been anywhere else."

He raised his brows. "This was a big step for you, then."

The baby closed its eyes and stopped sucking on the bottle. "Has it had enough?"

She touched the nipple to the baby's mouth and it roused a little and drank a bit more. Then Elizabeth set the bottle down, covered her shoulder with a clean cloth and placed the baby on it. She patted his back gently and a loud burp sounded in the quiet kitchen.

"Nice work," she murmured to him, then looked at Saul and smiled at him.

"We say 'nice work' now, and in a year or two scold them for burping."

"*Ya*," she agreed. She turned the baby in her arms and wiped a drop of milk from his mouth with the cloth.

"You're good with him."

"I should be," she muttered.

"How many *kinner* in your family?"

"Nine."

"I'll fix you a cup of coffee and hold him while you drink it."

She nodded and watched him pour it and bring it to the table. As he did, he heard his stomach growl.

"Well, we know it wasn't little Daniel's stomach."

Saul grinned. "You must be getting hungry, too."

"A little."

He held out his hands. "Give him to me and drink your coffee."

She leaned over and transferred the baby to his arms. As she did his hand accidentally brushed her arm and her eyes flew to his at the contact. He watched her blush, then turn her face away once he safely had the baby.

He was used to holding a *boppli*. People in his community loved children, saw them as a gift from God, so there were always *kinner* around. He and Lavina had talked about having *kinner* but it was over now and they had decided they weren't suited.

He wasn't worried. After all, he was only twenty-six. But he couldn't help thinking about how recently he'd thought he would be getting married in the fall, settling down, and maybe starting a family in the next year or so.

If anyone who didn't know them walked in right now they might have thought they were a family sitting like this around the table, sharing coffee and watching a baby sleep.

"If you're really hungry, I'm sure Miriam wouldn't mind if you fixed yourself a sandwich or something."

"True," he said. "Do you want something?"

She shook her head. "I can wait. I think Leroy's parents will be here soon, don't you?"

He nodded. "I do."

"I wonder what's wrong with her," Elizabeth said, biting her lip.

Saul reached into his pocket and checked his cell phone. "I guess it's too soon to hear anything yet."

"Maybe I should go pack a bag for the baby. You know, so he'll have everything he needs at his *grosseldre's* house. They might keep Miriam at the hospital."

She didn't say it, but the words hung unspoken on the air: she might not come back.

Elizabeth stood. "I'll go get them."

She found little sleepers, a pack of newborn disposable diapers, wipes, and toiletries and placed them in the diaper bag she found hanging on a peg. The room was furnished simply, as was the Plain way, but love was evident everywhere from the hand-carved crib Saul had given them, to the baby quilt folded over the side, to the rocker set in the corner.

When she returned to the kitchen, a buggy was pulling into the drive. Soon an older man and woman were rushing inside.

"Elizabeth, this is John and Linda, Leroy's parents."

Linda stared at the baby for a moment and tears filled her eyes. She touched his hand. "*Grossmudder's* here. I will take care of you."

Saul carefully handed the baby to her.

"Where's Leroy?" the man asked Saul.

"He went with Miriam to the hospital."

"I don't understand how they felt Miriam was well enough to come home and now she's back at the hospital." Tears rushed into the woman's eyes.

John patted her back. "I'm sure she'll be back soon."

"I packed some of the baby's things for you to take home," Elizabeth said. "The tote bag from the hospital there on the counter has enough formula to last for a day or so."

"*Danki.*"

"Elizabeth is helping us at the store while Miriam's out on maternity leave."

"Samuel and Saul have been *gut* to Miriam," Linda said with a nod.

"Well, we should be getting home," John said as he opened the door.

"Oh, you'll need the baby's car seat, too." She rushed back to the baby's room, retrieved it and carried it to the kitchen.

"We never had these when the *kinner* were growing up," the woman said, handing it to her husband. "Well, we'll be going."

Saul followed everyone out and locked the door behind him.

"How are you getting home?" John asked. "I don't see your buggy."

"My driver was called away for an emergency, but he'll be back soon," Saul told them. "We'll just wait out here for him."

He gestured for Elizabeth to sit in one of the rockers lined up on the front porch, then sat in one beside her. "Are you going to be warm enough?"

She buttoned the jacket she'd worn into work. "I'm fine." She waved at Leroy's parents as their buggy headed down the road. "Phil will be here soon."

He nodded, stretched out his long legs, and tried to focus on something other than his growing hunger. "Nice night."

"Was that your cell?" she asked him.

He pulled it out. "No. I could text him but I think I'll wait a little longer."

"My *mamm* always said 'no news is good news' but I'm having a little trouble with it."

"Phoebe would say worry is acting like God doesn't know what He's doing."

"Phoebe?"

"A friend of mine." He rocked for a moment. "Elizabeth, has anyone invited you to attend church?"

She stiffened, and it seemed to him a shutter came down over her expression. "No."

"I just thought maybe you missed it. I could pick you up."

"*Danki*, but . . . *nee*."

"I—okay," he said slowly. He didn't know what to say. A refusal was the last thing he'd expected. Why didn't she want to go to church?

Or was it she didn't want to go with him?

Car headlights approached. The van pulled into the drive.

Saul stood. "It's been a long day. It'll be good to get home, get something to eat, and relax."

"*Ya*," she said fervently.

"And even better, to hear how Miriam is doing. Thank you again for helping. I'm not sure Leroy or I would have known what to do if you hadn't been there to notice something was wrong."

He glanced at her as they walked down the porch steps. "Did you ever think about becoming a midwife?"

Elizabeth stumbled, and he reached out to grasp her arm and steady her.

"Have you ever thought about it?" he asked her as they approached the van.

"No," she said with such vehemence his brows went up.

"No," she said more quietly. "I've never been interested in it at all."

As held open the door to the van, he felt at a complete loss.

⌘

Paula looked up as Elizabeth walked into the apartment.

"You're home! Is everything all right?"

Elizabeth set her purse down on the sofa and sat down. "We still don't know. What do you think is wrong with Miriam?"

She hesitated, biting her lip. "I don't want to worry you."

Elizabeth frowned. "Now you've got me worried."

"It could be anything from something minor to something major. Anemia, infection, blood clot. I really wouldn't want to speculate. I'm just a nursing student, not a doctor."

"I've been at the hospital when my mother went in to have the last two babies. The nurses seemed to know as much as the doctors."

Paula grinned. "I can't wait to tell my instructors you said so. Listen, Bruce called. I told him I wasn't sure when you'd be in."

"I'll call him tomorrow."

"Is everything okay between the two of you?"

Elizabeth nodded. "We had fun at the movie."

"Have you had dinner?"

"No. I'm starved."

"Well, you're in luck. Mom and Dad stopped by. They brought a pan of her lasagna. I kept some warm for you."

"Oh, I'll get it," Elizabeth said when Paula started to get up.

"It's no trouble," Paula told her. She looked at Elizabeth. "Do you find it hard to let someone do something for you?"

Surprised, Elizabeth nodded.

"Well, I haven't been on my feet all day like you and then had to help with an emergency. C'mon, I'll keep you company while you eat." She chuckled as she pulled the food from the oven. "I'll just have another little piece. Well, maybe not so little. Mom's lasagna is one of my favorites."

Elizabeth poured them both a glass of iced tea and took a seat at the kitchen island.

"You're awfully quiet," Paula remarked a few minutes later. "Quieter than usual," she amended. "You seem sad."

"I'm just a little tired, that's all."

"You sure?"

Elizabeth put her fork down and swiveled in her chair. "It's just it reminds me of why I left Indiana," she blurted out.

"Okay," Paula said slowly. "Tell me."

"You'll think I'm an awful person."

Paula's eyes widened. "I wouldn't think that of you. What could you have possibly done?"

Elizabeth pressed her hands to her face, then dropped them into her lap. "Everyone back home—everyone Amish—they love babies and see them as a blessing from God. But I got to where I felt . . . smothered. All I did was help *Mamm* with them and the chores."

Her throat felt dry. She took a sip of tea. "Working at the fabric store was an escape."

Paula looked at her sympathetically. "I'm sorry. I always wanted a brother or sister, but I guess if you feel you have too many and you're a babysitter, it's no fun, either."

"I felt so guilty—so selfish—about wanting to get out for a little while," Elizabeth confessed, reassured Paula wasn't judging her. "We're supposed to help each other."

"You didn't have anyone to talk to about it?"

She shook her head. "Not after I graduated from school. So it just built and built inside me. I had to get away."

Paula took the plates and loaded them into the dishwasher. "You want some pineapple upside-down cake? Mom brought some."

"Maybe later."

"C'mon, let's go sit in the living room."

Elizabeth took her glass of tea and sat on the sofa. She glanced at the laptop Paula had been working on. "How's your paper going?"

"Almost finished. I'm taking a break, and then I hope to get the draft done before bed. It's due day after tomorrow."

"How did you decide you wanted to be a nurse?"

Paula smiled. "I've wanted to be one since I was a little girl. My dolls were always covered with Band-Aids and getting their arms splinted." She studied Elizabeth. "Why do you ask?"

Elizabeth shrugged. "Saul asked me if I'd considered becoming a midwife, because I seemed good at knowing something was wrong with Miriam."

"You don't sound happy about him suggesting it."

"I wasn't," she said flatly. "It's the last thing I want to do."

"Then you shouldn't. You have to love what you do or work is unpleasant. And who needs someone unhappy around them when they're having a baby? I'm curious. When you were a kid, did anyone ask you what you wanted to be when you grew up?"

"My teacher did, but we don't have as many choices as you do in the *Englisch* world." She glanced at the clock on the wall and stood. "I'm tired. I think I'll go on to bed and let you get your paper finished."

"Okay." Paula said. "Let me know if you want to talk about it. You don't have to . . . settle . . . if you don't want to."

"I will." She started to walk away and then turned. "Paula?"

She looked up from her laptop. "Yes?"

"Thanks."

Paula smiled. "No need for thanks. I'm glad you're here."

8

Elizabeth was finishing up with her last customer of the day when Bruce walked into the store.

She fumbled with the shopping bag she was handing to the customer but managed to recover and smile at her.

Bruce strolled up to the counter and grinned. "Hey there. Thought I'd stop by and see if you wanted to get something to eat, maybe do something."

Elizabeth glanced around. Saul. Where was Saul? Then she remembered. He'd gone into the back room to work on ordering supplies. "I can't. Paula's coming to get me."

"I could call her," he said as he pulled his cell phone from his pocket.

"I can't. We're having supper with her parents. I haven't met them yet."

"But—" he began.

"Bruce, I'm at work. I can't talk to you now."

"It's nearly time to close," he said as he checked his watch. "There can't be any harm—"

"Bruce!" She saw Saul enter the store space and smile at a customer. She needed to get rid of Bruce. "Really, I can't talk to you now. I'm new here and there's my boss!"

He backed away. "Okay, okay. But I can be a customer." He turned and looked around at the shelves.

"Everything okay?" Saul asked as he came to stand near the counter.

"It's fine," she said brightly. "I sold another quilt."

"Wonderful," he said. "We had a good day. It's time to close up. Why don't you go on since your . . . friend is here?" he said, his attention clearly on Bruce.

Elizabeth flushed with embarrassment. "I told him I can't talk during work. I'm sorry, I didn't ask him to come here. Paula is picking me up and we're going to her parents for dinner."

"It's *allrecht*, Elizabeth. But I meant it. You can leave now. Just turn the sign to CLOSED as you go out."

"I'm not leaving until you do," she said, lifting her chin. "I work a full day."

Saul lifted his hands and let them fall. "Have it your way. Go turn the sign around and lock the door. I'll make out a deposit slip."

She did as he asked, and on her way back to the counter, Bruce stopped her. "Can you ring this up for me?"

"You want a child's wooden pull toy."

"Yeah. I'm getting it for a nephew. He'll be one a few weeks after Christmas."

"You're sure?"

He handed it to her. "Yes. Do you have some moral objection to me starting my Christmas shopping early?" he asked, his eyes twinkling.

She tried to hold back a smile but couldn't resist his charm. "No, Bruce. Cash or charge?"

"Charge."

Elizabeth stepped behind the counter to make the transaction. "I have one more sale for the day," she murmured to Saul.

"I see." He nodded at Bruce. "Do you have children?"

Bruce laughed and shook his head. "No, it's for my sister's boy."

"Saul, this is Bruce, a friend of mine and Paula's."

"Nice to meet you," Bruce said. "You have great stuff."

"Thank you."

Elizabeth handed Bruce the credit slip to sign, wrapped the toy in tissue, and tucked it into one of the store bags. She turned to Saul. "I guess I'll go get my purse if you don't need anything else from me."

"Actually, I do have a question for you," Saul said. "Bruce, if you'll excuse us for just a moment,"

"No prob," Bruce said. "I guess I'll be going." He strolled toward the door.

Curious, Elizabeth turned to Saul. "A question?"

"I'm sorry I was late getting payroll together today," he said. "It doesn't happen often."

"It's no problem." She watched him open the cash drawer, withdraw an envelope, and hold it out to her.

"It's too late to get to the bank right now," he said. "I can cash it for you if you like. Or you can take it to the bank tomorrow since you have the day off."

"Cash would be good. I haven't opened an account here yet."

He nodded. "Just sign it and give it back." He began counting out money and handed it to her after she handed him the check. "Just be careful, *allrecht*?"

"I will."

"Did you think about going to church on Sunday?"

She stood there, biting her lip. It was hard to say yes—not to the man, but to the idea of walking into a new church. She told herself it was church, not a date. It didn't mean she had to commit to either for more than the three hours that the church service lasted. . . .

Church had always been important to her. She'd left her home to find a place of peace for herself. Going to church might be the road to finding it here. She knew Saul and his parents. It would be three people she'd know. . . .

She nodded and he smiled at her. Saul had such a nice smile. "I'll pick you up."

Elizabeth went into the back room to get her purse. She remembered his caution about carrying the cash so she tucked the bills into her pocket instead of her wallet in her purse.

When she emerged, Saul was zipping up a night deposit bag. "Have a good evening."

Elizabeth smiled and wished him one, too. Her steps were light as she walked toward the front door. Her first paycheck! she thought.

Then she stopped. Her first paycheck here and she didn't have to hand it over to anyone. Well, she owed some to Paula.

But she didn't have to hand the check over to her parents. A thought struck her and she headed down the aisle to a shelf near the front door. Smiling, she picked up the little carved wooden bird she'd been admiring and carried it back to the counter.

"You okay?"

She grinned at him. "More than okay," she told him. "My money's mine!"

"Well, of course it is," he said, staring at her with a frown of confusion. Then after a moment, the frown cleared. "Oh, I see. Well, I'm sure you'll spend it wisely."

Chuckling, she nodded. "*Ya.* On luxuries like my share of the rent and something called utilities. I can't wait to tell Paula!" She pushed the bird toward him. "I'm buying this. I get an employee discount, right?"

He smiled at her. "Of course. So you like sparrows, eh?"

Elizabeth counted out the money and insisted on wrapping it in tissue herself and tucking it into a store bag. The little bird would sit on the desk in her room and be a reminder to her how God provided.

She said good night to him and walked out of the store. She'd just gotten paid. And she had a day off tomorrow. Now she felt like skipping. A day off with nothing to do. Imagine. What did people do on a day off? She'd never had one. There were always chores to do on an Amish farm. Cooking to be done. Babies to be cared for. What would she do with herself tomorrow?

Paula pulled up just as she walked outside. She could ask her about what to do on a day off although she didn't think Paula did a lot of relaxing because she was attending school and doing something called a clinical, at the hospital several days a week. Well, she'd figure it out.

⟳

Saul watched Elizabeth get in Paula's car and drive away. He looked around and saw Bruce walking toward a car. He must have waited outside for a last chance to talk to Elizabeth, Saul mused.

The other man had the easy, confident walk of an *Englischman*—like he didn't have a care in the world. He'd overheard Elizabeth telling Bruce she couldn't go out with him that night. Evidently, the rejection hadn't bothered Bruce.

As he nodded at his driver and got into the van for the drive home, Saul wondered why Bruce was interested in Elizabeth. Not that he didn't have good reason, of course. She was pretty and very sweet.

But Saul hadn't heard good things about why *Englisch* guys dated Amish girls. And he cared about her too much to see her hurt.

He had some thinking to do.

"You're kind of quiet tonight," his mother said as she served him a second bowl of stew. Then she passed him the plate of cornbread.

"Everything okay at the store?" his father asked.

Saul nodded and took a sip of water. "We had a really good day today. Maybe later we should talk about Christmas inventory."

"No work talk at the supper table!" Waneta admonished. "We run the store, the store doesn't run us!"

His parents made a great team, but his *mamm* got the last word at the supper table, insisting it was family time. And since she was the heart of the home, they listened.

"I'm picking Elizabeth up for church this Sunday," Saul said casually after there had been silence for a few minutes. "Just wanted to let you know so you won't be surprised."

His parents exchanged a look.

"I just thought she might like to attend," Saul said. "It doesn't seem to me she's ready to give up being Amish. I thought inviting her might make her feel more comfortable."

"I wonder if her family is related to Matthew Bontrager? Samuel, didn't one of Matthew's great-uncles move to Goshen back in, oh, the '40s?"

Samuel nodded. "You'll have to introduce them Sunday, Saul."

"Good idea." He polished off his cornbread and cleared the dinner plates, so his mother could cut slices of her sour cream chocolate cake.

He found himself thinking about Elizabeth's remark earlier in the day about her check belonging to her. Many Amish children contributed a portion of their paychecks to the family when they continued to live at home. It sounded like Elizabeth had done it, too—maybe more—and was happy to have it for herself. She didn't strike him as selfish. And if she lived with a roommate now, she certainly needed all of her check.

Saul contributed a portion of his check to his parents for room and board. And considering how much he ate, he didn't think they were making money on him.

"Something funny?" Samuel asked, breaking into Saul's thoughts.

"Not really."

They heard a knock on the door. Saul went to the door and welcomed in their next-door neighbor.

"I'll come back and do the dishes," he promised and Waneta nodded and began talking with the neighbor. They settled at the kitchen table and he and his father took their mugs of coffee into the den.

"About those orders," he said.

His father cast a wistful look at his armchair and newspaper. "We have to do this tonight?"

"You know we do. A wise man once told me to look ahead."

"And you listened too well," his mother said, startling Saul as she entered the room. "You think too much about work lately. Go do something else."

"Like what?"

She shook her head. "You've done nothing since you came back from visiting Lavina. Go take a walk or something. Visit a friend. Shoo!" she said, flapping her hands.

Saul cast a look at his father, but the man was nodding.

"Fine," he said. "I'll go take a walk."

"*Gut*," his father told him.

"You're only agreeing with her because you want to read your paper. I guess you'll help her with the dishes, since I offered."

His mother brightened. "Right. Come on, Samuel. I'll wash and you can dry."

Saul grinned as he headed for the door. It would serve to teach his father not to join forces with his mother against him.

Grabbing his jacket, he stepped outside and felt how the temperature had cooled. He pulled his collar up around his neck and shoved his hands in his pockets. His mother was right. She usually was. He knew he'd been working too hard and not getting out much. When he thought about it, he couldn't remember the last time he'd done anything with his best friend. He'd spent too much time courting Lavina and neglected him. It was time he fixed that.

A buggy rolled past on the road and a neighbor who lived a few houses away waved at him. "Need a ride?" he called.

Saul shook his head. "Enjoying a walk, thanks!"

The buggy reminded Saul he should see if his needed cleaning before Sunday. A man should pick up a woman in a buggy that wasn't dusty or needed attention whether she was a friend or a woman you hoped would become your *fraa*.

The sun's rays turned the low-lying clouds rosy pink and gold, signaling the night would turn cooler. Dusk fell and the gentle glow of gas lamps and battery-powered lights shone in windows. Families settled in for the night.

And Saul suddenly felt the pang of loneliness in his heart. He looked away from the homes, turned back in the direction of his own and trudged home.

Elizabeth woke at her usual time and started to bound out of bed as usual.

Then she remembered: it was her day off.

Her day off! She breathed in the wonder of it and savored the feeling of lying abed. She'd always secretly envied the princesses in the storybooks she read as a girl and always felt like Cinderella toiling while her stepsisters enjoyed a life of leisure. It wasn't helped by the fact Mary, the second oldest, never seemed to want to help at home.

This must be what it felt like.

She drifted back to sleep for a few minutes, but years of rising early and being dutiful and hard-working—and Amish to the bone—had made her feel lazy lying in bed.

So she compromised by getting up, pulling on her robe, and going to the kitchen to quietly make herself a pot of coffee.

Paula staggered out, bleary eyed and yawning a half hour later.

"I smelled something amazing," she mumbled as she hauled herself into a bar stool. Elizabeth turned from the stove to hand her a mug of coffee. "Are you making blueberry pancakes?"

Little bubbles formed at the edges of one of the pancakes. Elizabeth nudged at it with a spatula then expertly flipped it over.

"I have a day off, remember? So I'm fixing pancakes for us."

"Awesome." She slid off the stool and got the maple syrup.

Elizabeth flipped a pancake, then another, onto a plate and set it before Paula. She did the same with two for herself and joined her at the island.

"Mmm," Paula said, rolling her eyes as she put the first bite of pancake in her mouth. "So, what are your plans today, oh Lady of Leisure?"

She laughed. "I don't know. What does someone do with a day off?"

Paula stopped chewing a bite of pancake. "You're serious?"

"Very much. I have no idea what I'll do with it. Maybe clean the apartment and—"

"Don't you dare! You should have fun." She tilted her head and considered Elizabeth. "Do you know how to have fun?" She clapped a hand to her mouth. "Oh, I shouldn't have said that! It sounds so critical!"

"It's okay. I guess we do look pretty serious to outsiders," Elizabeth told her. "But we do know how to have fun. We even know how to turn work into a work frolic and have fun." She hoped she didn't sound defensive; she knew Paula was teasing.

"Promise me you'll do something to have fun today. I'll be home by four and if you haven't got plans with Bruce we can go to dinner or a movie or something."

"That would be great. Or as the Amish here say, *wunderbaar.*"

Paula started to pick up her empty plate, but Elizabeth shooed her off to get dressed. She found Paula's travel mug and filled it with coffee, adding the milk and diet sweetener her roommate liked, and set it on the table by the front door next to the bowl for their keys.

"Thank you!" Paula called, saluting Elizabeth with the mug as she opened the door. "Be thinking of what you want to do when I come home!"

Then the apartment became quiet. Elizabeth hummed as she loaded the dishwasher. She poured the dishwasher soap into the dispenser but only a few grains of the stuff fell into it. Sighing, she threw the empty box into the kitchen trash can and wrote "dishwasher soap" on the grocery list on the refrigerator. Paula had a habit of putting almost-empty things like cartons of juice and soda bottles back in the refrigerator. She didn't know why, but figured it was just one of Paula's quirks.

She looked around the kitchen and spied the bottle of dishwashing liquid sitting on the sink. It should work. She poured some into the place where you put the powder dishwashing stuff, snapped the lid on it and closed the dishwasher door. A push of a button and the dishes were soon getting washed without any work. She'd never minded washing dishes but this certainly made things easy.

More time to enjoy a day off . . .

She walked into the bathroom to brush her teeth and saw the bottle of bubble bath sitting on the edge of the tub. Paula loved relaxing in a bubble bath, but Elizabeth had never had time for one. Back home in Goshen, she was lucky if she got to take a quick shower with just the one bathroom and so many other people in the family.

But there was time on a day off. She started the water running and wandered back to the kitchen. A cup of tea in the tub sounded like pure luxury.

That's when she saw the bubbles pouring from the dishwasher.

Screeching in alarm, she ran into the room, slipped and slid into the counter. Rubbing her hip, she frantically punched the stop button and then turned to grab several dishtowels from a drawer. She threw them down and mopped up the excess water, wringing them out in the sink several times.

Walking carefully so she wouldn't slip again, she got the mop and quickly mopped the floor. Oh well, the job was done for another week.

Then she heard running water. The bathtub! Clutching the mop, she ran for the bathroom and found the water slipping over the side. She sloshed through the water and turned off the spigot. Once again, she found herself mopping. When she finished she returned the mop to the storage closet in the kitchen and sagged against the door. The morning wasn't over and she felt exhausted. Well, it had been a morning full of water. She might as well go sit in some of it.

So, she fixed a cup of tea and went to soak in the tub, reveling in the vanilla-scented bubbles. Candles sat on the edge of the tub, but she decided not to light them after her misadventures.

She reluctantly got out of the tub and toweled dry after her toes and fingertips turned pruny. No need to get dressed yet. She wrapped up in her robe and wandered back into the living room.

What now? Paula had teased her calling her a lady of leisure. Television was a favorite leisure activity of the *Englisch*. Elizabeth had watched a few shows with Paula, but since Paula had to study so often the television usually got turned off early.

She plopped down on the sofa and spent the next ten minutes figuring out the remote. Paula had shown her how, but there had been so much to learn about this way of life, she'd forgotten.

After she learned how to start the television, she pressed the control and flipped through the channels. Oh, the things she saw. Commercials for sexy underwear she'd never known existed. Shows with couples arguing and someone seeming to urge them to do more . . . someone who called himself a counselor. And, oh my—couples taking off their clothes. She quickly changed the channel and found a show about puppies on Animal Planet.

A little while later she realized she was hungry. She didn't want to eat too much because she and Paula were planning to go out, so she found a can of soup, opened it, and put it in a pan on the stove. Paula had shown her how to use the microwave but she didn't feel comfortable with the appliance and besides, she'd put the soup in a metal pan before she thought about it and it couldn't go into the microwave.

So many new things to learn. So much to remember. She found herself wondering what was happening back home and decided to go check the mail. Maybe her mother had gotten her letter and answered her. She went to check the mailbox, careful to lock the door behind her, and found a handful of bills—and a letter from Goshen!

Thrilled, she carried the mail back to the apartment and sat happily on the sofa to read it. Her smile faded when she opened it.

"I can't believe your utter selfishness," she read. "Your mother needed your help, and you didn't care. You need to come back where you belong and do your duty to your family. God is frowning on your behavior. I'm praying for you."

Elizabeth knew the name of the letter writer before she glanced down at the signature. Her *grossmudder*—her mother's mother had always been a very stern woman, never showing her or any of her brothers and sisters any affection.

She blinked back tears rushing into her eyes, refusing to let them fall. Then she realized her eyes were burning. A shrill siren sound came from the kitchen. Jumping up, she ran into the room and found the pan of soup smoking. She grabbed at the handle, yelped when she burned herself, and turned off the burner underneath the pan.

Panicked, her ears ringing from the alarm, she looked wildly around for something to turn off the noise. She flapped at the smoke with a kitchen towel, but the alarm kept shrieking. Throwing down the towel, she ran from the apartment and knocked on the first door she came to.

An older lady opened it. "Yes?"

"Please help me," she said quickly. "I don't know how to turn off the smoke alarm."

"Oh, no problem, dear." The woman walked to the apartment with her, opened the kitchen closet, and pulled out a broom.

Broom. Now Elizabeth felt dumb. She remembered Paula turning off the alarm with the end of the broom handle when smoke poured from the toaster.

The woman turned to Elizabeth. "Are you sure you want me to do this?"

Elizabeth felt unnerved by the racket. "Yes!"

"If you say so." She lifted the broom and used the wooden end to nudge the center button on the alarm. It immediately went silent. "I just think you might have enjoyed the cute firemen from the local station."

"Well, well, what's going on?" Paula asked with a grin as she walked into the apartment. "Looks like you've been having some excitement here."

9

Elizabeth jumped when she heard a knock on the door.

"He's here!" Paula sang from her perch on the living room sofa. Then she frowned. "You don't look very happy."

She bit her lip, then blurted, "I changed my mind. I don't want to go."

"Why not?"

"I won't know anyone."

"The only way to know them is to meet them," Paula said practically. "C'mon, you'll enjoy it."

"Why don't you join us?"

Paula pulled another tissue from the box beside her and wiped her nose. "I don't think I'd be welcome with this cold. You go and tell me all about it later."

"I should stay home and make you some soup."

"I have a can of chicken and stars in the cupboard."

Elizabeth wrinkled her nose. "I'm sure it's not as good as my chicken soup."

"Then you can make me some when you come home. Now get the door," she said as they heard another knock.

Then, just as Elizabeth put her hand on the door, Paula hissed, "And smile!"

Elizabeth summoned up a smile and opened the door. And then she blinked at the sight of Saul. He looked so handsome in his Sunday best white shirt, dark jacket, and pants.

"*Guder mariye*," he said, giving her a big smile. "How are you today?"

They heard a big sneeze just as she shut the door. "*Gut*, unlike my roommate," she told him. "I'm afraid she has a very bad cold."

"I'm sorry to hear it." He began walking down the hallway with her. "The cold and flu season seems to be getting an early start this year."

Elizabeth didn't expect the reaction she had when they walked outside and she saw Saul's buggy. She stood there, hesitating for just a moment and then he was holding out his hand to help her inside, evidently taking her inaction for the need for help.

She glanced around the interior as he walked to his side, noting how clean and well-kept it was.

He noticed her looking around and lifted one eyebrow at her. "Everything okay?"

"Of course." She smoothed her hand over the skirt of her dress. "I just haven't ridden in a buggy since I left Goshen."

"I see."

He lifted the reins and the horse began moving out into the road. "It's a fine day for a buggy ride," he told her. "Not a cloud in sight."

Elizabeth found her nerves settling a bit as the buggy rolled along, the movement and the sound of the wheels on the road and the horse's hooves clip-clopping a reminder of traveling back home. Memories of riding with her parents and her brothers and sisters, riding to church on Sunday morning, suddenly swamped her.

She must have made a sound because Saul touched her hand, asking, "Are you okay?"

"Fine," she managed, grateful the bonnet she wore kept him from scanning her face. "Will your parents be there?"

"Of course. So there's two—make it three—people you know. Oh, and Katie and Rosie."

She glanced at him. How had he known she'd been a little uncomfortable about walking into church and not knowing anyone?

"I expect things will be a little different from what you're used to back home, too," he said. "Every district is a bit different from what I hear."

He was right. Her clothing would mark her as someone who'd come from outside Pennsylvania. She much preferred the distinctive organdy *kapps* with their heart-shaped backs— some called them butterfly shapes, but she thought they looked like hearts—the women wore here to her own stiff, pleated one.

If she stayed—and when she had the money—she'd change her *kapp* and clothing to the style of the Lancaster County Amish women. The dresses here were very similar to the Indiana and Ohio dresses. Some Indiana Amish women wore dresses with tiny pleats on the skirts while the Lancaster County skirts were just gathered at the waist.

The biggest difference she hoped to make in her appearance would be to one day own more than three dresses she'd worn for years. There had been little money for new, and even when her boss at the fabric store offered her a wonderful discount, Elizabeth hadn't been able to find the time to sew anything for herself.

"Did you have a good day off?"

She tried not to grimace. "It was different," she said finally. "I'm not used to having time on my hands."

"Enjoy it while you can," he told her. "Leroy called me and Miriam may need more time off. I didn't ask for specifics—it's private. But she needed a few days for treatment in the hospital, so it's possible we'll need you longer."

Elizabeth felt a mixture of emotion at hearing the news . . . it was good for her to have the job longer, but she didn't like that Miriam being ill was the reason.

"We'll be getting busier at the shop soon. You could be asked to work overtime."

"It's fine. I don't mind."

The site of the home hosting the church service came into view. The homes in this area looked as large as those back in Indiana. The Amish believed in big families so many of their homes featured additions as the number of their *kinner* increased.

Home would always be big, too, because so much took place there—most importantly, church services. Faith began in the home and so it was natural for services to take place there. And hundreds of years didn't erase why the Amish had emigrated to this country to begin with. Elizabeth could vividly remember the lessons she'd learned in *schul* about how the Amish had been persecuted for their religion in Europe.

Saul pulled into the drive behind other buggies. Men and boys unhitched horses and led them into the barn so they didn't have to stand in harness for the three hours of the church service. Women and girls made their way inside the home. Just like Goshen, she thought as Saul stopped the buggy and she got out. It gave her comfort. She'd missed church—the message, the singing, the fellowship afterward sharing a light meal and talking.

"You should have gone inside," Saul said when he joined her on the front porch.

She opened her mouth to confess that she felt reluctant to meet so many new people at once—there looked to be about seventy-five men, women and children attending—but then a woman rushed up.

"Elizabeth, Saul, *guder mariye!*"

At last, a familiar face. Elizabeth smiled at Saul's mother. "*Guder mariye,* Waneta."

"It's *gut* to see you here. Let's go in, shall we?" She didn't wait for an answer but slipped her arm in Elizabeth's and sailed along to the front door with her.

Elizabeth glanced helplessly at Saul and saw him grinning at her.

"Samuel will be along as soon as he parks the buggy," Waneta called over her shoulder.

Within a few minutes, Elizabeth couldn't say she didn't know anyone. Waneta introduced her to everyone she passed, so by the time they sat with the women waiting for the service to begin, Elizabeth wondered how she'd remember them all.

Saul took a seat in the men's section and looked in her direction. He raised his eyebrows in a silent question and she nodded. His quiet smile warmed her heart.

The service began. Voices rose in pure harmony around her—hymns she'd sung at her church for as far back as she could remember. She began singing and felt peace settling over her. Paula had been right; she'd needed this.

One of the lay ministers spoke about Jeremiah 29:11: For I know the thoughts that I think toward you, says the Lord, thoughts of peace and not of evil, to give you a future and a hope.

Elizabeth liked it. From the moment she had remembered the words about God providing for sparrows, she had felt comforted she would be provided for. She didn't expect to just sit around without doing what she should for herself, but if He cared about little creatures like a sparrow, she felt He'd provide for her, too. Parents did it for their children and He was, after all, her Father.

All her life Elizabeth had heard about God's will. Her grandmother had talked about it like God wielded his will like a giant whip to keep His children in line. But Elizabeth had been so unhappy she hadn't been able to stay in Goshen. She'd run away, taken a road that led her here, and if this hadn't been His plan for her, well, surely He would have stopped her, wouldn't He?

Instead, she had a safe, warm place to live with a wonderful friend who treated her better than her family had. She loved her job, even though she knew it was temporary. And instead of one man, she had two who seemed interested in her.

Life is good, she thought, and she found herself exchanging a smile with Waneta as they began singing hymns once again.

Saul walked over to them after the service. "I hope you're glad you came." He turned to his mother. "We're going to go have lunch. I'll see you at home later."

"Oh, no, don't go rushing off!" Waneta exclaimed. "I have a few more people I want her to meet. Just a few more minutes!"

"It's okay," Elizabeth reassured Saul.

"Let's go help with the food," Waneta said as the men began moving benches around and creating places for people to sit and eat.

But just as they approached the kitchen someone called to Waneta, and she turned to Elizabeth. "I'll be right there."

Buoyed by the friendly reception she'd had so far, Elizabeth walked into the kitchen by herself. Two women her age had their backs to her as they unwrapped plates of food.

"So what do you think of the Indiana woman?"

Elizabeth stopped in the doorway. Were they talking about her?

"I can't imagine Saul being interested in her. Lavina was much prettier. Wonder what happened to her."

Someone touched her elbow and she jumped. She turned and found herself staring into the sympathetic gray eyes of a middle-aged woman.

"If you think that's bad you should have heard how they used to talk about me," the woman whispered. "Come on, let's go outside and talk."

Mystified, Elizabeth followed her.

❧

Saul talked with a friend for a few minutes and then he looked around. His mother had promised she'd keep Elizabeth for just a few minutes, but it had now been fifteen.

He poked his head into the kitchen, but didn't find either of them there.

"Saul!" Lillian turned and smiled at him. "How are you?"

"Uh, fine, *danki*," he said, staying in the doorway. She was either flirting with him or she had something in her eyes. "Have you seen Elizabeth?"

The eye fluttering stopped and her voice turned cool. "Is that the girl from Indiana I saw your mother sitting next to?"

He nodded. "Have you seen her?"

"*Nee*. So how have you been, Saul?"

"*Gut*. Uh—oh, *Mamm*, have you seen Elizabeth?"

She looked around. "I thought she was in here."

"I'll look outside." He hurried away.

He found her standing near the front door, talking with Jenny Bontrager. He wasn't surprised. Jenny would reach out to newcomers since she'd been something of one herself once. Although her father chose to reject the Amish faith, Jenny came here a few summers before she went off to college and to work for a big network in New York City.

Then a terrible bombing overseas changed everything for Jenny. Her grandmother, Leah King, invited her to recuperate here and Jenny married the man next door she'd loved as a teenager. Saul knew the story because some in the congregation hadn't accepted Jenny at first and they hadn't been convinced she'd really convert to the Amish faith—or stay.

They looked up as he approached.

"Elizabeth, there you are," he said, relieved. "And you've met someone I was going to introduce you to. Jenny, Elizabeth here is a Bontrager. *Daed* said some Bontragers from this area moved to Indiana. He wondered if Elizabeth could be a cousin of your husband, Matthew."

Jenny beamed at Elizabeth. "Wouldn't it be wonderful? I'll ask Matthew. He's out of town for a few days." She looked around. "Did your parents come with you today?"

Saul watched Elizabeth's expression grow shuttered. "No, they're back in Goshen. I'm here by myself."

"Oh," Jenny said. "I didn't realize. Have you visited this area before?"

"No. I'm staying with a friend and working at Saul's store. He brought me to church today."

"I see," Jenny said, and she gave Saul an assessing look.

A toddler squealed and ran toward Jenny. She scooped her up and planted kisses on her cheeks. "Elizabeth, this is Rosanna, my granddaughter. Say, Rosie, where's your *mamm*?"

She glanced at Elizabeth. "I loved having children, but having grandchildren is even better!"

"Rosanna, you're wearing me out!" a woman cried as she rushed up.

"And here's my daughter, Mary," Jenny said, smiling at her. "Ready to go?"

"More than," Mary responded.

Jenny turned to Elizabeth. "I'll be talking to Matthew. It'd be so nice to find out we're all related. Have a wonderful day." She nodded at Saul as she walked out the door.

"Are you ready to go?" he asked Elizabeth.

She glanced at the kitchen and frowned, then nodded. "More than."

He looked back at the kitchen. "Something wrong?"

"It's nothing."

"I'll go get the buggy."

"So, I finally get to buy you the Big Mac I promised you when I first met you," he said as they rolled along the road to town.

"It's not a date," she reminded him.

"I remember." He tried not to mind how firm she sounded about it.

She looked at him, then away. "It seems like such a long time ago, but it was just last month."

"Still happy you're here?"

"Of course. How much farther is it?"

"Not much. Are you hungry—or wanting me to stop asking you questions?"

She jerked around to stare at him. Then she pressed her lips together as if trying to suppress a smile. "A little of both."

"I thought we could get it to go and eat at a park not far from here."

"The park sounds nice."

"Big Mac, fries, Diet Coke? Anything else?"

"Sounds good."

She said it wasn't a date but it felt like one to him as he drove them to the park and they got out to eat their meal at a picnic bench overlooking a pond. The park was small and few people were here today.

They talked about the week at the store, about the church service, and how fall was in the air. A mother walked with her little girl to the pond's edge.

"So how did you fare talking to Jenny?" he asked her as he ripped open a packet of ketchup and squeezed it over his French fries. "Jenny's notorious for asking questions. She was a television reporter years ago."

"Jenny?"

"Before she came here to stay with her grandmother and married Matthew, she worked overseas. She used to be *Englisch*."

She glanced over at the pond. The little girl giggled as several ducks ran up onto the grass and seemed to argue with each other who was going to be first to get the piece of bread she held.

He popped a fry in his mouth and chewed. "Bet Jenny could get you to talk, mystery lady."

"I'm not a mystery lady," she said quietly. "And if I told you about me, you wouldn't think much of me."

"Not true."

She met his gaze. "I ran away from home because I got so tired of helping my family," she blurted out. "There. What do you think of me now?"

❦

The apartment was quiet when Elizabeth let herself in.

Paula snuggled under a blanket in the same corner of the sofa she'd been in when Elizabeth left for church. She clutched a handful of tissues and her face looked a little pink. Elizabeth thought about touching her forehead to see if she had a fever but was afraid of waking her.

She tiptoed into the kitchen, pulled a pot from a cupboard, and quietly placed it on a burner on the stove. Then she began assembling the ingredients for chicken noodle soup. The act of chopping onions and carrots and sautéing them in the pot soothed her. Soon the scent of simmering chicken noodle soup filled the apartment.

Paula sneezed and sat up. "Smells good," she said huskily. She shuffled into the kitchen wearing pink pajamas and a pair of fluffy bunny slippers.

"It'll be ready soon."

"Good." Paula took a carton of orange juice from the refrigerator and poured herself a glass, drank it down, then poured another.

"You look flushed. Have you got a thermometer?"

"Yeah." She slumped onto a bar stool at the kitchen island and watched Elizabeth stir the soup.

"In your medicine cabinet?"

"Yeah." Paula rubbed the glass over her forehead but she didn't move.

Elizabeth bit back a smile. "I'll go get it."

"Thanks."

She found the thermometer and when she returned to the kitchen she handed it to Paula. When Paula stared at it blankly, Elizabeth withdrew the thermometer from its case and held it out to her.

"I can't pick your tongue up and put it underneath," she said dryly. "You have to do it."

Paula laughed. "Sorry. I feel like a slug right now." She put the thermometer in her mouth. When she withdrew it she frowned. "It's 101. Guess I'll take something for it."

Elizabeth went in search of some ibuprofen, and when she returned she found Paula sound asleep on the sofa. She woke her to take the pills with a glass of water, got her to take off her slippers, and covered her with the blanket.

She returned to the stove and stirred the soup, then set the timer before she went into her bedroom to change out of her Sunday dress. The soup needed to simmer, so she lay down on her bed and read for a while.

When she walked down the hall to return to the kitchen she heard a male voice. Very strange. She hadn't heard anyone knock on the apartment door.

Then she stepped into the living room and saw Paula sitting up, leaning forward, and talking at her laptop screen. She saw the image of a man with short, blond hair dressed in the camouflage uniform of the military.

"Elizabeth! Come here!" Paula said, waving her hand. "Jason, this is Elizabeth, my roommate."

"He's in the computer?" Elizabeth murmured as she walked over and sat on the sofa next to Paula.

"We're Skyping," Paula told her. "He's sitting at a computer at his base. It has a camera on it just like this one. Say hi."

"Hi, Jason."

"Hey, Elizabeth!" Jason grinned. "I hear you're taking good care of my girl."

"I haven't done much." She glanced at the pot on the stove, not wanting a repeat of what had happened the other day. "If you'll excuse me, I'll let you two talk. Nice to meet you."

"Nice to meet you, too," Jason said. "Now, Paula, wait 'til you hear my good news."

Not wanting to eavesdrop, Elizabeth hurried into the kitchen and peered into the pot. It smelled delicious.

But even though she tried not to eavesdrop, she heard kissy noises coming from the living room. She grinned and put the lid back on the pan.

Paula wandered back into the kitchen. "Jason had some great news. He's getting some R and R—vacation time—next month. I can't wait for you to meet him."

"How wonderful. Are you ready for some soup?"

"Love some." She climbed back onto a bar stool.

Elizabeth carefully ladled soup into a bowl and set it in front of Paula. She fixed herself a cupful and joined her at the island.

"That's all you're having?"

"I had lunch out after church."

Paula lifted a spoonful of soup to her lips and blew on it, then she put it into her mouth. "Mmm. This is good."

She concentrated on the soup for a few minutes. Elizabeth ate her own soup and decided to go for another cup.

"I didn't get a chance to ask you how things went today," Paula said. "Did you enjoy going to a new church with Saul?"

"It was nice." Before she overheard the other women in the kitchen. And before she'd blurted out what she had to Saul.

"Are you going to see him again?"

"Saul? Every day at work."

"You know what I mean."

"I'm not dating him." She set her spoon down and sighed. "Paula, I don't think Saul would ever want to date me after what I said to him today. I told him I ran away from home because I got so tired of helping my family."

"It doesn't make you a bad person if you get tired of being a caretaker."

"No?"

"No," Paula said definitely. "A person can suffer caretaker burnout."

"Even nurses?"

"Especially nurses." She pushed her empty bowl away. "Do you remember the story of Martha? From the Bible? She complained to Jesus because Mary got to sit at his feet and listen to him, but she had too much to do. She told Jesus her sister had left her to do all the work by herself, and she wanted Him to tell Mary to help her."

Elizabeth gestured to the empty bowl. "Want more?"

When Paula nodded, she got up and filled the bowl again.

"Anyway, Jesus didn't tell Martha she was a bad person, did he?"

"No. But the Amish love children. I'm not sure I'll ever want them. It doesn't make me good material to become a good Amish *fraa*—wife" she said. "And it's the reason the Amish date. To find the person we want to marry."

"What did Saul say?"

"Nothing. He just looked at me, kind of stunned."

"It doesn't mean he thinks you're terrible," Paula pointed out. "It just means you surprised him. I'd give him the benefit of the doubt. And if it's important to you, you could even ask him. If he's judgmental about it, then he's not the right guy for you."

"I'm not looking at him as a man to date." But she had thought about it . . .

"But you do see Bruce that way?"

Elizabeth shrugged. "Bruce is fun."

"And you just want some fun at this point. I can understand that. But just be careful. Bruce is a little self-centered, and *Englisch* guys seem more interested in getting what they want from a girl than Amish guys, if you know what I mean."

She paused and ate more soup. Then her spoon clattered in her bowl and she looked at Elizabeth with a stricken expression. "Elizabeth, you're not thinking of—of—"

"Of?" Elizabeth supplied helpfully.

"Of—oh, don't make me spell it out!" Paula stared at her, looking exasperated. "You know what I mean! You're not going to do anything with Bruce, are you?"

"We're going out tomorrow after I get off work."

"Elizabeth! Stop being dense!"

She laughed. "Sorry. It was too much fun to tease you. I'm Amish, not unaware. I was raised on a farm, Paula. I know about the birds and the bees."

"Oh, I didn't realize the Amish raised those," Paula said dryly.

Elizabeth stared at her for a long moment and then she laughed.

10

Elizabeth felt grateful the store was busy from what seemed like the moment she walked in on Monday.

All she got to do was say a quick hello to Saul and customers began arriving. It stayed busy for most of the morning.

"If it keeps up like this, I may call Katie and Rosie in early," Saul said.

She nodded at him, but before she could speak, a woman walked into the store and straight for her.

"My mother was in recently and she told me I needed to visit," she told Elizabeth. "I had the day off and thought it was a good time to start shopping for Christmas. I have a large family."

She lifted a full shopping bag she carried in one hand. "As you can see I've already gotten a good start today."

Elizabeth saw the Stitches in Time store logo on the bag. "I haven't been there yet. I'm new to town."

The woman looked around. "If you like this store, I think you'd like it."

She chose a quilt for her grown daughter, a carved horse paperweight for her husband, and a wooden pull toy for her first grandson. When she left, she carried a second shopping bag as full as the one from Stitches in Time.

Finally, just before lunch, the stream of customers became a trickle.

"Go take a break," Saul told her.

She nodded. A quick trip to the ladies room and then a cup of coffee sounded too good to refuse.

In the act of pouring herself a cup, she saw her cuff was fraying. She frowned. Her clothes were starting to look a little shabby. No wonder. She had just two dresses and a good church dress. But even if she could squeeze out the cost of fabric from next week's paycheck, she didn't have a sewing machine to make a dress. When she got home, she'd have to ask Paula if she knew anyone she could borrow one from. She could set up the machine on the desk in her room and sew it in the evenings after work.

Saul joined her just as she sat down with the coffee and poured himself a cup.

"Katie and Rosie just got here."

"One of my customers said she was shopping for Christmas. She bought a lot."

Saul sipped his coffee. "I think we're going to have a really good season. I've ordered extra inventory, so I'll be busy unpacking it in the next week or two."

She nodded and blew on her coffee, trying to cool it so she could drink it and get back to work. And away from him.

"Don't be in such a hurry," he said, giving her a rueful grin as if he knew what she was doing. "I'm not going to dock you for taking a break. You work hard."

"*Danki*." She bit her lip and thought about what to say.

"I—" they spoke at the same time. Stopped. Then did it again.

"I'd say ladies first, but I want to clear the air," Saul said. "I'm glad you were honest with me yesterday. It couldn't have been easy for you to leave home."

"My family thinks I'm selfish."

"I'm sorry," he said quietly. "I'm not judging you, Elizabeth. But it sounds like you're being very hard on yourself."

"I don't know anyone who's done what I did," she said quietly. "Would you have?"

When he hesitated, she persisted, "Would you?"

He glanced at the doorway, then back at her. "I had some . . . reservations about taking over the store. I always enjoyed working here, but I wasn't sure I wanted to do this the rest of my life. "

She stared at him, surprised. "You seem to enjoy it."

He shrugged. "I grew to like it. Well, everything except doing inventory. The important difference is I felt like I had a choice, Elizabeth. It doesn't sound like you feel like you had one about staying there."

Katie stuck her head in the door. "Saul, Mervin is here."

"Tell him I'll be right there."

"I need to get back to work," Elizabeth said and she stood.

"Elizabeth!"

He held out his hand, but she pretended she didn't see it and hurried from the room.

The twins were helping customers. Elizabeth walked to the front window and looked out. The day had turned gray and drizzly. It usually meant people wouldn't be out shopping.

A woman hurried toward the store holding an umbrella. Elizabeth opened the door and was pleasantly surprised to see Jenny Bontrager.

"Hello," she said with a big smile. She shook the rainwater from the umbrella outside before she entered the store. "The weatherman is finally right. He's been predicting rain for two days and we have it at last."

She put the umbrella in the big ceramic pot near the door intended for just such a purpose. "I spoke to Matthew and he said to tell you the two of you are indeed cousins. Second cousins. He's looking forward to meeting you soon."

"I'm looking forward to it, too."

Jenny glanced around. "Well, then, I have to stop by Stitches in Time for some thread."

"I haven't been there yet."

"Is it near your lunch hour? You could go with me."

Elizabeth felt warmed by the invitation. "I'll have to ask Saul."

He was just coming out of the back room with Mervin when she started there. He nodded and walked past her.

"Would you mind if I went to lunch a little early?"

Saul waved at Jenny. "Of course not."

She proceeded to the back room, retrieved her purse and jacket, and went back to Jenny. "I'm ready when you are."

"How nice!" Jenny said. She glanced out the window. "Why, look! The sun's out."

Elizabeth reached for the umbrella. "Don't forget this. You might need it later."

"True. *Danki*." She opened the door. "I'm hoping Mary Katherine will be working today. I'd like the two of you to meet."

"Oh? Why?"

Jenny gave her a mischievous grin. "Oh, you'll find out soon enough."

Saul had said Jenny would be able to find out about her, calling her a mystery lady. Elizabeth decided Jenny had a mystery of her own. Intrigued, she followed her out of the store.

෴

Saul watched Elizabeth leave and thought about the conversation they'd had in the back room.

They had so much more in common than she knew. But he could never tell her. Because when his mother had needed him, he'd stayed and Elizabeth had—in her own words—run away.

It wasn't because he was a better person than her. Someone—something—had made up his mind for him.

Its name was cancer.

From the moment his mother came home with the diagnosis, he'd known he couldn't leave the area to go to another county to work with a friend on a construction job. Who would run the store?

And so he'd called his friend and shown up at the store bright and early the next day. He'd never looked back. His father spent his days going to chemotherapy appointments with his wife, traveling to a cancer center in a neighboring state when the first round of chemo didn't work. Cancer sucked the life out of hours, days, weeks, months—years of time, energy, and money.

Saul knew he'd given his father the freedom to concentrate on helping his mother fight the battle of her life—the battle for her life.

He figured it was a small thing to do when the woman had given him life.

She'd won the battle and recent tests had shown she was in remission. Saul waited for his father to say he wanted to come back to the store and told himself he'd be happy to hand the reins over to him even though he'd come to love running it. His father surprised him by saying he wanted to retire.

Saul smiled at the memory.

"Something funny, boss?" Katie asked him.

"Nothing important," he said. "I think I'll go eat my lunch if you don't need me for anything."

"We can run the store without you," she said confidently.

"Thanks," he said.

He strolled into the back room and got his lunch from the refrigerator. His mother insisted on packing his lunch so he reached into the lunch box and spread a feast out on the table: cold sliced roast beef and bread from last night's dinner, potato salad, dill pickles she'd canned from cucumbers grown in her garden. A handful of peanut butter cookies for his sweet tooth. She'd even included a thermos of lemonade.

While he ate he read through the latest issue of *The Budget*, the national Amish and Mennonite newspaper and caught up on what was happening in the community. Before long, he was reaching for the batch of invoices he needed to take care of before the end of the day. Working while eating was a bad habit he'd tried to break, but other than talking briefly with his father about Christmas orders he didn't take his work home with him.

He glanced at the clock and wondered where Elizabeth had gone with Jenny Bontrager. Elizabeth had left her lunch in the refrigerator, so she was either going to return to eat it or they were going to a restaurant and she'd eat it another time.

The holidays were coming up soon and he couldn't help wondering if she would return home—or if she would even be welcome after what she'd said about leaving the way she had. His *daed* had been correct when he'd said one day Elizabeth was running away from something, not running around.

Maybe Jenny and Matthew would ask her to join their family for Thanksgiving and Christmas dinner. Maybe he should ask his parents if they would. No, it might be a bad idea. He wouldn't want his mother to get the idea he was interested in Elizabeth as anything more than an employee.

Rosie walked into the room and frowned at him. "Working while you're eating is bad for the digestion."

"It's called multitasking."

"I'm familiar with the term. I believe it's why many *Englischers* have ulcers," she informed him breezily.

"Did you need me for something?" he asked mildly.

She chuckled. "*Ya*. Barbie is here to see you."

"Great. Show her back."

Rosie glanced at the door, then back at him. "She's got Lillian with her. I swear, I think the girl lives to flirt with you."

Saul kept his smile in place, but it was hard. So Rosie had noticed, too. "Great. Show them back."

He quickly cleared away his lunch remains and wiped down the table. Then he unlocked the cabinet where he kept the business checks. Seeing Lillian with her mother might not make his day, but he was about to make her mother's day. Her first delivery of quilts had sold out and he couldn't wait to tell her he'd raised the prices after a customer's comments. She'd not only be getting a check today, but it would be one for more than he had estimated.

He couldn't help thinking this might be the start of a long and prosperous business relationship for them both. The fact the store not only prospered him and his family but the lives of others in his Plain community had become his favorite part of his job.

His mother's cancer might have seemed like an awful thing—and it had been. But it had been part of God's mysterious plan and he thanked Him for it every day.

Elizabeth stepped into Stitches in Time and her eyes widened in delight.

The shop looked like a kaleidoscope full of color: walls of bright yardage, tables of fabrics of cotton, silk, and other fibers. Women sat in a circle around a quilt and stitched and chatted before a cozy fireplace. A very pregnant woman knitted a baby cap, while resting her feet on a footstool.

And in a corner, a baby napped in a crib near a woman whose loom made a soft, rhythmic clacking noise as she wove a striped throw.

"I knew you'd love it," Jenny said as Elizabeth stood there just drinking in the scene.

"Jenny!" an older woman said as she walked toward them. She took Jenny's hands in hers and studied her with kind, faded blue eyes. "*Wilkumm*! How are you?"

"I'm doing well," Jenny told her. "This is Elizabeth. She's a cousin of Matthew's who's working at Saul's store. Elizabeth, this is Leah."

"You have the look of Naomi Bontrager," Leah said, eyeing her with interest. "She moved away to Goshen so many years ago."

Elizabeth's heart warmed. "I'm so glad you remember her! She was one of my grandmothers." The nice one, she thought, but didn't say it.

"I always wished she'd made it back for a visit. Have you time for a cup of tea? I'd love for you to catch me up on her and the family."

"I'm on my lunch break."

"Well, then, tea and a sandwich," Leah said. "We have plenty left from lunch. Even with some of us eating for two," she said with an indulgent grin at the pregnant woman near her.

"This is Anna," she told Elizabeth. "And Mary Katherine is at the loom. Naomi isn't in today."

She was greeted with welcoming smiles before Leah led the way to the back room. Leah bustled around making tea, while Jenny with the ease of a frequent visitor, found a plastic container in the refrigerator and brought it to the table.

"Roast beef, tuna, or egg salad," she announced as she set it before Elizabeth.

She chose half a roast beef sandwich and put it on her plate. Jenny shook her head and added another, telling her she needed to eat more than that.

Then Jenny chuckled. "Sorry, I'm a mother."

"I don't mind," Elizabeth told her. She really didn't. Her mother was usually so busy with the younger children she didn't have time to tell her eldest to eat. And truth be told, Elizabeth had always been a healthy eater and needed no urging.

"There are cookies as well," Leah said, bringing the cookie jar to the table.

They sat and chatted easily and Elizabeth liked how comfortable Leah made her, never asking her why she'd left Goshen.

Jenny glanced at her watch and said she had to get home. Leah got called away for a customer who came asking for her. She got up and left Elizabeth to finish her lunch promising to return as quickly as possible.

Mary Katherine came in, fixed herself a cup of tea, and sat down at the table. "Leah asked me to come in and keep you company until she gets back."

"I appreciate it, but you don't need to. I mean, you looked busy," she stammered, hoping she didn't sound unfriendly.

"I do most of my weaving at home," Mary Katherine told her. "I only come in two days a week now since I have little Isaac. We leave in time to be home for his brother who's in *schul*."

She opened the cookie jar and withdrew two chocolate chip cookies, then held out the jar to Elizabeth who gratefully took two. They were her favorite.

"Jenny thought we should talk," Mary Katherine said.

"Really? Why?"

Mary Katherine took a sip of her tea. "When Jenny found out you were here without your family, I think she thought we have something in common. You see, years ago I wasn't sure where I belonged—I was in my *rumschpringe* like you. I didn't get along with my *dat* and I felt a lot of pressure to join the church. I just felt so frustrated."

"I get along with my father, mostly," Elizabeth said. "It was my mother. And it wasn't as if we didn't get along. I just got overwhelmed with helping at home. I have eight brothers and sisters—all younger than me. I started thinking I'd never get out and date and get married one day."

"I almost turned away Jacob—the man I ended up marrying—because I was afraid of being trapped in a marriage like my parents," Mary Katherine told her quietly.

She got up, picked up the teakettle, and filled her cup with more hot water. "Do you have time for another cup?"

Elizabeth glanced at the nearby clock, nodded, then took another tea bag and dunked it in the cup.

"What made you come here? I mean, it's not a small distance from Goshen. Do you have relatives here?"

Elizabeth smiled. "I'd heard I had relatives here, but I didn't know them. Matthew Bontrager is a second cousin. I'm living with an *Englisch* woman my age I met when her family visited Goshen."

"And you're working for Saul at his store?"

She nodded. "Just until Miriam comes back from maternity leave."

"Come talk to Leah when the job is over," Mary Katherine said. "She may know someone who needs a hard worker."

"How do you know I'm a hard worker?" Elizabeth asked curiously.

"Saul wouldn't have hired you—or kept you—if you weren't," Mary Katherine told her with a grin.

Leah walked in holding the baby Elizabeth had seen napping earlier. The baby looked about six months old and Elizabeth could already see she looked like her mother.

"Somebody woke up and wanted her *mamm*," Leah told her.

"Do you want your lunch, *liebschen*?" Mary Katherine asked her with a chuckle as she held out her arms to take her.

Elizabeth stood. "I need to get back to work. I enjoyed talking to you."

Mary Katherine turned her attention from the baby in her arms to Elizabeth. "I hope we'll talk again."

"I'd like that."

As they left the room, Leah closed the door and turned a small sign to read "Do not disturb."

"I wanted to get some fabric to make myself a dress," Elizabeth told Leah. "But I don't have a sewing machine here."

"You're welcome to use one here any time," Leah told her as they walked back into the shop. "But it doesn't really fit into your schedule, does it? You can't sew much in a lunch hour. I could loan you a machine to take home if you like."

"I would love that," Elizabeth said fervently.

"Stop by here on your way home and I'll have it ready for you."

"I don't think my ride will mind stopping for it. Thank you—*danki*," she said in the Pennsylvania *Dietsch* she'd been learning since she'd lived here.

Leah showed her some dress material and Elizabeth fairly fell onto a bolt of polyester cotton in a color that could only be described as morning glory blue.

"Wonderful choice," Leah approved. "Let's go cut it. Do you need a pattern? We have them."

She did have one in mind and quickly chose it, looked up the yardage needed, and Leah cut it. When Elizabeth left the shop she felt so satisfied. She'd met several wonderful people who welcomed her, especially Mary Katherine, enjoyed a lovely lunch away from work, and she now had the makings for her first brand-new dress in more than a year. And the loan of a sewing machine. Maybe she could squeeze out some money to get fabric to make another before she returned the machine.

When she left the shop—spending less than she'd thought she might have to—she walked with a lighter step. It was a very good day and only a few hours into it. And after work, she and Bruce were having dinner and going to see a movie.

Ya, a very good day indeed!

11

$\mathcal{Y}$ou need to stop for what?"

"A sewing machine. It's on the way to the restaurant. I hope you don't mind."

Bruce shrugged. "Okay."

But he didn't seem particularly happy about it. She directed him to the store and he parked in front of it.

"I can get it," she said and she got out of his car.

"I'll help."

He got out of the car and walked inside with her.

"There you are!" Leah said as she left the counter and walked toward them. "I put the machine right up here for you."

"This is Bruce," Elizabeth told her. "Bruce, this is Leah."

"Nice to meet you, Bruce."

"You, too." He lifted the handle of the portable machine. "This isn't heavy at all."

"Thank you again, Leah," Elizabeth said. "I'll have it back to you in a week."

"Do you have to rush off?"

"We have dinner plans," Bruce told her. "I'll take this to the car."

He walked out and Elizabeth watched him set the machine in the trunk of the car.

"We're having dinner and then going to a movie."

Leah hesitated for a moment, and then she said, "I was kind of hoping you and Saul . . ."

"Saul and I what?"

"*Grossmudder*, are you matchmaking?" Anna asked her as she came to stand near the door.

"Anna, are you eavesdropping?"

"It's not eavesdropping if you just happen to overhear something," Anna retorted with a grin. "Let Elizabeth get going. Looks like her friend is impatient."

A car horn honked outside as if to reinforce her words.

"And from what I heard, she's been working for Saul for a while now," Anna added before Elizabeth could walk out the door. "Maybe he needs to know someone else is interested so he should get cracking."

"I better go," Elizabeth said, feeling her face redden. "Thank you again, Leah."

When she reached the car, she saw Bruce had his hand over the horn ready to honk it again. She got in and buckled her seat belt.

"'Bout time," he muttered as he started the car. "We're going to have less time to eat because we stopped here."

"Sorry. But I appreciate your picking up the machine. I really need it. I can't wait to sew a new dress with it."

"I thought you people didn't care about that sort of thing."

You people?

"What do you mean?" she asked, not wanting to misunderstand.

"Well, you're not supposed to care about material things, right? I figured it was why you wore the same couple dresses."

He couldn't have hurt her more if he'd hit her. Her face flamed. What could she say?

After a long moment when she didn't speak, he glanced at her. "What, did I say something wrong?"

"I come from a big family," she said quietly. "There wasn't a lot of money to have a big wardrobe."

"Oh," he said.

Just oh? she wanted to say.

"What about your family? Do you have brothers or sisters?"

"One of each. It was enough."

"Enough?"

"Yeah. Having a lot of kids costs a lot of money these days."

She knew it was true. But children were a gift from God and even if it all got to be too much for her, you couldn't tell God what to do, could you? Maybe the big family had been part of His plan for her and she just couldn't see it . . .

"You're being quiet."

"Long day."

He parked outside an Italian restaurant and they got out. As she did, she saw a bag with Saul's store logo lying on the back seat.

"What's that?"

"The toy I bought the day I stopped at the store, remember?" he said carelessly as he slipped his arm around her waist. "Your boss was frowning about me stopping by. He should chill."

Elizabeth stopped in her tracks as she felt his arm. He'd never touched her this way before.

"What?" he asked.

She glanced down at his arm. "I—"

"Geez, Elizabeth, I can't put my arm around you? What, are you frigid or something?"

"Frigid?" She stared at him.

"I thought you were out for a good time. I mean, you're on your *rumschpringe* and all."

"We don't suddenly go wild, you know."

"No? Some of the Amish kids around here do."

"Some isn't me," she said quietly.

He shoved his hands in the pockets of his jeans and frowned at her. "Well, I just can't say anything right tonight, can I? What, have you got PMS or something?"

Her eyes went wide. Where was the charming Bruce she knew?

"Look, let's just forget about it, okay?" he said. "Too many fish in the sea, you know?"

Then he stomped off to his car, got in, and the tires on his car squealed as he pulled out onto the road too fast.

Elizabeth stood there on the sidewalk, gaping as she watched the car disappear into traffic.

෴

Saul saw the guy who'd been taking Elizabeth out after work lurking around the sidewalk in front of the store.

Just how often was she seeing him anyway?

As soon as he thought it, he shook his head. It was none of his business. He'd been attracted to her on the bus and he hadn't acted fast enough.

"See you tomorrow," she said with a big smile.

Her step was quick and light as she walked toward the door swinging her shopping bag with a jaunty air.

He didn't know if her good mood came from her time with Jenny at Stitches in Time or the prospect of going out in the evening.

Rosie locked the door after the last customer and turned the sign to CLOSED. She wandered back and leaned against the counter, watching him as he made out the day's deposit slip.

"We had a *gut* day," she said.

"*Ya.*"

"So why are you frowning?"

He straightened and cleared his expression. "I wasn't aware I was."

"So why were you frowning?"

"No idea. Anyway, it's not important. You're working tomorrow, right?"

"Of course. Katie will be back, too. Her cold's much better. Really nasty one going around. Be glad you haven't caught it."

"Uh, *ya,* I am." He turned his attention back to the deposit slip.

He was grateful when she went to the back room to get her purse. He'd had enough questions.

She left and the quiet after a long, busy day was welcome.

Someone rapped on the door. A man pressed his face against the glass window.

Bishop Stoltzfus!

Saul shoved the bank deposit bag in the drawer and hurried to the door.

"*Gut-n-Owed,*" he said as he opened the door. "This is an unexpected pleasure."

His mother had taught him never to lie, but he felt she'd forgive this one. Tall, stern-looking, with his bushy dark eyebrows beetled over sharp black eyes, he was an imposing presence.

The bishop glanced around him. "Everyone's gone?"

"Er, *ya,*" Saul said. "Did you want to see someone? *Daed's* retired, you know."

He nodded. "Of course, I know that. I was looking for the new young woman who's working for you. Elizabeth?"

Surprised, Saul stared at him. "You wanted to see Elizabeth?"

"What do you know about her?"

"She's from Goshen. Been here for about a month. Why?"

The bishop shook his head. "I'm not at liberty to say."

That didn't sound good. "Nothing's wrong with her family, is there? Because I have her address and home phone if you need to contact her."

He hesitated and then he shook his head. "No. It can wait a day."

"She'll be in tomorrow morning. Shall I have her call you then?"

"I'll stop back then." He started to turn and then stopped and looked at Saul over the top of his bifocals. "What do you know about this young woman?"

"I checked her reference—the last place she worked."

"But I mean her character?"

"They said she was honest and trustworthy," Saul said, not liking the sound of this at all. "But it wouldn't have mattered what they said, if I didn't think she was a good person. I think I'm a pretty good judge of character and *Daed* interviewed her with me as well."

Careful, he told himself. Now you're sounding defensive.

"But what do you know about her? About why she came here?"

"Her reasons are personal," Saul told him carefully.

He wouldn't betray her confidence—especially since the bishop asked questions, but wouldn't give him any answers.

The bishop placed his hands on the counter and stared at him directly. "Are you interested in this young woman?"

"She's an employee."

"It's not an answer to my question."

"No, I'm not dating her, if you're asking." It wasn't something the bishop should be asking. . . . Couples dated very privately. Sometimes their own families didn't know they were dating or engaged until the wedding date was announced in church.

What was going on?

"As I said, she'll be here in the morning." Saul knew he sounded a little stiff, but he couldn't help it. The man was getting his back up.

"*Danki.*"

He escorted him to the door and watched as the man walked to a waiting van. He didn't envy Elizabeth the man's questions in the morning.

A million questions raced through his mind. Was Elizabeth's family looking for her? Why? Were they going to apply pressure to make her come home? He'd heard of parents doing it to their *kinner* who had run away.

He closed the door, slowly walked back to the counter and made quick work of finishing the deposit.

His driver pulled up at the curb just as he stepped outside.

"Sorry I ran a little late."

"It's all right. I had a last-minute visitor."

"You mean customer?"

"No, visitor."

They had been driving for about ten minutes when Saul happened to glance out the window at a familiar figure. Was that—? He leaned over and stared. No, it couldn't be Elizabeth. Why would she be standing on the sidewalk outside a restaurant? She was supposed to be out with Bruce and he didn't see the man anywhere.

It must be some other Amish woman.

"Phil? Could you circle the block? I thought I saw someone I know."

"Sure."

But when they circled the block the woman was gone.

"You want me to go around again?"

Saul shook his head. "No, thanks. I must have been wrong."

"No problem."

⌖

"Bruce did what?!"

The restaurant was noisy, but Elizabeth could hear the outrage in Paula's voice.

"He left me in front of the restaurant!" Elizabeth cried. She bit her lip and tried to stay calm. "They let me use the phone. I hate to ask, but can—can you come get me?"

"Of course. Give me the name of the restaurant and I'll be right there."

Elizabeth told her and then hung up.

"What a jerk!" said the waitress who'd let her use the phone. "Sorry, I couldn't help overhearing."

She shrugged. "Well, I don't know much about men."

"Take it from me—they all only think about one thing."

The woman appeared to be in her early twenties, but she sounded old and cynical.

"Here, honey, sit down and have something warm to drink," she said, waving her hand at a table near the window. "It's too cold for you to wait outside. You can keep an eye out for your ride from in here."

Elizabeth didn't really want to sit there in the restaurant with all the people around her sitting together in couples enjoying supper together. But the waitress was right.

"Could I have a cup of tea instead of coffee?"

"Sure thing. Be right back."

When she returned, she set a little teapot of hot water and a cup and saucer down on the table. On the saucer, she'd placed a biscotti.

Elizabeth thanked her and enjoyed the tea and the biscotti and finished them just in time before Paula pulled up outside. She counted out the money and the tip—then added to the tip for the waitress letting her use the phone to call Paula—and slipped on her jacket.

"I didn't want to call you," she told Paula when she got into her car. "You shouldn't be out with your cold."

"It's no problem," she said. "You'd better call me if you get in a jam again. I was thinking on the way here we need to get you a cell phone. What if you'd been stuck somewhere and couldn't get to a phone?"

"I can't really afford one yet."

"We'll find a cheap one. It doesn't have to be fancy. Just one for emergencies."

The talk of money made Elizabeth remember the way she'd felt when she and Bruce talked in the car. She'd felt embarrassed to admit she only had two dresses because her family didn't have much money.

Bruce. The car. *The sewing machine!*

She must have gasped, because Paula glanced over at her.

"What?"

"Leah loaned me a sewing machine and it's in the back of Bruce's car."

Paula muttered something under her breath. Elizabeth didn't want to know what she said.

She pulled over on the side of the road and got out her cell phone. Frowning, she dialed a number. "Bruce? This is Paula. Don't talk, just listen. I'll be by your apartment in about ten minutes. Be outside with the sewing machine. Understand?

Yeah, sewing machine. Did you forget it's in your trunk? Uh-huh. Well, never mind. I'll be there in ten minutes."

"Oh, and my shopping bag!" Elizabeth blurted out, suddenly remembering. "It's in the back seat."

"And her shopping bag in the back seat," Paula added.

Tucking away her phone, she pulled back onto the road. After a few minutes, she glanced at Elizabeth. "I know where he lives because several of us had a study group there one day."

"Oh."

"It's not because we dated."

"I didn't think so."

Paula sighed. "Yeah, because you're just so innocent."

"I know." Now it was her turn to sigh.

"Well, I suppose it's better than being cynical."

Just what Elizabeth had thought the waitress sounded like.

Bruce was standing on the sidewalk beside his car when they got to his apartment.

"You can put the machine and the bag in the back," Paula told him.

He did as she directed, and then he looked at Elizabeth. "Look, I'm sorry—"

"Forget it," Paula told him coolly. "We need to get home."

As they drove away, Elizabeth stole a look back and saw him standing there, looking after the car.

"The waitress said men were after just one thing," she said.

Paula's laugh didn't sound like it had any humor in it. "Yeah, well, I heard once they think about it—you know, S-E-X— every twenty-seven seconds. But there are nice guys out there."

"Like Jason?" she asked with a smile.

"Yeah, like Jason." Now she was the one smiling. "You'll meet someone just right for you one day." She fell silent. "Do you believe God has a plan for you, Elizabeth? He sets aside the right man for you?"

Surprised, she nodded, then realized Paula couldn't see because she was driving. "Yes."

"Well, it's not Bruce."

"No, it's not Bruce."

Paula pulled into the apartment complex parking lot. "But it's all right, right?"

"Right."

They got out of the car and Elizabeth retrieved the sewing machine and the bag of fabric.

"What are you going to make?" Paula asked her as they walked to the apartment.

"A new dress," Elizabeth told her. "For the man God's set aside for me."

Paula laughed and patted her back. "That's the spirit. Come on, I'll fix you some supper."

"Scrambled eggs and toast?"

"My spec-i-al-i-ty," Paula told her with a big grin.

12

"I'm glad you got here early," Saul told Elizabeth when she walked into the store the next morning.

She glanced around. "Do we have customers already?"

"*Nee.*" He shut the door, leaving the CLOSED sign on it. "*Kumm*, I made coffee."

Elizabeth walked to the back room, hung up her jacket, and locked her purse away in the cupboard.

She sat down and studied him as he poured her a cup of coffee. He seemed distracted. Did an employer give you coffee when he was firing you?

"Have I done something wrong?"

Startled, he stared at her. "Of course not. Why do you ask?"

"You look . . . grim. Is everything okay?"

He set her mug before her and took a seat. "I don't know. Elizabeth, the bishop stopped in yesterday after you left. He wanted to talk to you."

"Me? Why?"

"I have no idea."

Elizabeth stared into her coffee and then looked up at him. "I think I do."

"You do?"

She nodded. "He must have heard from my family back in Goshen."

"Perhaps they're just concerned about you and they contacted him."

"If they cared—" she stopped.

"I'm sure they care."

"I sent my mother my new address and said I hoped she'd write me but instead I heard from my grandmother. She let me know she thinks I was a bad daughter to leave and says I should return home."

He laid his hand over hers on the table. "I'm sorry. I had no idea."

She blinked back tears. "I—I can't talk about it."

"You don't have to."

Elizabeth stared at him. He seemed surprised at what he'd said himself.

"If you don't want to talk to him, you don't have to," he said decisively. "I'll tell him, if you want. After all, you're not a member of the church here. And you're working."

She couldn't believe he'd stand up for her. The bishop was an important man. Saul barely knew her, after all. Emotion swamped her.

"No," she said finally. "It's very nice of you but I don't want you to have any trouble over me. I'll talk to him, but not here. It isn't right he'd come to where I work and talk to me while you're paying my wage. I'll talk to him another time."

He spread his hands. "It's up to you."

Someone rapped at the door. "I'll get it," she said quickly, grateful for the excuse to get away.

She took a deep breath and felt composed by the time she got to the door to greet the first customer to the store.

Every time the door opened and the bell above it jangled the presence of a visitor, she jumped and cast an apprehensive look in its direction.

"Enough!" she muttered.

Her lunch break came and she ate half her sandwich in the back room, then put the rest back in the refrigerator. Egg salad just didn't mix well with butterflies.

And then the door opened, the bell jangled, and in walked the bishop.

Saul must have noticed her apprehension, because he moved behind the counter where she was finishing up a purchase for a customer.

"Get it over with now," he said quietly. "Talk to him in the back room."

"You're sure?"

"Positive."

So, she walked up to the bishop and invited him to accompany her to the back room. Saul caught her eye as the man walked past him and gave her a nod of encouragement as she passed.

He seated himself very deliberately at the head of the table.

"Would you like some coffee?"

"*Ya,*" he said. "Two sugars."

The sugar was sitting in a bowl on the table before him, but she merely nodded and fixed it the way he ordered. He obviously considered his stature as a religious leader to mean he deserved to be waited on. Besides, she'd learned from experience to pick her battles with toddlers in her home. Why make a fuss over something so minor when she didn't know what she was up against yet?

She sat at the table, her hands folded in her lap, and waited for him to say why he'd come.

He stirred his coffee even though she'd done it, took a sip, and stroked his beard as he looked at her, his black eyes piercing. "I heard from your family back in Goshen," he said finally. "They're worried about you. They asked me to speak to you."

"They?"

"Your grandmother wrote me for your family."

"I see."

"You need to go back home. You need to return to your church." His tone was stern and final.

"I can't do that."

"Can't—or won't?"

"Won't. I need some time away to know what's best for me."

"God knows what's best for you."

Her hands tightened in her lap. "If it is true, wouldn't God have stopped me from getting on the bus?"

"I won't debate this with you."

Won't or can't? she wanted to ask him. How did he know what God considered best for her? she thought with a touch of rebellion.

He pushed the cup of coffee away and a little slopped over the rim onto the wooden table. She reached for a paper napkin from the holder on the table and dabbed it up.

The phone rang, the sound jarring in the tense atmosphere.

"Excuse me," she said as she got up to answer it.

"Don't say anything, just listen," Saul said quickly when she said hello. "Do you want me to come rescue you?"

"No."

"You're sure?"

"I will check and see if we can order the item and get back to you."

She hung up the phone and returned to her seat. "Sorry for the interruption."

"I want you to think about what you're doing and call your parents and tell them you're coming home," he told her, his eyes boring into hers.

"I appreciate your concern," she said, working hard not to be intimidated. Her bishop back home was a much milder man than this one. "Now I have to return to work. It isn't fair to the man paying my wages to have me conducting personal business on his dime."

"You should be more concerned about being at risk of God's displeasure with you and see the error of your ways before it's too late. Remember what the *Ordnung* says about obedience."

She rose. "Thank you again for coming."

He rose stiffly, glaring at her the whole time, and stalked from the room. She followed him out and saw him give Saul a curt nod as he left the store.

"How are you?" Saul asked her quietly.

She turned to him and lifted her chin. "I'm *gut*," she said, and she gave him a smile she hoped wasn't as shaky as it felt. "Thank you for calling me and offering to come to my rescue. I didn't expect that."

"You're welcome. It strikes me, though, you didn't need rescuing." He walked away.

Elizabeth wondered if it was her imagination he sounded a little disappointed. She thought about last night. If he only knew . . . she'd been lucky Paula had been able to come for her. What would she have done otherwise?

⋘❧⋙

Saul had never had a problem with keeping his mind on business.

It wasn't pride. After all, *Der hochmut kummt vor dem fall*— pride goeth before a fall. No, it was simply a matter of being able to work when at work. It was what a man did. Especially if he wanted to prosper. And wanted to make his business successful for his son to take over as he'd taken over from his father.

One of the things his father had taught him about the business was to take care of the people who created the crafts for their store. They were the heart and soul of the store—the reason it existed. But it was more than that. The store meant the people in their community could carry on traditions and stay there to take care of their families and friends.

And being paid well and promptly, so they could feed and clothe their family was at the heart of Samuel's business philosophy.

So when Barbie didn't show up to pick up her second check, Saul knew he could drop it in the mail or wait until church to give it to her. But he also knew her family needed the money more than usual right now with her husband sick and unable to work. The sooner she received the money the sooner she could use it.

The errand wouldn't take but a few minutes and he'd be free of his obligation. His driver didn't have any problem waiting for a few minutes while he walked up to the door of Barbie's house and handed over the check.

Now Saul stood there waiting for his knock to be answered and found himself praying Barbie would greet him.

The door opened and Lillian of the fluttering eyelashes appeared.

"Saul! *Gut-n-Owed*. So nice to see you!"

He shook his head. "*Gut-n-Owed*. Is your mother at home?"

She opened the door. "She's in the kitchen. Come in!"

Saul wanted to just hand her the check and be on the way.

"Lillian! Is it Saul? Ask him to come in!"

He waved at his driver to indicate he needed a minute, and Phil nodded.

"I brought your check," he announced. He pulled it from his pocket.

Barbie's cheeks were pink from the heat of the stove as she turned from stirring a pot on a burner. "*Danki.* You could have just mailed it." She tucked it safely into the pocket of her apron. "Can you stay for supper?"

"I made a snitz pie," Lillian said.

Saul hadn't realized she'd come to stand so close to him. So close he could see her fluttering her eyelashes.

"Uh, no, I need to be getting home. But *danki.*"

"Maybe another time," Lillian said.

He nodded and hoped she wouldn't pin him down on when.

Barbie's *mann* walked in then, leaning heavily on a cane. Saul waited until the man switched the cane to another hand and held his right one out for a handshake.

"Glad to see you up and about," he told him.

"He starts physical therapy next week," Barbie said.

"Work would be therapy," Stephen muttered.

Barbie sighed and shook her head.

"Well, let me know when you have a delivery," Saul told her. "I'll send someone or stop by for it myself."

"Maybe I'll be able to do it," Stephen said hopefully.

"We'll see," his wife said.

"I'll walk you to the door," Lillian told Saul.

He walked quickly, but she still got in an invitation to the next singing.

"*Danki,*" he said. "But I'm not going."

"You never go to them." Her tone turned sulky.

"I'm feeling kind of old for them. But I hope you go and have a good time." He smiled at her, hoping it would lessen any rejection she might feel.

He walked quickly to the van and climbed inside. Narrow escape, he couldn't help thinking.

Phil started the van. "You didn't need rush."

Saul took a deep breath. "Didn't want to keep you waiting any longer."

As the van pulled out of the drive, he saw Lillian standing there staring after it. He felt a moment of guilt but he just wasn't interested in her. Once he'd been flattered at her flirting with him, but a friend had let him know Lillian's interest was in his ability to provide for her rather than in him as a man.

It was the bad thing about living in a small community—you sometimes knew too much about someone. Or was it a good thing? Everyone grew up together, knew each other. But he just couldn't muster up any interest in any of the *maedels* he knew.

His thoughts went to Elizabeth—conflicted thoughts. He'd been alternately attracted to her and somewhat disturbed by hearing she'd come here to get away from what she felt was a burdensome duty to her family.

Well, it didn't matter. She didn't seem interested in him. So that was that.

He was relieved when Phil asked him about his schedule for the rest of the week. He didn't need to be thinking about Elizabeth.

❧

As soon as supper was over and the dishes were put into the dishwasher, Elizabeth got out her shopping bag with the new fabric.

"I've been looking forward to cutting out my new dress all day," she told Paula. "Do you mind if I cut it out on the dining room floor?"

"No, but wouldn't you rather do it on the table?"

"Not enough room," Elizabeth said, kneeling on the wooden floor.

"Do you mind if I watch?"

"Not at all. It's not very exciting, though."

Paula sat cross-legged on the floor and put her chin in her hand, propping her elbow on her leg. "I think it is. I've never sewed a dress. We had a sewing unit in my high school life sciences class, but we made aprons. How silly. I mean, who wears aprons these days?"

Elizabeth just looked at her.

"Oh, right," Paula said. "I mean, very few *Englisch* women wear them."

"I don't understand why." Elizabeth cut out the pattern pieces and lay them on the floor. "They're so good for protecting your clothing."

Paula picked up the pattern envelope and studied the dress pictured on it. "So you're going to make an Indiana dress?"

"I'm from Indiana," Elizabeth pointed out with a grin.

"True. But you're in Pennsylvania now."

"Yes."

"You're not going to make one of the kind the Amish women wear here?"

Elizabeth concentrated on cutting out the next pattern piece. "I don't think I'm ready yet."

"Oh. I see."

She finished with the pattern pieces and spread the material out, smoothing it as she went. Humming, she pinned the pattern pieces to the material, careful to place them as close together as possible in order to save material. Every little bit of material was carefully used in an Amish home. She'd save the scraps in case she needed a patch for the dress. Or if she wanted to make a dress for a doll for one of her little sisters. Christmas was coming soon.

"What's the sigh for?"

"Hmm?"

Paula tilted her head and studied her. "You sighed and looked a little sad when you'd been so happy cutting out the material."

"I was thinking I could use some of the scraps of material to make a dress for a doll for one of my little sisters. Christmas isn't so far away."

"Are you going to go back home for Christmas?"

Elizabeth bit her lip, then shook her head and concentrated on cutting out the pattern pieces. "I don't think I'd be welcome."

She heard Paula sigh. "I'm sorry."

Sitting back, Elizabeth met her gaze. "Thank you. It means a lot."

She looked around the apartment. The modern, nearly new space with stylish furniture and sparkling appliances was so different from what she'd grown up with. Not better. Just different. Something she'd never anticipated when she left home and knew only her pen pal waited to shelter her.

"Well, I'm selfish enough to say it'll be nice to have you here for Christmas. My last roommate went skiing for Christmas vacation."

"Jason will be here," Elizabeth reminded her. "I don't think you'll care who else will be around."

"I will, too," Paula said staunchly.

Elizabeth cut out the last part of the dress, folded all the pieces, and put them back into the shopping bag. She checked the floor for pins, picked up a few threads, and got to her feet.

"How long will it take to make the dress?"

"It's been a long time since I got to sew and then it was in just bits and pieces of time. It might take more than an evening."

They decided to set the machine up on the dining room table so Elizabeth could join Paula in watching a television show.

Elizabeth missed using her mother's old treadle machine but after she figured out the difference in threading the needle between the two machines she began sewing. She smiled as she guided the material under the presser foot and listened to the whir of the machine as it stitched. It was a task and a sound she'd missed.

"You're really enjoying yourself, aren't you?" Paula asked when the program they were watching ended.

She nodded. "I always liked sewing. And I'm going to love having another dress to wear."

"Every girl appreciates having something new and pretty to wear. I'm making a cup of tea. Want one?"

"Yes, it would be nice." She sewed another seam and set the piece aside. The top of the dress was already coming along.

Paula brought over the tea and they sat and sipped it.

"So can I ask you something?" Paula asked her.

"Sure."

"Have you ever wanted to wear *Englisch* clothes?"

"Yes. Jeans," Elizabeth confessed. "They look so comfortable."

"They are! What size do you wear?"

"I don't know. I've never bought clothes."

"I bet you're around my size," Paula said. "C'mon."

Before she knew what was happening, Paula had grabbed her hand and dragged her, laughing and protesting, into her bedroom. "Sit down, I'll find a pair for you to try."

She pawed through a closet crammed with more clothes than Elizabeth had ever seen and tossed her a pair of jeans.

"Hmm. You need a top, too." She gave Elizabeth a critical look over. "The blue fabric you got was a good choice. It's a good color for you." She found a blue cardigan sweater and tossed it at her as well.

"They're yours if they fit and ever want to wear them."

Elizabeth took them to her room to try on, then returned to Paula's room to look at herself in her full-length mirror. She'd never seen herself in such a mirror before. Mirrors hung over bathroom vanities in Amish homes and she'd used a small mirror for grooming in her bedroom but she'd only seen these full-length ones in store changing rooms.

❧

The jeans fit a little tight—she must be a size bigger than Paula—but felt so strange she wasn't sure she'd ever wear them.

"They look great on you," Paula said. "What do you think?"

Elizabeth bit her lip. "They'll take some getting used to. I love the sweater. Thank you."

Paula nodded. "You're welcome."

Elizabeth changed back into her dress and returned to the dining room table. Paula watched her sew for a few minutes and then went to check her e-mail.

"Nothing from Jason tonight," she said and frowned. "I hope he's okay. When he came home from his last deployment I tried to get him to talk to me about what he did, what was going on, but he didn't want to. Said I'd just worry. Well, I watch the news, I read things on the Internet. I already know, so, of course, I worry."

Elizabeth couldn't imagine being separated from someone she was in love with the way Paula seemed to be with Jason. People in her own community stayed so close to home. Jason was thousands of miles away.

She'd be happy when he was home for the holidays to see Paula.

She glanced at the clock on the wall and decided she could sew for another half hour or so and then should be getting to bed. It was another work day tomorrow.

Paula looked up from her laptop. "Say, did you know there's a bunch of dating websites for the Amish on the Internet?"

"No, really?"

"Yeah. Maybe you should take a look at it."

Elizabeth wrinkled her nose. "I don't think so."

Paula became absorbed in it. "Oh honestly!" she said after a few minutes. "They have a photo of a supposed Amish guy and he's wearing a mustache! Amish men don't wear mustaches!"

She glanced over at Elizabeth. "I don't know why, I just know they're either clean-shaven when they're single or they wear a beard when they're married. But I've never seen an Amish man with a mustache. Why don't they wear them."

She removed a pin from her mouth. "Mustaches are forbidden because they're too reminiscent of what soldiers wore many, many years ago."

"Hmm. Didn't know that."

Elizabeth shook her head and smiled as she continued to sew. She finished the seams of the main part of the bodice, set it beside the sewing machine, and rolled her shoulders. They felt a little stiff from bending over the machine.

She felt a sense of accomplishment she hadn't experienced in a long time. Oh, she knew she was good at her job at the store. Saul had let her know he was pleased with her work the first day. She knew she was good at taking care of her brothers and sisters, too.

But sewing the dress—she'd seldom had time to sew back home and yet here she was creating—well, she'd been raised not to show pride but surely feeling a sense of accomplishment at a job well done wasn't wrong . . .

And while she didn't envy Paula her closet full of fancy *Englisch* clothes, she was girl enough to want to have a beautiful new modest dress to wear. She got ready for bed and smiled when she put her head on the pillow and drifted off to sleep.

13

$\mathcal{J}$enny sounds really sweet," Paula told Elizabeth. "I certainly didn't expect to be invited to a family meal just because you're my roommate."

"I'm sure she wouldn't have invited you if she didn't want to." She held the directions to Jenny's house in her hand as Paula drove. "Are you sure you don't need to look at the directions?"

Paula shook her head. "I recognized the address when you told me." She glanced over. "Your dress turned out really nice."

Elizabeth smoothed the skirt of the new dress she'd finished a couple of nights ago. Being invited to dinner with a local family seemed a good occasion to wear it the first time.

"The color's pretty on you."

Elizabeth pulled down the visor on the car and checked her appearance in the mirror. She smiled, refusing to think it was wrong to feel pretty in something new. She couldn't remember the last time she'd made herself a new dress. Some might hate hand-me-downs, but as the eldest in the family she never got them, so when money was tight as it frequently was, she had to make do with what she had.

They pulled into the drive of the address Jenny had given them. Several buggies were parked outside. Elizabeth wondered how many people were inside. A couple of butterflies fluttered around in her empty stomach.

"You coming?" Paula asked her when Elizabeth hesitated about getting out of the car. Then she tilted her head and studied her. "You okay?"

"I'm just a little nervous," Elizabeth confessed. "I don't know anyone here but Jenny."

"Well, you're about to meet some of your family. I'm sure they're nice. You said Jenny is."

"Families aren't always friendly."

"I know." Paula patted her hand. "You just say the word if you want to go home early."

"What word?"

Paula's forehead wrinkled as she thought about it. "Party girl."

Elizabeth laughed. How lucky she was to have a friend like Paula. "That's two words. But they're as good as any."

As they walked up to the front door, Elizabeth couldn't help thinking how close she'd grown to Paula in such a short time.

Jenny greeted them at the door and introduced them to Matthew, her husband and Elizabeth's second—or was it third?—cousin. He stood more than a head taller than his wife and his strong features and blue eyes reminded her so much of her family back home. His face bore the signs of a farmer: traces of the tan from late summer harvesting and a crinkling around the eyes from facing the sun in the fields nearly every day.

"*Wilkumm* to our home!" he said and he enveloped her hand in both of his. "How nice to meet one of the Goshen Bontragers."

"I hope you don't mind—I invited some of the family," Jenny said. "They wanted to meet you after I told them about you."

"I'd like to meet them, too," Elizabeth said. She wasn't just being polite. She *did* want to meet them—she was just nervous about it.

"My *grossmudder* Phoebe wanted to meet you, but she's been called away to take care of a sick friend," Jenny said.

Jenny and Matthew had four children. They ranged in age from what Elizabeth estimated was late thirties down to teenage: Joshua, Annie, and Johnny. Mary walked in carrying Rosanna. Interesting, thought Elizabeth. Mary was the name of one of her sisters.

"Rosanna!" Jenny plucked her from her mother's arms.

Matthew chucked her under the chin and held out his arms, but Jenny refused to part with her.

"Mine," she said, and then teased him by holding out Rosanna and then leaning back with her.

"Don't you need to go put supper on the table?" Matthew asked her.

"Mary, would you mind putting everything on the table?"

Mary turned to Joshua and Johnny. "You two can help me." She frowned at her daughter in her mother's arms. "She's been so fussy this afternoon, I'm wondering if she's getting another tooth."

"Your *mamm* is telling tales about you," Jenny chided. She smiled at Rosanna, then Elizabeth. "Would you like to hold her?"

There didn't seem to be any graceful way out of it, so Elizabeth held her for a few moments and then handed her back saying, "I should help."

Several leaves had been inserted in the kitchen table to make room for them all. One of the walls—a moveable partition really—had been pushed back the way it was so often done to make room for large groups for church. When Jenny's family left, the partition could be returned to its position for a cozier kitchen.

Elizabeth watched the way brothers and sisters cheerfully squabbled with each other as they placed serving dishes on the table and took seats. It reminded her of her own brothers and sisters although they were younger . . .

Annie glanced at the lock. "Aaron said he might run a little late."

"Wish my *mann* didn't have to be out of town," Mary said. She looked over at her mother cradling her daughter in her arms and smiled. "He got the chance for a little extra carpentry work and wanted to take it."

They prayed over the meal and then began passing the serving dishes.

"Elizabeth, I thought I'd let each of us tell you a little about ourselves, so you could get to know us. Joshua, why don't you start since you're the oldest?"

"Uh, that would be *Daed*," he said and they all laughed.

"Eldest child," Jenny emphasized, sending him a mother's look. "And head jester of the family."

"I have a small horse-breeding business and I'm engaged," he said and he reddened a bit.

"Finally," Mary said and Joshua stopped in the act of handing her the basket of bread and turned to give it to Johnny instead. "Hey!" She looked at Elizabeth. "The family thought Joshua was going to marry one of his horses for a while there."

"It wasn't my fault," Joshua defended himself. "God took a long time to set my intended before me. Now it's your turn to tell Elizabeth about yourself."

"I'm a new *mamm* as you can see," Mary told Elizabeth and Paula. "I used to be a teacher before I got married."

"Annie?"

"Hmm?" She looked up from scribbling a note on the back of an envelope. "Sorry, I just got an idea I needed to jot down. I'm a writer, like *Mamm*," she explained. "My first book is out later this year. It's about—"

Groans went up around the table.

"Just because you all have heard about it doesn't mean Elizabeth and Paula don't want to hear about it," she said in an aggrieved tone. But she grinned. "Writers get no respect. Anyway, it's about the Amish and their changing world."

Johnny made quick work of his introduction, mumbling about working at his first job with his brother, Joshua. Then he went back to eating, as if he hadn't seen food for a week. He reminded Elizabeth of her brothers who she always wondered if they had hollow legs because they ate so much.

"And now you, Elizabeth?" Jenny prompted.

"I work at Saul's store and I came here from Goshen, Indiana. Jenny came in one day and asked if I was related to your family and we are and it's why I'm here," she said all in a rush.

"And, last but not least, Paula, please tell us about yourself," Jenny invited.

"I'm finishing up my studies for a bachelor's degree in nursing," Paula told them as she helped herself to the bowl of mashed potatoes with browned butter on top.

"I'm a writer and Matthew is a farmer," Jenny said. "And Rosanna is our first grandchild."

"Let me hold her for you so you can eat," Matthew suggested.

"In a minute," Jenny told him and she looked around the table at her family. "I'm not in a hurry to eat. Supper's not just about eating. It's also about enjoying family and making memories."

Saul found a surprise on the store doorstep when he opened the door for business the next day.

Elizabeth walked in wearing a dress that reminded him of a morning glory blooming on a vine.

"You look very nice this morning," he told her and she beamed.

"*Danki.*"

"Harumph!"

Elizabeth turned and they both saw the bishop stood on the doorstep behind her.

He looked past her to Saul. "I'd like to speak to you."

Saul experienced a sinking feeling in the pit of his stomach. Could the man look any more stern and forbidding? He glanced at Elizabeth and she looked stricken.

"Certainly. We can go in the back room. Elizabeth, would you like to put your things up first?"

She nodded and walked ahead of them to store her jacket, purse, and lunch.

"Call me if you need anything," he told her and then he turned and gestured for the bishop to precede him into the back room.

"I'd offer you coffee, but I haven't made any yet," Saul said as he sat down at the head of the table.

The bishop appeared momentarily disconcerted at his action and glanced, frowning, at the percolator sitting on the cold stove, but Saul didn't care. This didn't look like a friendly visit so better the man say what he had to say and be gone.

"I came to ask you to fire Elizabeth."

Of all the things Saul had expected him to say, that hadn't been it.

"Why would you ask?"

"Obviously, if she has no job she'll have to return to her family where she belongs."

"You don't think she'll just go find another job?"

"If she does, I'll know about it soon enough and go talk to whoever hires her."

Elizabeth had been hired to fill in for Miriam while she was on maternity leave, but the man didn't need to know her employment was short-term.

"You can't do this sort of thing," Saul said. "Not only is it wrong, because she's been a good employee, but it's against the law."

"Not our law."

"But one we have to follow. And I don't agree in any case, because it has to be her choice if she goes back to her family."

"I saw how you looked at her when you opened the door," the bishop said. "If you care about her, you should care about her soul. I'm not trying to punish Elizabeth. I'm trying to bring her back into the fold."

He stood with some stiffness, nodded at Saul, and left the room.

Saul got to his feet and started the coffee. He stood staring out the window, listening to the blip of the coffee perking. When it stopped, he fixed two mugs and carried them out to the counter.

Elizabeth handed a woman a shopping bag and thanked her, then as the woman walked to the door, she turned to him.

He handed her a mug and indicated she should have a seat on the stool behind the counter.

"So, what did he want? It was about me, wasn't it?"

"Everything's not about you," he teased.

When she stared blankly at him, he shook his head. "It's an *Englisch* expression. 'It's all about you.' As if things are only about the other person. It has to be said with the appropriate amount of sarcasm."

Her face closed up. "I'm sorry," she began stiffly and she set her mug down without drinking from it. "I thought he came to talk about me."

Saul touched her arm. "I didn't mean to hurt your feelings. He did come to talk to me about you."

"Why would he do that? What did he think you could do?"

He hesitated, not sure how much he should say. "He thought I should fire you, so you'd have to go back home."

She'd picked up the mug and now she set it down so hard coffee slopped over the sides onto the counter.

"Ow!" she cried and shoved her burned fingers into her mouth.

Saul stood, grasped her other hand and led her into the back room. There, he turned on the cold water tap and persuaded her to put her burned hand under the cool stream of water.

"Better?"

She looked on the verge of tears, but she nodded. He found a plastic bag in the cupboard, filled it with ice and gave it to her to press against the burned hand.

"Why don't you sit in here for a few minutes and take care of that?" he said, drawing out a chair and waiting pointedly until she sat. "I'll go get your coffee."

"No, thanks," she said quickly.

"Something cold?" he asked. "There are soft drinks in the refrigerator."

"I'm fine." She cocked her head. "Sounds like someone just came in."

"I'll take care of it. You stay here."

The visitor was the mail carrier with a handful of mail and a package. Saul followed him to the door and locked it, then turned the sign around which read "Back in five minutes."

Elizabeth looked up when he returned.

"I put the sign up we're taking a break," he explained as he fixed himself another mug of coffee.

He sat down at the table opposite of her and searched her face, trying to find the words. She met his gaze, looking confused.

"Elizabeth, this isn't easy for me to say—"

"You are firing me!" she cried in disbelief.

He held up his hand and shook his head. "No, I'm not firing you. It's the furthest thing from my mind. The bishop said something to make me think. He said he saw how I looked at you when I opened the door."

She blushed and lowered her gaze for a moment, then looked up at him again. "That's none of his business."

"No. But it's ours. I've been attracted to you from the time I walked onto the bus and sat next to you. I haven't said anything, because I didn't want to make you uncomfortable working here. But I'd like to start seeing you outside of work. If you feel the same way. If you don't, we can forget we ever had this conversation and I promise you I won't say another word ever again."

"I felt the same way when I met you," she said honestly. "But I haven't dated and I didn't know what to say to you."

He reached over and squeezed the hand she didn't burn. "I'm glad."

They sat there looking at each other for a long moment. The only sound was the ticking of the clock on the wall. Then they heard someone banging on the front door.

Saul sighed. "Back to real life. Maybe we can have lunch together when Katie and Rosie come in."

"It would be nice."

"Maybe supper after work one night—"

She nodded.

"I'll go open again. You stay and keep ice on your hand."

"It feels fine now," she said, getting to her feet and following him. "I wouldn't want the boss to think I'm taking advantage of him."

Saul tried not to think about her words as he went to unlock the door. He didn't need his mind going in that direction—not now!

Dating was a new experience for Elizabeth, one she'd wanted for so long.

Knowing things had changed between them seemed to make work hours flash by. They ate lunch together whenever the twins could take care of the store without Saul. He took her to supper a couple of times a week and once, when they happened to be in the storeroom looking for something at the same time, she swore she thought he was going to kiss her and then he didn't.

She let him persuade her to go to church again—well, she let him think he persuaded her. While she didn't want to see the bishop again, she did want to see Jenny and Matthew and their family.

He invited her to Thanksgiving dinner with him and his family. She was grateful it was their custom not to discuss it with family until—*if*—they decided to become engaged. It was a big *if* for her right now. Dating was such a new experience for her.

One day when she was eating lunch alone, while Saul ran an errand to the post office and Katie handled customers, Rosie came into the back room and got a soft drink from the refrigerator and sat at the table.

"So how are you?" Rosie asked her.

"Good," she said as she put her plastic salad bowl back into her lunch carrier. "You?"

"Not as good as you. I'm not dating Saul."

Elizabeth's hands stilled on the handle of her carrier. "Who says we're dating?"

Rosie gave her a coy smile. "It doesn't take a detective to figure it out. We've seen the way you two look at each other."

"I see," Elizabeth said slowly. "I didn't realize we were being so obvious."

"That's because you care about each other," Rosie told her. "I think it's sweet. Katie does, too."

"I wonder if anyone else has noticed . . ." Elizabeth trailed off, thinking hard.

"I saw Samuel watching the two of you when he came in last week."

Elizabeth winced. She'd have to talk to Saul about that, see what he thought they should do when they had Thanksgiving dinner with his family.

Katie stuck her head in the door. "Rosie? I need help."

"I'm done with lunch," Elizabeth said as she got up. "Rosie, you take your break."

Grateful for the excuse to be away from her questions, she hurried from the back room.

Saul reassured her his parents wouldn't make her uncomfortable with nosy questions when she came to Thanksgiving dinner.

"How can you be so sure?" she asked him as they ate supper together after work one evening.

A thought struck her. "Is it because you've brought other women to supper?"

He laughed and shook his head. "No. Are you jealous?"

"No," she said, lifting her chin.

But she remembered those two young women she'd over-heard at church the first day and how they talked about him seeing a woman. She didn't feel comfortable bringing up the subject yet. How did you do that when you dated without sounding jealous—or nosy? she wondered. Maybe she'd ask Paula.

Thanksgiving. She wondered if her family would be cele-brating the way they had always done. There was always lots of food, lots of noise with so many crowded around the table. Always so many little mouths to feed, while trying to eat as well.

"Are you thinking about your family? About not being with them for Thanksgiving?"

"How is it you always seem to know what I'm thinking?" she asked quietly, staring into his eyes.

"Of course, I know what you're thinking. I care about you."

She cared about him so much, too, but men—this man—was still a mystery to her. He held out his hand to her on the table and she put hers in it.

On Thanksgiving, she found herself welcomed with a hug as she entered his house carrying one of the pecan pies she had baked the night before (the other went to Paula's parents with her). Saul's brother and his wife were having Thanksgiving dinner with her family and his sister and her family were down with the flu. So it was just the four of them at the table. Elizabeth felt a little relieved at not having to meet more new people.

Saul was right about his parents, she found. While she caught his mother looking thoughtfully at her as they sat at the table and ate turkey and stuffing and what felt like a dozen side dishes, she didn't cast hints about or ask nosy questions. Samuel didn't either despite what Rosie had said at work.

Instead, she thought he seemed quiet, not his usual jovial self, eating so little his wife asked several times if he was okay.

"Is your shoulder hurting again?" she asked.

"I'm *allrecht*," he insisted. "The woman worries," he confided to Elizabeth.

"Did you strain your shoulder somehow?" she asked casually. Something niggled at her memory, something from the first-aid course she'd taken.

"Must have, but I can't think how." He turned and nudged Saul. "Are you going to eat everything so I don't have any leftovers tomorrow? Best part of Thanksgiving is the leftovers."

"As if there are ever leftovers in this house," his wife remarked, winking at Elizabeth. "Samuel, do you want a slice of pie now or wait for supper to settle?"

"I think I'll wait," he said, patting his stomach. "Maybe I'll just have another cup of coffee."

"Let me get it, you've been cooking all morning," Elizabeth told Waneta.

Elizabeth fetched the percolator and served them all coffee. Just as she was about to sit down, Samuel's face changed color.

"Samuel? Are you all right?"

He stared at her, started to say something and then suddenly slumped at the table. His cup fell from his hand and coffee spread across the tablecloth.

14

Samuel! *Mein Gott*, what's wrong?" Waneta cried.

Elizabeth set the coffeepot on the stove and hurried to his side.

"Saul, help me lay him on the floor," Elizabeth said quickly.

He lay his father on the floor and loosened his collar. Elizabeth knelt beside him and checked to see if he was breathing.

"Call 911," she told Saul. "Tell them we need an ambulance."

Waneta knelt beside her. "Is he breathing?"

Elizabeth shook her head. She mentally ran through the steps to perform CPR she'd taken in the first-aid course: checking to make sure his airway was clear, then placing her hands on his chest to begin compressions.

"Is he having a heart attack?" Waneta cried. "He's never had any trouble with his heart."

Elizabeth glanced at Saul and heard him telling the dispatcher someone was doing CPR.

"They're on their way," he said. "They want me to stay on the line."

Busy counting out the compressions, she nodded and kept going. As much as she wanted to reassure Saul's mother, she had to focus.

She heard sirens and wanted to weep with relief.

"I'll go let them in," Saul said. "*Mamm*, why don't you sit at the table so the paramedics can get in here and help *Daed*?"

Moving almost like a robot, Waneta got to her feet and did as he suggested.

The paramedics streamed in, one of them taking over the CPR while Elizabeth moved out of the way and another paramedic asked her what had happened and made notes.

They gave Samuel oxygen and a shot of something and loaded him onto a gurney. Within minutes, he, Waneta, and all of the paramedics who had come to help were gone, leaving Elizabeth standing there, drained, staring after them.

Saul put his arms around her and hugged her for a long moment. "I don't know what we would have done without you here tonight," he said. "You're a good person to have around in an emergency. You're a good person, period."

"He's going to be all right," she said, knowing he needed reassurance. "They got here quickly."

Still he held her. She absorbed the comfort, the gratitude, and then became aware they shouldn't do this—they were alone and the events of the evening had affected them too much.

She stood back. "You need to get a ride to the hospital."

He nodded, pulled out his cell phone, and made arrangements. "Phil says he can drive you home after he drops me at the hospital."

They cleared the table, setting the dishes in the sink to soak in soapy water and put away the leftovers.

"There's some coffee left," she told him. "If you have a thermos you could take it to the hospital."

A van pulled into the driveway.

"No time. We have to go."

"Sorry to hear about your father," Phil said when Saul opened the passenger-side door for Elizabeth.

"I appreciate you being able to drive me to the hospital."

"No problem. The wife's praying for him. I'll have you to the hospital quick as I can, then I'll take Miss Bontrager home."

He nodded at Elizabeth. They'd met when he drove her and Saul on some dates.

The drive was silent. Saul looked drawn as he stared out the window. His fingers tensed on the seat between them. Elizabeth reached over and touched his hand. He looked up and smiled slightly at her.

Then he frowned. "The store. I should give you a key in case I can't get there in the morning to open up." He pulled his keys from his pocket, selected one and began working it off the key ring.

Elizabeth drew back in her seat. "I—I'm sure you'll be there—"

"If I am, I'll just be waiting for you to open up." He handed her the key.

It touched her how he trusted her with the key to the store but it felt like a big responsibility. "I'm not sure I'll know what to do if you're not there."

"Of course you will. And Katie and Rosie will be there around noon like usual. If you get too busy before then, you know where their phone numbers are to call them."

Phil pulled into the hospital parking lot and drove up to the emergency room entrance.

"I'll be praying for your *daed*," she told him and squeezed his hand before he got out.

The apartment was empty when she got home. She took off her dress and hung it up, then pulled on her nightgown and robe. Restless, she wandered into the living room, lay down on the sofa and turned on the television set. She could see why people talked about becoming couch potatoes. It was nice to lie here on a soft sofa and watch something on the television. But she was too restless and soon she was up again, looking for something to do.

"You're home already?" Paula asked when she came home a few minutes later. She carried a shopping bag into the kitchen. "Did you have a nice time?"

Elizabeth slid onto one of the stools at the kitchen island and watched Paula unload Tupperware containers and store them in the refrigerator.

"We won't have to cook for days. I always take these to Mom's for leftovers. Wait until you taste her green bean casserole. Oh, by the way, the pecan pie you made was amazing. Did Saul and his parents like it?" She stopped and grinned at her. "Sorry, I'll let you get a word in."

"You remember how you were watching a CPR video for class one night and I watched it with you, even though I said I took a class at the fire station last summer? Well, Samuel— Saul's *daed*—I think he had a heart attack."

"Oh, no!"

"I performed CPR on him until the paramedics arrived. I'm not sure if I would have remembered what I learned last summer if I hadn't seen that video recently."

She glanced at the clock on the wall. "I'm hoping Saul will call soon and let me know how he is."

But hours passed with no word, and finally Elizabeth went to bed.

Saul sat in the waiting room of the hospital and couldn't take his eyes off the door.

He prayed the next person walking through it would have good news about his father. When he'd arrived at the hospital, his father was already in surgery, and he found his mother shredding a tissue and praying as she rocked back and forth in a hard plastic chair.

An hour passed, then another. His father was the rock of the family and now he lay, vulnerable, under the knife of the surgeon.

Saul had managed the store his father started and made into a thriving business. He turned it over to Saul without a qualm when his wife fell ill, and Saul knew he'd run the store as well as anyone could have. But he'd relied on his *daed* for advice and always knew he could go to him for anything he needed.

Now, if it was God's will for him to leave, Saul didn't know what he'd do. Surely God hadn't helped heal his mother and given her a chance for more years with her *mann* only to lose him?

"I'm going to go get us some coffee," he told her. "Can I bring you anything else?"

She shook her head. He patted her hand and went in search of the cafeteria. When he returned bearing two cups she still sat in the same place, her gaze trained on the door as his had been.

"No word?"

She shook her head and accepted the cup he held out.

"The hospital smells the same as it did three years ago," she said. "I guess it never changes." She sighed.

"You got through chemo. *Daed*'ll get through this. He's strong." He hoped he sounded more certain than he felt. "You said they told you having someone start CPR right away was a big factor in his survival."

They'd prayed and then prayed some more. Saul went for coffee but his mother would drink just a sip and then set it down and walk away to stand and look out the waiting room window.

Finally, the door opened and the doctor walked in looking exhausted. "One of his arteries had a 90 percent blockage. We did a bypass and now it's just a waiting game."

"When can we see him?"

"He'll be in recovery for a while yet. The nurse will let you know." The doctor patted his mother's shoulder and left them.

They sat again.

"*Gut* news," Saul said.

His mother nodded. She closed her eyes and her lips began moving in what Saul thought was a silent prayer.

Saul felt her hand on his shoulder a little while later. He blinked, sat up, and realized he must have dozed off. When he checked his watch he saw that a half hour had passed since the last time he looked at it. His mother had left him some time during his unexpected nap and he was alone in the waiting room.

A nurse came in. "Your mother's with your father. Would you like to go in for a minute?"

He jumped up. "I sure would."

She led him down a corridor to a small room in intensive care. There, she gestured through the window at Saul's mother and she walked out.

"They said one at a time," his mother told him as she nurse walked away. "And we're not to try to wake him."

"I don't want to keep you from—" he began.

She squeezed his arm. "He's my *mann*, but he's your *daed* as well. Go in and see him. "

Saul walked into the room and winced as he saw how pale his father's face looked against the pillow. Fancy machines beeped and pulsed around him and he looked so much smaller lying here in bed.

He touched his father's hand and wondered if it he imagined he felt his father's fingers tighten imperceptibly around his. Shaking his head, he stayed for a few minutes, hoping his father's eyes would open and then finally, he released his hand and walked out.

His mother looked at him with hope in her eyes. "He's looking better than I thought he might."

"I agree," he said, trying to make his voice sound hearty and reassuring. "I'm feeling much better about him."

"I'm selfish," she confessed, her voice shaky. "I talked to God and said I would understand His will but to please let me have more years with Samuel."

He patted her hand. "I'm praying you get them." He sighed and glanced at the clock on the wall.

"I'm staying," she said firmly before he could speak. "You can go home if you want to. I know you'll have to open the store in the morning."

He waved away her words. "I gave Elizabeth a key. She'll open the store. I have complete faith in her. We're staying, but we need to get something to eat."

Saul could tell she wanted to argue with him, but to his surprise she nodded and picked up her purse. He took her hand and tucked it into the crook of his arm as they walked.

"I hope this place isn't bringing back bad memories," he said as he punched the elevator button.

"Why no," she said, looking at him with surprise. "Everyone was wonderful here and the chemo saved my life. And the hospital worked with us to give us a discount in the cost."

Saul knew the payment had still been significant and without the Plain community sharing the financial burden they could have lost everything.

The hospital never closed but now as it grew near daylight it seemed to be coming awake. They joined the line to get coffee and breakfast.

"It isn't the breakfast my *mamm* makes for me," Saul said when they were seated at their table.

"Sssh," she said. "They do the best they can with so many to cook for." But she smiled.

After they asked for a blessing for the meal, Saul began eating his eggs. "Wonder how long it'll be before *Daed* wakes up?"

"Don't know. But I don't want to leave before he does," Waneta said.

He looked at her nursing her cup of coffee. She hadn't touched her own breakfast. When he simply gave her a direct look she smiled slightly. "I'll eat in a minute."

"You'll fall on your face if you don't take care of yourself."

He buttered a piece of toast and dug strawberry jelly out of a little container to spread over it. The stuff tasted very much like chemicals—nothing like the jelly his *mamm* had made from the harvest.

"I'll be *allrecht*. I'll go home after Samuel wakes up." She set her coffee down and picked up her fork. "You think a lot of Elizabeth to have her watching the store."

He nodded.

"I'm so grateful to her," she said quietly. "I don't know what we'd have done tonight without her. I was too panicked to do anything."

Saul glanced up from his breakfast and saw the tears rolling down her cheeks. Reaction had finally set in. He reached across the table and took one of her hands in his. "I think maybe God put her in just the right place, don't you?"

She smiled through her tears and nodded. "She's such a sweet *maedel*. I hope she's happier here than she was back home."

Was she? he wondered as he released her hand. He'd thought she was until the bishop had come to the store. But then it seemed to him she'd looked a little preoccupied and uncertain since then.

After his father was out of the woods he'd have to ask her how she was doing. It wasn't just because he and his family owed her a lot. He'd grown to care so much for her and her happiness was important to him.

Very important.

⟨ஐ⟩

The key to the store didn't work.

Panicked, Elizabeth tried it again and this time it worked. She turned and waved to Paula who was sitting at the curb in her car and her roommate nodded and pulled out onto the road.

Relieved, Elizabeth stepped inside and locked the door. She had about a half hour before opening and needed to store her jacket and purse. Start some coffee.

Get her nerves under control.

It was a big responsibility to be in charge of opening—maybe closing—the store until Saul felt he could leave his father at the hospital.

She walked into the back room, put her things away and started coffee in the percolator. While it perked, she stepped back into the store, looked over the shelves and nodded. Everything looked neat and tidy. She knew some deliveries had come just before Thanksgiving and in the afternoon when the twins arrived, she'd see if they had time between customers to get them unpacked, tagged, and on the shelves.

The approaching holiday season was an important one for this and other area stores. Not the best time to have its owner distracted by urgent family matters like illness. But then again, when was there one? She just hoped Samuel had gotten through the night and was recovering . . .

She returned to fix herself a mug of coffee—her stomach had been jumping too much back home to have one—and her fingers itched to call Saul on his cell. She glanced at the wall clock and decided if she didn't hear from him in a couple of hours she'd do so, if for no other reason than to reassure him the store was fine. She told herself no news was good news.

As she sat behind the counter, she surveyed the store and drank her coffee. What would it be like to do this every day? She'd never opened or closed the fabric store back in Goshen. And really, this might just be for today, she told herself. So, she needed to stop with the mix of terror and elation she'd felt ever since she'd been given the key. She'd barely slept last night.

Saul worked hard to have a good store and while Plain folk such as them didn't believe in *hochmut*—in pride—she knew he cared very much about stewarding the shop successfully after his father turned it over to him.

She found herself wondering about her own father. Although the man was the head of the home, the spiritual leader, her mother had always seemed more dominant to her. Maybe it was because she spent so much time with her helping with the house and with the *kinner*. And the latest *boppli*. Now she wondered how he was doing. Was he helping more with household matters? Was he making Mary, the next oldest, do more as she should have been doing all along?

Someone rapped on the door. She set down her coffee and hurried to see who it was.

Leah, the owner of Stitches in Time, stood smiling on the doorstep.

"I heard about Samuel," she said when Elizabeth opened the door and invited her inside. "I came by to see if there's anything I can do to help."

"How very nice. Saul asked me to open the store and take care of things until he can leave his father."

Leah studied her and nodded. "It's good he knew he could rely on you."

"Oh, I'm sure he thought about asking others," Elizabeth said, shrugging. "He probably even called them from the hospital."

"Don't say such a thing," Leah chided her gently. "We're discouraged from being prideful, but the opposite—thinking we aren't worthy and good at what we do—well, it's not our way either, is it?"

"I haven't done my job here long enough to know I'm any good at it."

Leah patted her cheek. "Dear one, Saul wouldn't have you working here if you weren't good at your job."

"Well, um, *danki*." She stood there uncertainly for a moment. "Do you have time for some coffee? I just made it."

"*Schur*. Naomi and Jamie are working today. Which brings up something I'd like to talk to you about. "

She glanced at the door as a customer walked up and rattled the door. "I'll go get the coffee while you open up."

Elizabeth opened the door and greeted the woman who stood there. "*Wilkuum*. Come right in."

"You're open, right?"

She nodded. "You're my first customer. Is there something special you're looking for?"

"No, just starting my Christmas shopping and looking around."

"Let me know if I can help you in any way."

The woman, a prosperous-looking *Englischer*, glanced around. "I will. Thank you. *Danki*," she added. "That's right, isn't it?"

Elizabeth smiled. "It certainly is. Do you know much Pennsylvania *Dietsch*?"

"I know two words," the woman confessed with a laugh. "*Danki* and *ya*—yes. I'm just on vacation here."

"I know just a few more than you," Elizabeth admitted. She saw Leah take a seat on a stool behind the counter at the back of the store. "Please let me know if there's anything I can help you with."

She walked back to Leah, took a seat on another stool and picked up her own coffee.

"I came by to tell you we'd be happy to help you in any way while Saul's out," Leah began without preamble. She pulled a card from her pocket and pressed it into Elizabeth's hand. "I know Katie and Rosie will be in later today, but if you should need one of us to run over and help with anything I want you to promise you'll call."

"I will."

"I heard you were eating Thanksgiving dinner with Saul and Samuel and Waneta when Samuel had his heart attack."

Elizabeth nodded.

"It's interesting how God works, don't you think?" Leah asked her.

She frowned. "What do you mean?"

"You were there to help Samuel when he needed you. Not so long ago you didn't even know him."

"Saul would have helped his *dat*."

"Undoubtedly. But it sounds like you jumped right in and knew exactly what to do."

She shrugged. "It was something I learned in a class last summer, then my roommate was watching a video on it for a class and I joined her."

"There are no coincidences," Leah said sagely. "I'd say not just Saul is glad you came here."

"Well, I'm happy to help Saul—"

Leah chuckled. "Saul may be grateful for the help at the store, but it's not what I was referring to. I hear things." She slid from the stool. "Well, I'd best be getting back to Stitches. Stop by sometime after things settle down. I'd love to talk with you some more."

With that, she took their empty mugs to the back room, then waved as she left the store.

The customer who'd been browsing approached with a question. The door opened and another walked in.

The day had begun.

15

"What time is it?"

Saul blinked and sat up. His father was awake and staring at him, looking a little bleary. He glanced at the clock. "Nine a.m."

"Why aren't you at the store?"

He shoved aside the blanket someone had covered him with as he sat beside his father's bed. "I thought it was more important to be here."

Samuel shook his gray head. "People depend on you to be open."

"Didn't say we weren't open." He shoved his hands through his hair and stared down at his wrinkled clothes. "I gave Elizabeth a key and told her I'd be stopping in later."

"Elizabeth, huh?"

Saul tilted his head and studied his father. "You have a problem with her doing it? She saved your life. She knew CPR and started it before I could think what to do."

Waneta walked in, and when she saw Samuel was awake she brightened and hurried over to kiss his cheek. "How are you feeling?"

"Weak. Chest hurts."

She nodded and patted his arm. "Stay quiet. I'll ring for the nurse."

"Let Saul get her. I just want to look at you."

Tears sprang to her eyes. "Oh, you!" she cried. "Don't get me started."

Saul decided to walk to the nurse's station so they could have a private moment. When he returned from talking to a nurse, his mother was helping his father take a sip of water from a cup with a straw. The effort clearly cost him. He lay back against his pillow, wan and a little winded.

The nurse entered the room a few minutes later and checked her patient's vital signs. When she finished, she was smiling.

"He's doing very well but he's asleep again and he'll doze most of the day. It's a good time to go home, get a little rest and something to eat. When you come back this afternoon he should be more alert."

His mother glanced back at the door, clearly torn. "She makes sense. Let's go home for a little while and we'll come back. *Daed* wouldn't want you to make yourself sick worrying."

When she continued to stand there, he touched her arm. "Sitting there and watching his every breath won't keep him with us. We have to trust."

She choked up for a moment, and then she nodded. "We'll see you later," she told the nurse.

The woman patted her arm. "We'll take good care of him. I promise."

They stopped by the cafeteria and Saul convinced his mother they should order a sandwich while they waited for his driver to come for them.

It was tempting to stop by the store on the way home, yet Saul was determined to get his mother home to rest. But he gave Elizabeth a quick call and felt some relief when she answered the store phone quickly and with confidence in her tone.

"It's Saul. How are things going?"

"Very well. Leah stopped in this morning to see if I needed anything and the twins came in a little early. News spreads fast. A number of people have come by to ask how your father is doing."

"You can tell them he continues to improve. I'm taking my mother home to rest and we'll be going back again in a few hours."

"Good. Hold on for a moment, please."

Saul heard Katie ask a question and Elizabeth answered it, then came back on the phone. "Sales have been good."

They talked for a few minutes more about what she should do with the day's deposit. He couldn't help wishing he could be there at the store to talk to her. He was a grown man; he didn't need reassurance. But somehow her presence, her words, had been so comforting as she rode with him to the hospital . . . he longed for it again. With reluctance he said good-bye.

"Saul?" she said quickly before he could hang up. "Call me later if you'd like to talk?"

He felt himself smile. "I will. *Danki* for everything."

"She's very special, isn't she?" his mother asked quietly.

Saul had forgotten she sat beside him while he talked on his cell phone. He nodded.

"More than a friend?"

Their gazes met. "*Ya.*"

"You feel God's chosen her for you?"

"I do. I think He sent her all the way here from Indiana for me."

She sighed and smiled. "I am so happy for you, *sohn.*" She gazed out the window, then back at him. "Sometimes when we let go and stop trying to tell Him what's best for us we find it, eh?"

"We do," he said. "We do."

He'd gotten on the bus to go home, unhappy at realizing it wasn't going to work out with Lavina and walked right up to Elizabeth. What a perfect outworking of God's invisible, mysterious plan.

The van pulled into the driveway of their home. They went inside. The house seemed so quiet without Samuel's large presence and booming voice. Waneta took off her jacket and hung it on a peg. She touched Samuel's jacket beside hers, and Saul watched her shoulders sag.

"He'll be home before we know it."

She nodded. "I know. I'm going to go lie down now. You should, too."

"I'm headed there now."

He went into his room, lay down, and was asleep the second his head hit the pillow.

꧂

One day turned into two.

Things had gone well at the store and while she'd have liked to see Saul, she understood he'd gone back to the hospital and sat with his father some more yesterday afternoon.

Samuel had suffered a bit of a setback then, so Saul sounded a bit distracted when Elizabeth called at closing time. She quickly asked him what to do with the day's deposit, he told her, and then he hung up so quickly, she was left holding the receiver and staring at it.

Elizabeth felt more settled when she opened the store the next morning. Taking care of the shop the day before hadn't been as hard as she'd thought it would be.

Leah stopped in at lunchtime and glanced around. "Saul in?"

Elizabeth shook her head. "He's still at the hospital. Did you need to talk to him? Can I help you with anything?"

She smiled. "No, I came to see if you need any help. Things going *allrecht*?"

"Very well." She bit her lip. "Well, it sounds like he had a hard night. Samuel, I mean. So Saul and his mother are at the hospital today."

"Two men in the community had the same surgery. One of them recovered quickly and the other took twice as long to get over it."

Elizabeth straightened a shelf of quilts and sighed. "Samuel sounds like the second man."

"He might be. Before I go back to the shop we can say a prayer. I wanted to talk with you a few minutes. Do you have the time?"

The store was empty as it often was during the noon hour. Tourists enjoyed the Amish specialties at local restaurants before returning to shop the stores.

"Of course. Do you want some coffee or tea?"

Leah held up a tote. "I brought lunch. Sandwiches and iced tea."

"Katie and Rosie aren't due in for a while so if you don't mind eating at the counter."

"That's fine."

They walked back to the counter and Leah pulled the sand-wiches from the tote. Elizabeth brought paper plates and cups from the back room and they settled on the high stools to eat.

"The new dress came out well."

Elizabeth glanced down at it and smiled. "*Danki*. I love the color. I'm hoping to visit the shop and get more fabric soon. I was wondering. Do you know anywhere I could buy a sewing machine at a reasonable price? I can't afford a new one—I'd have to get a nice used one."

"I know someone who sells them. I'll contact him for you."

"I appreciate it." She bit into her sandwich. "And I appreciate the sandwich. I packed peanut butter and jelly today. I haven't had time to shop the last few days."

"About the fabric," Leah said as she unscrewed the top of the thermos of iced tea and poured it into the cups. "You could get an employee's discount."

"Really? But I don't work there."

Leah looked at her directly. "I know when you came here you were supposed to fill in for Miriam for her maternity leave. Do you know when she'll be back?"

"First of the year. Why?"

"I wouldn't want anyone to think I would try to steal you away from Saul," Leah said carefully. "But Jamie is leaving for a wonderful opportunity in New York City after the first of the year. I thought you might like to join us at Stitches in Time. If you've decided to stay here in Paradise for a while."

Elizabeth had tried not to think about what would happen after Miriam returned. Now it seemed she would be able to walk from one job to another.

"It would be *wunderbaar*," she breathed. "I mean, I'm sorry Jamie's leaving, but I love the shop. And yes, I intend to stay in Paradise. At least, I'd like to."

She didn't know where things might go with Saul but she was hopeful. And she liked it here.

Leah nodded. "You seem to love sewing. Maybe you can experiment with it around your work there."

"I can't do anything like the cousins," she said doubtfully. "They're all so creative."

"They started somewhere, too," Leah said. "And they became better at what they do. But the main thing is we all help run the shop. We wouldn't make any money if all we did was sit around and create. You think about it. Come visit again. There's time."

She folded the waxed paper from her sandwich, put it in the tote, and finished her tea. "I have one more question for you. It's kind of personal."

Elizabeth braced herself for a question about Saul. Each community was different. It was possible such things were considered less personal and more open for discussion here . . .

"We missed you at church last Sunday."

Surprised, Elizabeth didn't know quite how to answer.

Leah laid a hand on hers. "The Amish grapevine works quickly. I heard the bishop talked to you. I hope he didn't discourage you from attending."

"Not exactly," Elizabeth said. She met Leah's concerned gaze. "He heard from my grandmother. He thinks I should go back home."

"And what do you think you should do? What is God telling you, *kind*?"

Elizabeth felt tears rushing up at the quiet question, at the sincere caring she saw in Leah's gaze. "I think I'm supposed to be here. When I left Goshen, it was sort of an impulsive decision. I hadn't planned it out for a long time. But from the moment I met Paula and thought about it, things started happening to make me think I had to come here."

She balled up the paper her sandwich had been wrapped in. "I sat on the bus and I was so scared. I kept looking for a sign to help me know if I was supposed to go or get off and stay in Goshen. How was I going to provide for myself? I didn't know if I'd find a job here. But something—Someone?—kept me on it and the bus started rolling and that was that."

She slid from her stool, found a little carved sparrow on a shelf, and brought it back to show Leah. "I bought one of these with my first paycheck from the store. I have it on my bedside table. It reminds me of the little birds I saw outside the bus window when I was so worried about how I'd take care of myself. I remembered something from the Bible about God provides for the sparrow and realized He'll take care of me."

Leah smiled. "It sounds like He spoke to you. Please don't let the bishop keep you from joining us and hearing other messages from Him."

"I won't."

"I can talk to him if you like. Matter of fact, I'd enjoy it."

"I don't think we need to. Saul spoke to him."

Leah raised her eyebrows. "He did, did he?"

Elizabeth smiled. "*Ya.*"

"Well, isn't that interesting," Leah said.

She put the thermos in the tote and stood. Just as she did, a customer entered the shop.

"Perfect timing," she told Elizabeth with a smile. "But then He always has it, even when we think He doesn't answer us when we want. We'll talk again. Tell Saul I'm praying for Samuel."

"I will. And thank you." Impulsively, Elizabeth hugged Leah. "Thank you for everything."

Leah patted her back. "See you soon." She nodded to the customer as she left the store.

Elizabeth regarded the little carved wooden sparrow on the counter in front of her. Its head was tilted, its little beady black eyes seeming to stare intently at her.

He looked much like the one she'd bought but with the slight difference hand-carving created. She tilted her own head and stared at it. Maybe she should buy him to keep the one at home company. Make a pair. Like her and Saul?

She wondered if Paula would be willing to take her to visit Samuel at the hospital.

"Excuse, me, miss?"

Elizabeth came back to earth. "Can I help you?"

There was no time for daydreaming after that. The shop became busy with after-lunch shoppers and she was grateful when the twins came on duty in the afternoon.

Paula arrived a little late to pick her up and seemed a little distracted. "Sorry, I was trying to get Jason on the phone, but it kept going to voicemail."

"He's due home this weekend, isn't he?"

She slanted Elizabeth a wry look. "As if I've talked about anything else."

Elizabeth smiled. "It's okay. I just wish you weren't so worried."

Paula's fingers tightened on the steering wheel and then she relaxed them. "He got through two tours in Afghanistan. I just don't want anything to happen to him on the way home."

"I'm sure it won't," Elizabeth said. She decided she'd say an extra prayer for him tonight.

"What do you have in the bag?"

She grinned. "Another sparrow. I decided the first one needed company."

"If only it were as easy to get a mate for us," Paula said with a laugh. "My guy's who-knows-where right now and you haven't seen Saul in days." She sighed as she signaled to pull into their parking lot. "I'm bushed. Thank goodness I have no homework tonight. I'm going to be a couch potato."

Elizabeth was about to say she thought it was an interesting name for a lazy person when she climbed the last step and saw the man seated—slumped, really—in front of their door. She stopped abruptly.

"What is it?" Paula asked when she bumped into Elizabeth. Then she saw what Elizabeth had seen.

"Jason!"

He blinked and woke. "Paula! Hey, baby, don't cry! I'm home!"

Elizabeth smiled as she edged around them, unlocked the apartment door, and went inside to cook supper for the three of them.

❧

Saul felt strange opening the store after being away for a couple of days.

Nothing had changed and yet there was something different. He stepped inside, turned, and locked the door behind him. The stock was neatly arranged on shelves, the floor didn't show a speck of dust, and when he peeked in the storage room the recently delivered boxes were gone—evidently marked and stocked on the shelves.

Then he saw what was different: there was a vase of red and white carnations on the counter. Elizabeth's touch?

He walked into the back room and started coffee. The brew he made wasn't the best, but it sure would be an improvement on the stuff he'd been drinking at the hospital.

The store was so quiet he heard when a key was inserted in the front door. When Elizabeth stepped into the back room, she gasped and clutched her chest with one hand.

"I'm sorry, I should have called out I was here," Saul said.

"Second time I've walked up on a man," she muttered.

"What?"

"Nothing. It's *gut* to see you. How is your *dat*?"

"Better. I think he's out of the woods."

The coffee finished percolating. "Want some?"

"Yes, please."

She took off her jacket, hung it on a peg and stowed her purse. He fixed her coffee the way she liked, set both mugs at the table and took a seat.

It was so good to look at her face again. "I missed you."

"I missed you, too," she said with a shy smile.

"*Mamm* and *Daed* wanted me to tell you thank you again."

"Please, it was nothing," she told him, shrugging. "You should thank Paula for having me watch the nursing video. It was a good refresher for the class."

"I think it would be a good idea for me to watch it sometime," he said quietly. "The doctor thinks *Daed* will be fine, but you never know."

"God provides." She reached across the table and touched his hand. "You look tired."

"I am."

"Maybe you can leave early today. After all, you're the boss."

He laughed shortly and sipped his coffee. "Everything go okay?"

"Very well. Leah stopped by to offer her help and the twins came in a little early. We've got all the stock on the shelves."

"I saw that."

"I have some ideas about some Christmas gifts," she began.

His cell phone buzzed. Frowning, he looked at the display, praying the call wasn't from the hospital. Instead, he saw a text message from his bank warning several checks had overdrawn the store account.

He glanced up at Elizabeth. "Did you make the day's deposits?"

She blinked. "Of course."

"You're sure?"

"Of course, I'm sure. I wouldn't leave the money in the store overnight."

He got to his feet. "I have to leave for a few minutes. Open up when it's time."

Grabbing his jacket, he rushed from the room. A business couldn't afford not to meet its obligations—especially in a small town. Reputation was everything.

The bank manager greeted him by name when he arrived and asked how he could help him. Saul explained about the text message and the man waved to him to take a seat and began pulling his account up on his computer.

Saul didn't like how the thought came to him Elizabeth might not have deposited the money . . . at least not in the business account. Had he trusted her with more responsibility than he should have? Thought she was more honest than she was?

His stomach rolled over.

"Ah, I see the problem," the manager said.

"The money wasn't deposited?"

"Oh, no, not to worry, I see daily deposits the last two days," the man was quick to reassure him. "But you made them to your store savings account, not to your checking account."

"An employee must have made a mistake," he explained. "I was with my father in the hospital."

"Oh, sorry, hope Samuel is okay?"

"*Ya*, he is. But this was a bit of a scare for me. I was asking myself if I'd misplaced trust in my employee."

"I see. Listen, I don't know why you don't have overdraft protection on your account."

Saul shook his head. "It was mentioned to me when I took over the store after *Daed* retired. But I don't believe in over-drawing my accounts, in spending money I don't have."

The manager nodded and pulled some papers from a drawer. "I understand. But it's more a protection for times just like this. A mistake happens and suddenly checks don't clear and there are overdraft charges."

"Overdraft charges?" Saul winced.

"We can waive those this time. But let's have you sign up for the protection for the future."

A few minutes later, Saul walked back into the store. Elizabeth had turned the sign on the door to OPEN and stood rearranging a shelf near the back of the store.

She turned when she heard the door open and regarded him silently. "Everything okay?"

"*Ya.* You deposited the day's receipts to the store savings account, not checking, so some checks bounced."

"I'm sorry. I haven't had to do it before."

"It's *allrecht.* The manager fixed it."

She clasped her hands in front of her and continued to watch him. He realized there was hurt in her blue eyes.

"I don't think it's *allrecht*," she said slowly. "Not really. I think you thought I didn't put the money in the store account, but maybe into my own pocket."

16

Saul recoiled at her words, but Elizabeth didn't back off.

"I didn't think that." But he didn't meet her gaze. "Well, just for a moment. But it didn't make sense."

"Because I was still here."

Now, he looked at her. "Elizabeth—"

"Then again, I didn't know you were coming in this morning. I could have thought I had another day or two to steal." She turned on her heel and started walking away.

"You're blowing this all up," he said, and he followed her. "I didn't think you were a thief and I didn't think you would run away."

He stopped her, his hand on her arm.

"Why not? I've done it before."

Startled, he stared at her. "I didn't even think of that," he repeated.

She gave him a disbelieving look and shook off his hand.

The bell over the door rang as a customer entered the store. Elizabeth used the distraction as a way to distance herself from him, leaving him standing near the store counter.

Fortunately, the woman wanted her help and they spent a good deal of time choosing a quilt for her daughter's wedding present.

Elizabeth wrapped the quilt in tissue and tucked it into a shopping bag. She handed it to the woman with a smile. "I hope your daughter has a lovely wedding."

The minute the woman turned to exit the shop Elizabeth moved away from the counter.

"Elizabeth, we need to talk."

She shook her head. "I need to fold the quilts we disarranged."

He shoved his hands in his hair. "You don't understand what pressure I've been under for the past few days."

Her steps faltered and she turned. She tried to push past her hurt feelings and saw he looked exhausted and worried.

"I do understand," she said quietly. "But you immediately ran out of here like I'd done something awful."

"I'm sorry for how it looked."

His words sounded stiff but he seemed sorry. Maybe he didn't have to make apologies often. Troubled, she stood there, not knowing what to say, what to do.

Saul's cell phone rang. He answered it, and he frowned as he listened. When he finished, he sighed as he put his phone away. "I have to go back to the hospital."

"Is your father worse?"

"He's had an allergic reaction to some medication. I think *Mamm* needs someone to sit with her for a while more than anything. I may not be able to come back. Can you close up again?"

"Of course."

He walked over to the counter and pulled out a bank deposit slip. "Let me show you what to do and then I'm going to go call for a ride."

She stood beside him as he went over what she needed to know, then he called his driver. Minutes later, as she was ringing up a sale for a customer, he left.

"Tough day?" Paula asked when she picked her up after the store closed.

"Work was okay," Elizabeth said. "But Saul and I—" she touched her bottom lip with her fingers to still the trembling—"Saul and I had a fight."

"Oh, sweetie, I'm so sorry!" Paula sat there looking at her with sympathy. "First one, huh?"

She nodded. "First one, with my first boyfriend."

"The first one is always rough. Tell you what, let's go home and get in our PJs and order in a pizza and you can tell me all about it."

"What about Jason?"

"It'll be girls only night. He's spending the evening with his parents. I have to share him on his leave. The four of us are having dinner tomorrow night so I'll see him then. And meet his parents." She bit her bottom lip. "Little nervous about it."

"They'll love you."

"I hope."

An hour later, they were eating pizza in their PJs on the sofa and Elizabeth was telling her what had happened.

"I know you're upset, but it doesn't sound so bad now, does it?"

"I don't know." Elizabeth set the slice of pizza she'd been eating back on her plate. "I didn't feel he trusted me. I might not know much about dating and men, but trust is important."

"It is."

"Maybe it's just that he feels he doesn't know you well yet. After all, don't most Amish date and marry someone right in their community they've known for years? He hasn't known you long."

She picked up the slice of pizza again. "You think that could be it?"

"I don't know. Why don't you think about it, maybe ask him?"

"When I see him again," she said glumly. "He had to rush back to the hospital." She set the slice of pizza back on her plate. "Now I feel guilty I'm even thinking about how I feel when his father isn't doing well."

"He's going to be fine. Recovery isn't something that's a straight incline. It can be a lot of ups and downs, particularly with major surgery."

"Really?"

"Really. Now eat your pizza and let's pick out a movie."

"Oh, I almost forgot I got some good news yesterday," Elizabeth said suddenly. She told Paula about Leah's visit and the job offer. "It's so nice to think I might have a job after this one at the store ends. I didn't know what I was going to do. I mean, I don't have a lot of skills. I don't know a lot."

"You know plenty. Don't sell yourself short."

Elizabeth shook her head. "I know about taking care of babies." She looked at Paula. "No. I do not want to take care of babies."

"Ever?"

Elizabeth blinked. "I—I haven't thought about it. Maybe my own one day. But I just got so tired of doing nothing but the same thing day after day. And cleaning house. I never got to do anything but baby care and housework and work. Never got to go to a singing or go for a buggy ride." She sighed. "You know this. You let me whine in my letters often enough."

"You didn't whine."

"I did."

Paula laughed. "It's okay. People need to vent. Then at some point they can decide to change things. When people don't make a change in the things bothering them, then it's not healthy."

"But what if they don't make the change in a good way?"

"What do you mean?"

Elizabeth shrugged. "I ran away."

"I could tell you weren't happy about it," Paula said sympathetically. "It didn't sound like you thought you had any other choice."

"I didn't think I did."

"But now you wonder?"

She nodded.

"So what are you going to do?"

"You think I should do something?"

Paula patted her hand. "It's more important what *you* think."

"Life's not easy sometimes," Elizabeth complained.

Fwap! A sofa pillow smacked her in the face.

"Now you're whining!" Paula said, laughing at Elizabeth's surprise.

Elizabeth picked up the pillow. "Pillow fight!" She smacked Paula with it.

They acted like a couple of kids chasing each other around the room, hitting each other with pillows until they collapsed, giggling on the sofa.

⁓

Saul went into the store the next afternoon and closeted himself in the back room to go over paperwork. Elizabeth and the twins were doing a good job running the store, but only he could manage it. He'd had to come up to speed quickly when his mother needed treatment for her cancer and his father turned the store over to him.

Now when he felt needed by the two of them he had no one to give the responsibility of ordering inventory, checking on shipments, and all the big and small aspects of the store.

And every so often the specter of the mounting hospital bills sneaked up on him. He knew his mother thought about it as well, since she'd mentioned it to him outside his father's room. The community had helped share the costs of the che-motherapy, so he knew they'd have help. Still, he'd heard the heart surgery, the specialists, the around-the-clock care—the complications his father had suffered—were undoubtedly going to be staggering.

He sighed. As soon as things got on an even keel with his father, with the store, he needed to talk with the church lead-ers. If he could, he'd try to make the discussion without his mother. She had enough to cope with.

There was a knock on the door. "*Kumm.*"

Elizabeth opened the door and stuck her head in. "Sorry. I need to get my lunch."

"It's time already?"

"*Ya.*" She slipped into the room and retrieved her lunch from the refrigerator.

"Let me move these papers," he said, reaching for the neat stacks he'd made on the table.

"No need," she said, slipping on her jacket and getting her purse. "I'm going to go eat it at Stitches in Time with Leah."

"Oh. Well, then, have a *gut* time."

"*Danki.* I'll be back soon." She bit her bottom lip, started to say something and then shook her head. Turning, she started to leave and nearly ran into Miriam. She blinked. "Well, hello."

"Hello." Miriam grinned. "Hello, Saul."

"Miriam! It's *gut* to see you! What are you doing in town?"

"I'm ready to come back to work."

His gaze flew to Elizabeth. She looked stricken. Then she was mumbling something about going to lunch and she was gone.

"Have a seat, Miriam. Can I get you some coffee?"

"*Nee, danki.* Is everything *allrecht*? Elizabeth looked upset."

"Well, your news might have had something to do with that. Remember, I hired her to fill in for you and you're saying you're ready to come back early."

"Oh, no. I'm sorry!"

"Don't worry about it. I'll talk to her when she comes back."

Miriam bit her lip. "I guess I won't be coming back early, then. I don't want to take Elizabeth's job away from her."

Saul shook his head. "It's fine. You've heard my *daed* is in the hospital?"

"*Ya.* Oh, now I really feel selfish. I intended to ask you about him when I walked in here."

"It's fine," he said again. "I could use some extra help, especially with Christmas coming up."

She brightened. "Well, then, it all worked out! I'll see you tomorrow morning, then?"

He nodded and sat back with a sigh after she left. Yes, it had all worked out for him. But he didn't like the idea Elizabeth looked upset. He glanced at the clock. She'd be back soon and he'd explain.

Determined to get caught up, he focused on the paperwork in front of him. Before he knew it Elizabeth was walking into the room and hanging up her jacket.

"*Gut*, you're back—"

"I have another job to go to, so if you don't need me to finish out the week I can go there," she said, lifting her chin.

"You what?"

"I got another job. So if you don't need me because Miriam will be here I can go work there."

"Why did you go get another job?" he demanded, exasperated. "I never said I wanted you to leave."

She put her purse away and stared at him. "I was hired to fill in while Miriam was out. Now she's back."

"She wanted to come back early, but it didn't mean I was going to let her!" He heard his voice rise and took a deep breath.

"Well, are you saying you didn't?"

"No, but—"

"Then you should be happy I have another job to go to, so you don't have two of us."

Saul counted to ten, praying for patience. "It would have been fine. I wouldn't ask you to leave before your time. And we could use the extra help since I've been out so much with my parents, and we're having extra Christmas traffic."

"Well, I didn't know you'd want me to stay."

"You got a job while you were out on your lunch hour?" he asked her. "This has to be some kind of record—a person finding a job in less than an hour."

"You don't think I'm good enough to find a job quickly?" She crossed her arms over her chest and glared at him.

"It's not what I said. It's just amazing, that's all. Sometimes people look for jobs for weeks. Years."

"Well, I didn't really find it during my lunch hour," she said, looking less angry. "I got offered the job before today, but it wasn't supposed to start until after the first of the year."

"I see. So what do you want to do?"

"What do you mean, what do I want to do? I want to work. I have to work. I don't have anyone supporting me."

Saul wondered what she'd do if he banged his head on the wall.

"Anyway, maybe it's better this way since we're not getting along," she said quietly.

"We had a fight. There's no need to overreact, Elizabeth."

"I didn't overreact."

"No? Even if you didn't then, what do you call now? You go rushing out and grab at another job, so we don't see each other?"

"So we can only see each other if we work together?"

That stopped him. He'd grown to really enjoy working with her. Maybe he hadn't come to the point of envisioning a future with her, but now the idea was there, he wondered if the possibility was lost forever.

It hurt more than he wanted to admit. "You didn't have to get another job," he blurted out before he could stop himself. "Is this what you do when things get hard?"

"It's what you think, isn't it?" she asked slowly. "I just run away from my problems?"

Saul sensed whatever he said was going to decide if they ever saw each other again. Why had he opened his big mouth and stuck his foot into it?

"Let's not talk about this now," he urged. "It's too important."

She bit her lip, a habit of hers when she felt uncertain. Then she glanced at the clock and her eyes widened when she saw the time.

"Fine. I'm going back to work." She turned and started out of the room.

"Elizabeth?"

She stopped but she didn't turn. "What?"

"Can we go somewhere after work and talk?"

"I can't tonight."

He wanted to ask her who she had plans with, but he didn't have the right. "Sunday? After church?"

"I'm not sure I want to go. The bishop—"

"Don't worry about him. He's not going to say anything to you if you're with me."

She hesitated for a long moment and then she nodded. "See you Sunday."

It was all he could ask. Maybe by the time they talked he'd know what to say.

❧

Elizabeth heard giggling.

She perked up, listening, but it stopped. Shrugging, she returned to reading her book.

The giggling began again.

Kicking off the afghan she'd tucked around her legs, she left the sofa and tiptoed over to the front door. She peeked out the peephole in the door and her eyes widened. Paula and Jason were kissing!

Embarrassed she'd accidentally seen something so private she backed away and climbed back onto the sofa. No, better to go to her room. Paula might invite Jason in for a cup of coffee or something.

She was just getting up again when she heard a key turn in the lock and they walked in.

"Oh, hi, Elizabeth! You're still up!"

"Well, it's Saturday," she said lamely, wishing she'd moved faster.

Maybe if she faked a yawn.

"I'm glad you're up," Paula told her. She took Jason by the hand and led him over to the sofa. "I have something to tell you."

She turned to smile up at Jason and he looked at her with such love Elizabeth knew Paula had gotten the engagement ring she hoped for—early before Christmas. "We're engaged!" She held out her hand to show Elizabeth her ring.

Elizabeth didn't have any experience with engagement rings—the Amish didn't wear engagement or wedding rings—but it was pretty and Paula and Jason acted so happy.

"It's lovely," she said, taking Paula's hand and studying it.

"I wanted to get her something bigger—" Jason began.

"Don't you start again!" she told him. "I love it. And we agreed to save the money for a down payment on a house."

"When are you getting married?

"June."

"How wonderful."

"Don't worry," Paula said quickly. "You can stay here. Nothing has to change."

"Oh, I couldn't do that. You two deserve to have the place to yourselves."

"You always think about others." She turned to Jason. "How about I start some coffee and go pack an overnight bag?"

"I can do it. I think I remember how."

"We're going to go to his parents' house to tell them and spend the rest of the weekend," Paula told Elizabeth. "Come help me pick out what to take."

Elizabeth followed her into her bedroom where she sat on the end of the bed and watched Paula go through her closet.

"So, how did it go today?" Paula called from her walk-in closet. "Did you get to talk and work things out with Saul?"

She bit her lip. Now wasn't the time to tell Paula she and Saul had argued again. "He wasn't in long. We'll talk soon."

Paula emerged from the closet with two dresses. "What do you think? The pink or the navy?"

"Pink. The navy's kind of . . ." she searched for the word.

"Boring?"

"No! It's just the pink is so pretty on you."

Her bag packed, Paula returned to the living room with Elizabeth trailing behind her.

Jason had made coffee and stood at the kitchen island pouring mugs for the three of them. "There's some really good-looking pie in the fridge," he said. "I really like pie."

"I'll get it for you," Elizabeth said. "Paula?"

She shook her head. "I'm too excited to eat."

Jason eyed the pie as Elizabeth took it from the refrigerator. "I've never had that happen." Then he looked up and reddened. "Sorry, honey, I didn't mean I'm not excited about us getting engaged. I just meant I never turn down food."

She laughed. "I knew what you meant. And it's Elizabeth's Dutch apple pie. I'll be lucky you don't want to marry her instead of me after you eat a slice."

"Stop," Elizabeth said with a laugh. "Shall I warm it up in the microwave?"

"Just hand it here," he said. "I'll warm it up eating it." He took a bite and rolled his eyes. "Oh, man, Paula, make her give you the recipe for this, will ya?"

Elizabeth cut a slice for Paula and then decided to have one as a bedtime snack.

Too soon, they were gone and the apartment fell silent again. Elizabeth loaded the dishwasher and took her book to bed. But instead of reading, she lay there on her side staring at the two little carved wooden sparrows sitting on her bedside table. They were lined up like a pair ready for Noah's ark, she thought.

It didn't feel like she was going to get engaged anytime soon. She knew she should be grateful she had a new job lined up because she certainly needed to support herself. But her heart ached and no matter how hard she tried to blink them away tears splashed down onto her cheeks.

She swiped at the tears with her hands, admonishing herself for a good old pity party. God was sure not going to think she appreciated Him by carrying on this way. She sat up, reached for a tissue from the box on the bedside table to dab at the tears and said a prayer, asking His forgiveness.

God had a plan for her. She'd thought she knew what it was but now she wasn't so certain. She lay back against her pillow and stared at the ceiling, wishing she could see His face and ask Him what His plan was.

Verdraue.

Trust.

She wasn't certain if the word drifting across her consciousness just as she was on the edge of sleep came from her own mind or His. But she smiled. She'd do her best to trust Him. She hoped her effort would be worthy in His eyes.

17

Elizabeth! It's *gut* to see you again! I missed you at the shop when you came in."

She looked up as she climbed the stairs to the porch and saw Mary Katherine beaming down at her as she bounced a toddler on her hip.

"It's *gut* to see you, too." She smiled at the toddler busy stuffing the ties to her *kapp* into her mouth and chewing on them and received a grin.

Mary Katherine waited until Elizabeth stood beside her then she glanced around her. "Leah asked me to see if you'd like to sit with me," she said quietly. "She told me she didn't want the bishop making you feel uncomfortable. I don't know if you know, but a different bishop kept pressuring me to join the church years ago. I wasn't ready and she defended me like a mama lion."

"I didn't know. This one wants me to go back to Goshen. I can't blame him. My *grossmudder* wrote him. She's . . . a very strong woman."

Mary Katherine lifted her chin and fire flashed from her eyes. "No one should pressure anyone to do something they don't think is right. I don't know you well, but what I do know is you have to do what's right for you. It's between you and God. No one else should be trying to tell you what to do."

The toddler reacted to her vehemence with a screech and slapped her own cheeks and giggled. Mary Katherine and Elizabeth laughed and walked inside to find seats.

Leah came in a few minutes later and nodded when she saw Elizabeth sitting with Mary Katherine.

Once during the service Elizabeth felt as if someone watched her and when she looked over, she saw Saul sitting in the men's section, looking in her direction. So much for separating men and women to eliminate distractions during the church service. She didn't need to sit next to him to know when he looked at her. There was a faint line between his eyebrows and his expression seemed serious.

When he realized she'd noticed him looking, he turned his attention back to the lay minister.

She focused her own attention on his message and smiled slightly when she realized he was talking about listening for messages from God about His plan for you.

Mary Katherine elbowed her. She turned to look at her and Mary Katherine grinned. "He agrees with me," she whispered.

Elizabeth smiled. She loved church. It seemed like when she felt troubled about something she heard just what she needed to do. Goshen or Paradise, God found a way to send a message to her listening ear, her waiting spirit.

She felt a hand tug on her sleeve and realized the hand belonged to Mary Katherine's daughter. The little girl gave her another of her winsome smiles and Elizabeth found herself holding out her arms.

"Lizzie," Mary Katherine whispered. "Don't bother Elizabeth."

"It was my nickname, too, when I was little," she whispered back. "And she's not bothering me."

The child clambered onto Elizabeth's lap. Her mother produced a little plastic bag with a handful of pretzel sticks. Lizzie reached up and pushed one at Elizabeth's lips, so she had to accept it and thank her. Then Lizzie settled back against Elizabeth and happily munched for the rest of the service.

Elizabeth found herself thinking about her favorite younger sister. She loved all of her brothers and sisters, but she'd always felt closest to one, Sadie. They seemed tuned to each other more than Elizabeth felt to the others. Maybe it was why Sadie had tucked her teddy bear in Elizabeth's suitcase when she wasn't looking.

It would have been so nice if she hadn't had to tear herself from the fabric of her family life in order to find some personal happiness.

Lizzie became still and the little plastic bag of pretzels slipped from her hand. Elizabeth caught it and handed it to Mary Katherine, then looked down and found Lizzie had fallen asleep. A tiny snore escaped her lips and the minister, pausing, heard it and looked in her direction. He smiled and then went on.

Saul caught the direction of the minister's look, and he regarded Elizabeth thoughtfully for a long moment before returning his attention to the service.

"I can take her," Mary Katherine whispered.

"I'm fine," Elizabeth whispered back. Holding the little body sleeping so trustfully in her arms felt oddly comforting. She'd missed this.

When the service concluded, the women got up and hurried to the kitchen to get the light meal ready while the men converted the seating for it. Elizabeth got up, holding the sleeping Lizzie, and walked over to a corner of the room to get out of the way.

And ran into the bishop.

"Have you thought about what we discussed?" he asked her.

She held a finger to her lips and glanced down at the *kind*.

"I'll find her *mamm* so we can talk," he said, frowning at her.

He turned and headed purposefully toward the kitchen before Elizabeth could think of a response.

"Elizabeth? Everything *allrecht*?" Saul asked her.

She looked up at him and winced. "He's gone to get Mary Katherine so we can talk."

Saul glanced in the direction the bishop had walked. There they could both see Leah standing in the doorway of the kitchen. She had her hands on her hips and she was shaking her head.

Elizabeth remembered what Mary Katherine had told her before the service—she'd said Leah wanted her to sit with her because she didn't want the bishop making her feel uncomfortable.

How had she described Leah when she did the same for her years earlier? Like a mama lion? When Leah glanced in her direction, Elizabeth wondered if she was doing the same for her. When Leah visited at the store, she'd said she'd talk to the bishop if Elizabeth wanted. It looked like Leah might be doing so now, without being asked.

The bishop shook his graying head and didn't look happy, but he didn't return to talk with Elizabeth.

Lizzie woke and puckered up to cry when she saw Elizabeth instead of her mother. "Let's go find your *mamm*," she told her. "I think she's making you something *gut* to eat."

She looked at Saul. "I'll be back in a minute."

He nodded. "I thought we could go somewhere and get something to eat instead of staying here. Then we can talk."

"I'll be right back."

Leah looked up as she entered the room. "The bishop didn't try to talk to you, did he?"

"*Nee.*" Elizabeth couldn't help smiling. "*Danki.*"

"You're *wilkumm.*" Tsk-tsking, she turned. "Mary Katherine, look who finally woke up!"

Elizabeth surrendered the child and then, just as she started to walk toward Saul, something made her stop so abruptly a woman leaving the kitchen behind her bumped into her.

"Sorry!" the woman apologized.

"*Nee*, it was my fault." she said.

People who had started out as acquaintances and become friends now seemed like family, defending her when they felt she needed it, standing up to authority. And Saul—the man she'd come to feel so much for—he'd done these things as well . . .

She'd felt she had to leave Goshen, but it didn't mean she liked having to do it or felt good about it then or now. Especially now.

Maybe she was growing up.

Elizabeth found herself walking toward the bishop who was headed toward the front door.

"Bishop, I'd like to talk to you!" she called and smiled when she saw him turn and stare at her, surprised.

～✲～

"You did what?"

"I told the bishop to contact my *grossmudder.*" She put her menu down and looked at the waitress. "I'd like the chicken salad sandwich please. On a croissant."

Distracted, Saul shook his head. "The cheeseburger with everything."

"How do you want it cooked?"

"What?" He looked up at the waitress.

She grinned at him. "How do you want it cooked? The cheeseburger."

"Oh, sorry. Medium rare. And with everything. Thank you."

The minute the woman left, he turned back to Elizabeth. "I don't understand. Why would you suddenly say you'll go back home?"

"I didn't say home," she said in a low voice, so low he almost couldn't hear her. "I said Goshen."

"Elizabeth, why would you go there when you've always acted so glad to be away from it?"

She gave him a level look. "You're the one who thinks I shouldn't have run away." She sighed and rubbed her forehead. "You said you wanted to talk. But I'm not sure we can resolve the differences between us. I ran from my family. You stayed. What more is there to say?"

"You promised we'd talk," he said, searching for patience. "We were both upset and said things we shouldn't."

After a moment, she nodded. "*Ya.*"

"Let's get the work issue out of the way first," he said. "When do you start your new job?"

"After the first of the year."

He smiled slightly. "Are you going to tell me where it is?"

"Leah asked me to work for her at Stitches in Time since Jamie has a new job in New York City."

"I see."

"Don't be mad at her. She didn't come and try to hire me away while you were with your father."

He shook his head. "I'm not mad at her. And it's logical. You're good at your job and you used to work at a fabric store."

The waitress brought their food, but neither of them touched it.

"So do you want to work at the store until then?"

She nodded.

"We can use your help. This last week before Christmas is going to be very hectic."

The waitress returned. "Something wrong with the food?"

"It looks good," Saul said. He picked up his cheeseburger and took a bite.

Elizabeth did the same with her sandwich and the waitress nodded and left them.

"So what's your plan? You said you told the bishop you'd go back if your *grossmudder* sends the bus fare. What if she does?"

"I'll go visit for the holidays."

"Just the holidays?" He found himself holding his breath.

"Just the holidays," she said firmly.

He let out the breath he'd been holding.

"I'm sorry we argued. I care about you, Elizabeth Bontrager."

He watched her smile bloom slowly, like a flower coming to life after a long winter.

"I care about you, Saul Miller."

They smiled at each other and then began eating. Saul told her about how his father was doing—if he continued recovering as he was doing, he'd get to come home in a day or two. Elizabeth told Saul about how Leah wanted her to think about the sewing she'd been enjoying and how she might do it at the job.

Then Elizabeth hesitantly began telling him about some of her ideas for his store.

"Two people came in looking for gifts last week," she said. "But they said they couldn't spend much. I was thinking it might be nice to sell quilt squares Barbie could make and put them in simple wooden frames by Amos and his *sohns*. They could sell for a reasonable price and be a wonderful gift."

He thought about that. "Good idea. I'll talk to Barbie and Amos."

They talked about several other ideas she had, holiday shoppers, the weather, Paula and Jason's engagement—just about everything since they'd had so little time lately with Saul spending so much time at the hospital.

"Do you think your *grossmudder* will send the bus fare?"

Elizabeth nodded. "She'll probably tell me she shouldn't have to do it, but I can't afford it myself."

She cupped her chin in her hand and looked thoughtful. "I don't know what to do for gifts. I don't have time to make any and I don't have money to buy them."

"I can give you an advance on your wages."

"*Nee. Danki,* but *nee.* It's money I need for monthly expenses."

"Your being there will be gift enough," he said and felt warmth rush into his face when she looked at him with surprise. "What?"

"You are so sweet!"

He shrugged and reached for the check, embarrassed. "I have my moments."

She laughed and patted his hand. "*Ya*, you do." Her expression became serious. "I'm sure you'll be celebrating having your *dat* at home for Christmas."

"Yes, I will." He ran his finger up and down the condensation on the glass of water before him. "I'll miss you."

"You'll have a peaceful Christmas without me," she said lightly. But her eyes were warm when they met his.

Sandwiches disappeared, pie was ordered and eaten, and two cups of coffee consumed by each of them.

They climbed into Saul's buggy and went for a ride and talked some more. By the time he dropped Elizabeth off at her apartment, he thought they'd gotten back to where they'd been before their fight.

He prayed so.

⟡

The envelope postmarked Goshen arrived several days later.

Paula handed the envelope to her as she checked the mail. "Open it! Open it!"

Elizabeth smiled. "I will." She accepted the envelope, ripped it open and pulled out the bus ticket she found inside. She frowned. One ticket—a one-way ticket. She sighed.

Well, at least half of the trip was paid for. If *Grossmudder* thought sending a one-way ticket would make her stay in Goshen, she would be very surprised. Elizabeth didn't want to spend the money she'd saved but she had it to buy a round-trip ticket before she left.

"So are you going to go? Elizabeth?"

"What?" She looked at Paula.

"Are you going to go?"

"I am."

They walked to their apartment and after she shed her jacket Elizabeth immediately began poking in the refrigerator for the makings for supper.

"I'm going to miss you doing this."

Elizabeth looked over her shoulder. "I won't be gone long."

"You sure?" Paula slid into a stool at the kitchen island, put her elbows on the counter, and her face in her hands. She gave Elizabeth a hangdog expression. "I'm afraid you'll stay."

"You don't have to worry about that."

She pulled a package of pork chops from the refrigerator and placed them in a baking dish, then added a sauce made of cream of mushroom soup, ketchup, Worcestershire sauce, and chopped onion. She slid the baking dish into the oven and set the timer.

"What do you want with the pork chops?"

"Can we have mashed potatoes? I love the way you make them."

"I boil the potatoes and mash them," Elizabeth told her dryly. "And add a little milk and butter. You can do it."

"No, I can't. Mine always taste like glue."

Elizabeth handed her a bag of potatoes and a potato peeler. It didn't faze Paula. She happily began peeling the potatoes.

"I watched you make them," Elizabeth told her. "You were using baking potatoes. That's why they turned out gluey. And you added too much milk."

"I'll never cook as good as you."

"I'll write down some recipes for you."

"Especially the pie. Jason was nuts about it."

Elizabeth smiled. "Especially the pie."

Paula finished peeling the potatoes so Elizabeth handed her the wooden cutting board. "Aren't you afraid they'll pressure you to stay? Your parents, I mean."

"I'm expecting it." She was also expecting her little brothers and sisters would provide their own pressure, even though they wouldn't realize it.

"You okay?"

She looked up. Paula wore a concerned expression. "Yes, I'm fine. I promise you, I'll be back. I'm not taking all my things. Don't get a new roommate."

Paula laughed. "I won't. And how can you not take all your things? You only have a few dresses. You'll need all of them."

"True. But I'm leaving my little wooden sparrows I bought. And my books." She thought about it. She didn't actually own anything else. "I'll leave my Bible. I would never not come back

for my Bible. My other *grossmudder*—my father's mother—
gave it to me before she died."

"You promise you won't call or write me and ask me to send
it to you?"

"Promise."

"Pinky swear?"

"What?"

"Just an expression. Here, I cut up the potatoes."

Elizabeth scooped them into a saucepan, rinsed them, and
filled the pan with water before putting it on a burner.

"Green beans or broccoli?"

"Broccoli." She slid off the stool. "I'm going to go get out of
my scrubs. I'll be back in a minute to help some more. Don't
do everything."

Elizabeth put the broccoli into the electric steamer Paula's
mother had given her, added water, and set the timer. "There's
nothing else to do."

"Cool." She went off to change and a few minutes later,
Elizabeth could hear her talking on her cell phone.

She walked over to sit on the sofa and picked up a bride
magazine. Her eyes widened at the fancy dresses, veils, and
flowers *Englisch* brides evidently wore for their weddings.
The food pictured looked fancier than the simple fare served
at Amish weddings, too. There were lists of all the tasks the
brides had to perform before a wedding. It looked like a lot
of work to Elizabeth and that was saying a lot. Amish brides
sewed their own dresses, helped cook some of the food, even
helped clean up the day after the wedding. But there seemed
to be so much involved in an *Englisch* wedding. Maybe she
could help Paula with some of it when she returned.

Paula finished her call and returned to the living room
dressed in comfortable sweats. "Jason's coming over for a little
while after dinner."

"That's nice. I'll stay in my room. Give you some privacy."

"You don't have to do that. I have to tell you he asked if you'd baked another pie. He loved your pie."

"We have some apples. I could make another one."

"You trying to lure away my fiancé?"

She laughed and carried the bag of apples over to the island. "No. Here, you peel them and I'll make the crust."

"What's the latest with Saul?"

Elizabeth got a bowl and measured flour. "Things are better. But he doesn't want me to go to Goshen, either."

Paula frowned in concentration as she worked the knife under the peel of an apple. It fell in one long continuous red ribbon landing with a plop onto the counter. "I'm sure he's worried you're going to stay, too."

She started to tell Paula if he hadn't been critical of her leaving she might not have gotten the idea to return now. But someone was knocking on the door.

"Jason!" Paula squealed when she opened the door. "You're early." She threw her arms around him and they kissed.

Elizabeth looked away and dumped the pie crust onto the counter to roll it out.

"Look who's here!" Paula called.

She looked up and smiled at Jason.

"How could he know you were making a pie?" Paula asked, trying to sound suspicious.

"Really?" He walked over and grinned at her. "The same kind as the other day?"

Elizabeth stopped rolling out the crust. "Oh, maybe you don't want the same thing again."

"Are you kidding? I could eat it every day of the week and not get tired of it."

He settled onto a stool and Paula got back on hers and continued peeling apples. "She's not the only one making it, you'll notice."

Jason leaned over and kissed her on the cheek. "Thank you, sweetie."

She grinned. "You're forgiven. As long as you don't kiss Elizabeth for making it."

Elizabeth felt her cheeks redden. She was glad when the timer on the oven went off and she could turn and get the pork chops out.

Jason sniffed the air. "Man, you girls eat like this every night?"

"Whenever Elizabeth cooks. She's giving me some recipes."

"We have plenty, if you'd like to eat with us," Elizabeth told him.

"Great."

"I thought you were having dinner with your parents."

"Mom's not a very good cook," he confided. "We had a frozen lasagna. Trust me, I have room for a pork chop and a piece of pie."

So Paula finished peeling the apples and Elizabeth assembled the pie and put it into the oven and Jason set the table.

"So, Elizabeth, are you seeing anyone?" Jason asked as they sat at the table eating. "Ouch! What'd you do that for?" he demanded of Paula.

"You're not supposed to ask personal questions."

He looked so chastened Elizabeth smiled. "It's okay. Paula forgets how personal she gets with her questions."

"Well, he's a guy. I didn't think you'd want him asking them," she defended herself. "Say, why don't you invite Saul here for dinner one night this week? You said his dad's out of the hospital."

"I don't know," she said, hesitating. "It's your apartment."

"It's ours," Paula told her firmly. "We can have a kind of double date."

"Sounds like fun." Jason speared a bite of pork chop. "You'll make pie, right?"

Paula laughed and ruffled his hair with her hand. "Stop with the pie."

"I don't think I can," he said. "Will it be done soon?"

"Not for a while yet. Don't worry, I set the timer."

They talked and ate and Jason not only polished off a pork chop but two helpings of mashed potatoes as well.

The oven timer went off and Elizabeth got up to get the pie out and set it to cool on the counter.

"It needs a few minutes to cool," she warned Jason when he looked expectantly at her as she returned to the table.

"Cold, hot, I'll eat it any ole way," he said as he cleaned his plate. "It's some great pie."

18

7 appreciate you driving me here," Elizabeth told Paula as they pulled into the bus station.

"It's no problem. I'm just sorry something happened with Saul." Her cell phone rang and she picked it up and answered. She handed it to Elizabeth. "It's Saul."

"Yes?"

"I'm so sorry," he said quickly. "Phil called a friend to come get me since he's broken down and we're on our way, but I don't think I'm going to get there before your bus leaves."

"Saul, it's okay. Really."

"It's not," he said quietly.

"I'll see you soon."

"Not soon enough. And as soon as you call me and tell me you're on the bus coming back, I'm camping out at the bus station."

Tears stung her eyes. He was so sweet. "You don't have to do that."

"Promise me you'll come back, Elizabeth."

"I promise I'm coming back."

She hung up and they got out to walk into the bus station. Elizabeth's bus pulled in a few minutes later.

Paula hugged her. "Have a wonderful Christmas."

"You, too."

"If you don't come back, I'm getting in my car and coming up there to get you. I mean it."

"I've been warned." Elizabeth summoned up a smile for her.

She climbed aboard, found a seat, and settled in. It felt strange to sit with nothing to do after all the activity at the store in the days leading up to the trip. During her lunch hour and after work, she'd worked on making some presents for the family: an outfit for the teddy bear she intended to give back to Sadie, doll clothes for the other girls. She searched for inexpensive fabric at Stitches in Time and another fabric store and found muslin to make carriers for the boys to transport the little carved wooden buggies and spring wagons they so loved, then added a few of the colorful carved toys when she found some on sale at Saul's store.

There was no time or money to make presents for her parents. They'd have to understand. Who knew if they were even going to be very welcoming after she'd left home . . .

Then she and Saul had tried to fit in some time together, too, even though his father was home now. Saul took over a lot of the things his mother did since she helped his father while he recuperated. Elizabeth had been pleasantly surprised to find Saul knew how to cook although he said he kept making the same couple recipes he'd mastered.

Saul. She already missed him. Maybe it was because he was on her mind . . . but it looked like him getting out of a van in the parking lot. The man just looked like him because he was dressed in Amish clothing.

No, it was Saul. He searched the bus windows and when he saw her, he waved. She waved back.

The bus driver shut the doors and started the engine, then slowly pulled out of the parking lot. Elizabeth watched as Saul's hand fell and then she had to turn away from the window. She couldn't look at him again or she was afraid she would make the driver stop and let her off.

She closed her eyes and told herself she needed to do this. Saul would be there when she came back. The next few days might be unpleasant but she could get through them.

Then, just as she'd done when she got on the bus to come to Paradise, she experienced doubt she was doing what she should be. The bus stopped and her eyes flew open. Was God saying she was supposed to get off and stay in Paradise?

Then she saw that the bus had merely stopped for a traffic light and once it turned green, it began moving again.

Carrying her toward Goshen.

All roads lead to Goshen they said. Well, they'd led out of Goshen, too, and she couldn't wait to return to Paradise.

Exhausted, she slept on and off for much of the trip. Paula had insisted on packing her some food and in her tote bag she found a thermos of coffee, sandwiches, some fruit . . . and a slice of pie in a little plastic container. A note was taped to the top of the container. It was from Jason. *"I didn't eat the last slice, because I know you'll be back to make me another pie."*

She smiled. He was such a sweet guy. She was so glad Paula had him in her life.

The container went back into the tote for later. Her fingers encountered the stiff edges of an envelope. She drew it out and found Paula had tucked two twenty-dollar bills inside with a note for her to use the money to get herself something—food on the trip, something she liked at a store—but not to spend it on her family, because it was for Elizabeth.

Sometimes family was made of those you were connected to through birth and sometimes, she thought, it was made of people like Paula.

The trip felt longer than the one she'd taken to come to Paradise. There was no talkative woman curious about the Amish. There was no handsome man with friendly brown eyes who'd boarded the bus and become someone special in her life.

And when the bus finally pulled into the bus station at Elkhart, the town next to Goshen, there was no one waiting for her.

꒰꒱

She knocked on the door because she didn't feel she had the right to enter what had been her home.

The door flew open and Sadie stood there. Her eyes went saucer wide and she screamed, "'Lizabet!" and flung her arms around Elizabeth's knees.

She dropped her bags, lifted her little sister and hugged her. "Oh, I missed you, Binky!"

"I'm not Binky," Sadie corrected her. "I don't use a Binky anymore."

Elizabeth bet the pacifier was hidden somewhere in Sadie's room. She'd refused to give it up for years.

She set the child on her feet and rooted around in one of her bags, then held out the teddy bear. "Look who came back with me!"

"Brownie!" Sadie clutched the bear and ran into the other room yelling for her mother. "*Mamm*, 'Lizabet is back!"

Her mother hurried into the room, wiping her hands on a kitchen towel. She looked the same as the last time Elizabeth had seen her: a bit frazzled, her dark hair escaping her *kapp*, her apron spotted with flour.

"Elizabeth! You're here already. *Mamm*, Elizabeth's here!" she called over her shoulder.

Her grandmother strode out of the kitchen. A tall, spare woman, she looked at Elizabeth over the rims of her metal-rimmed glasses. "So you came."

She nodded and tried not to shiver. There was no warmth in those eyes, no welcome as she crossed her arms over her chest.

"*Danki* for sending the ticket."

"I wanted to arrange for a ride for you but *Mamm* said we didn't know when you'd arrive." Her mother waved her hands a bit ineffectually.

Elizabeth tried not to feel it would have been nice if someone had been waiting for her. Perhaps it had been unrealistic to expect such. But not only had it taken time to look up the name of a driver and call him, it had taken precious dollars she couldn't spare.

"Sadie, go get everyone so we can eat."

She ran to the stairs and yelled, "Supper's ready!"

Elizabeth's mother winced. "Well, I meant you should go upstairs and get them but whatever."

Nothing had changed. Footsteps pounded down the stairs and her *bruders* and *schweschders* came into view. They ran toward Elizabeth, their voices high and excited, everyone talking at once.

"You've all grown," she said as she bent to hug them. It was a good thing there had been no time to sew clothes for them. They might not have fit.

Mary, the second oldest, followed, wearing a sullen expression only a fourteen-year-old could. She shrugged when Elizabeth greeted her.

"Let's eat," her mother said and stepped out of the way as the *kinner* raced toward the kitchen. Mary let out a long-suffering sigh and followed them at a much slower pace.

"Nothing's changed," Elizabeth said, grinning.

Then her smile slipped as her grandmother walked toward the door. "Aren't you joining us?"

"I have to get home to your *grossdaadi*."

"Oh. Well, I'm looking forward to seeing him Christmas Eve."

She nodded and left.

Elizabeth felt a small hand slip into hers. She looked down and saw Sadie gazing up at her with big brown eyes.

"C'mon, 'Lizabet. Sit next to me."

Here was her welcome, she thought. She nodded and smiled and they walked into the kitchen.

Her father walked into the kitchen a few minutes later and looked surprised when he saw her. "You came."

She felt a little defensive. After all, she'd written them the date and time of arrival. But she bit her tongue and nodded. This was going to be a good visit.

The kitchen felt the same—warm and comforting, filled with the heat from the stove and the aromas from the food served in big dishes on the big wooden table.

"Mmm, everything looks so good," Elizabeth said, glancing around the table.

"*Mamm* made your favorites," Mary told her, shrugging.

Was it her imagination there was a hint of jealousy in her voice? Maybe not. Their father sent Mary a sharp look.

The family said grace and then bowls and platters were passed. The pork chops reminded Elizabeth of the night she'd cooked them for herself and Paula and Jason had shown up for supper. She'd have to go out to the phone shanty after supper and let her—and Saul—know she'd arrived safely.

The *kinner* began pelting her with questions about Paradise: Where was she living? Did she have a job?

And—to them the most important question: Had she brought presents for them?

She laughed. Nothing had changed.

Soon little heads were nodding over their plates. Despite Elizabeth's frequent naps on the bus, she found herself nodding as well.

Her mother clapped her hands. "Baths, then bed."

"Shall I help with baths or dishes?" Elizabeth asked her.

"Baths," said Mary.

In the first display of quick movement Elizabeth had seen since she returned, Mary jumped up and began clearing the table, even trying to take her father's coffee cup before he was finished with it.

"She doesn't like to help with the *kinner* as much as you did," her mother said as they followed the children upstairs. "The girl just doesn't have a servant's heart like you."

Elizabeth was glad to hear her mother hadn't noticed she'd tired of child care at the end . . . but she was bothered by the term "servant's heart." She didn't want her mother to think she lived only to serve others. She wanted some love, some affection, a husband, and maybe a family of her own.

Her father came upstairs once everyone was bathed and it seemed he'd taken over one of Elizabeth's old routines— reading the bedtime story. Tonight, though, when the *kinner* begged for Elizabeth to read, he cheerfully relinquished the honor to her and went out to do a final check of the horses in the barn.

"You're tired," her mother said before she left the room. "We'll talk tomorrow."

That night, Elizabeth lay in her bed in her old room and found herself homesick for the bed in the apartment she shared with Paula. Mary slept in the bed next to hers, but had barely talked to her before she went to sleep.

Footsteps padded toward the door and then it opened a little. Sadie stuck her head in. "Hi."

"Hi."

"Can I come in?"

Elizabeth nodded and pulled back the covers. Sadie slid in and she covered her up.

"Wow, your feet are freezing! Where are your socks?"

Sadie giggled. "In my room."

"Well, get those cold feet off my legs or I'm chasing you back to your room." It was an empty threat and Sadie knew it.

So she slept with Sadie snuggled up next to her, clutching her teddy bear to her chest.

Sometime in the middle of the night Sadie got up. She patted Elizabeth's head and then, carrying her teddy bear, went back to her own bed. Elizabeth smiled. Sadie had obviously thought she needed comforting on her first night back.

The next morning, when Elizabeth went downstairs she found her mother making breakfast. Her brothers and sisters were seated at the table busily eating oatmeal. Mary was nowhere in sight.

"Where's Mary?"

Her mother looked up from the pan she was stirring on the stove. "Probably primping."

Elizabeth sent Sadie upstairs for a hairbrush, and when she returned, helped brush her hair and braid it. The boys needed a quick grooming they tried to fight, swatting away the brush she wielded, but she prevailed.

Mary came down a few minutes later, turned up her nose at the oatmeal and helped herself to a piece of toast instead. "*Kumm*," she said impatiently to her brothers and sisters. "I don't want to be late."

"She doesn't want to be late to see a boy," one of the brothers said and he got up and pulled his jacket from a peg on the wall.

"That's enough," Mary said and the two of them stuck their tongues out at each other when their mother wasn't looking.

Elizabeth helped put coats on, handed out lunches, and gave everyone—well, everyone but Mary—a hug before seeing them out the door. Mary was already standing by the door impatiently tapping her foot.

"*Danki* for the help," her mother told Elizabeth. She poured them both a cup of coffee and sat at the table. "It's so nice to have you back." She glanced at the clock. "Your father will be in soon for his breakfast. Do you want some bacon and eggs or oatmeal?"

"Bacon and eggs would be nice."

Her mother nodded. "Then I thought we could bake *kichli* for the Christmas play they're having at *schul* later this week."

"Snickerdoodles?"

"Any kind you like. They'll all be eaten for sure."

The back door opened and her father walked in. He went to the sink and washed his hands.

"I'll start your breakfast now," her mother said.

"In a minute. Sit and drink your coffee." He poured himself a mug and then sat at the table.

"I was just telling Elizabeth I was glad she was back."

Elizabeth took a deep breath, then plunged ahead. "I came back because I wanted to apologize to you both for leaving the way I did."

They looked at each other, then back at her.

"I just needed to go off and make a life of my own."

"And have you done that?" her father asked her. He took a sip of his coffee and studied her with a calm, steady gaze.

She nodded. "I share an apartment with a nice *Englisch* girl who's studying nursing. And I work in a store. It's a temporary job while someone's out on maternity leave, but I already have a job lined up after the new year."

"New year? What do you mean, new year?" Her mother turned to her father. "What does she mean new year?"

He held up a hand to quiet her and turned to look at Elizabeth. "What are you talking about?"

"I'm here for a visit," she said, glancing from one to the other. "I didn't come back to stay."

"That's not what *Mamm* told me," her mother protested.

Elizabeth shook her head. "I said I'd come back for a visit."

They heard a knock on the front door, then it opened. "It's me."

"Well, looks like we'll get this straightened out right away," her father said calmly. He looked up at his mother-in-law as she walked into the room. "I thought you said Elizabeth was coming back."

"Well, she has, she's sitting right there," she said with some asperity.

"I said I'd come for a visit," Elizabeth corrected her politely but firmly. "I didn't say I'd come back for good."

"Of course, you will," *grossmudder* told her. "You'll do your duty like a good daughter."

❧

Something was wrong.

Elizabeth denied it but Saul could hear the strain in Elizabeth's voice every time he talked to her. He said good-bye and put his cell phone away.

"You haven't left yet?" Samuel asked as he entered the kitchen.

"Phil will be here in a few minutes. Sit down, I'll pour you some coffee."

"I can get my own cup," Samuel told him. "I'm not an invalid you know."

"Never said you were."

"Everyone's acting like it," he grumbled as he brought his mug to the table and sat down. He looked up as Waneta walked into the kitchen. "And I don't want oatmeal. I want some bacon and eggs. I'll cook 'em if I have to."

"Be my guest," she said. She poured her own cup of coffee, nodded at Saul, and left the room.

Both men stared after her.

"Uh-oh," Saul said when he turned his attention back to his father. "I think she's had enough of the bad mood you've been in for a couple of days now."

"Tired of hearing what I can't do," Samuel said, staring into his coffee. "It's not easy getting old."

"You're not old. You've just been shown you can't push your body around or it pushes you back. How about I scramble you some egg whites and fry up some turkey bacon?"

Samuel made a face but finally he nodded. "So why are you moping around?" he asked Saul. "Elizabeth not back yet?"

Saul shook his head. He got up, pulled a package of turkey bacon from the refrigerator and placed several slices in a skillet on the stove.

"She planned on returning on the twenty-seventh, but when I talked to her just now she wasn't sure when she was leaving."

"So, she's taking an extra day or two."

He put the bacon package back in the refrigerator, then returned to the stove and poked at the slices frying in the skillet.

"Saul?"

He turned and looked at his father. "What?"

"Are you afraid she's staying there?"

Saul's shoulders slumped and he nodded. "*Ya.*"

"You love her, eh?"

"*Ya.*"

"Then what are you waiting for? Get on a bus and go up and get her."

Saul turned to stare at him. "It's not that easy."

"*Schur* it is. You go buy a ticket and climb on a bus to Goshen."

"What about the store?"

"Miriam's back, right? Katie and Rosie still work there part-time?"

Saul flipped the bacon. "*Ya.*"

Samuel shrugged. "Seems to me everyone found a way to keep the store running when you sat with your mother and me at the hospital. So go get Elizabeth and bring her back here where she belongs."

Waneta walked into the kitchen and set her empty cup on the counter. "So what's this about Elizabeth?"

"I told Saul he needed to go get her and bring her back here where she belongs."

"Saul?"

He transferred the bacon to a plate lined with a paper towel and set about making the egg whites. "He makes it sound like I can just abandon the store and take off."

"You're not indispensable," she said briefly. She took the spatula from him and nudged him aside. "I'll finish your father's breakfast. You go pack and make your phone call to Miriam. Phil can drop you at the bus station just as easily as the store."

"The two of you planning something?" he asked, staring at them dubiously. "Is that why you're trying to run me off?"

"*Schur,*" she said. "With your father recovering and me running around taking care of him, we have lots of time and energy to get into mischief. Now shoo!"

Ten minutes later, Saul walked out to the van carrying his suitcase.

"Mind taking me to the bus station instead of the store?" he asked Phil.

"Of course not. Where you headed?"

"Goshen, Indiana."

"Where Elizabeth just went?"

Saul nodded.

"I see," Phil said. "How about that."

Their eyes met in the rearview mirror.

"*Ya*," Saul said. "How about that?"

He wondered if he was *ab im kop*. It felt a little crazy to be suddenly boarding a bus and going to get a woman who might not want to come home with him. *Lieb*—love—felt a little crazy.

He got the last ticket on the bus and found it crowded with passengers returning North after the holidays. What a different trip it was from the one when he met Elizabeth and they talked for hours on the way to Pennsylvania. This time he sat scrunched in a window seat while a young mother tried to keep a toddler entertained and quiet for hours. This time he ate sandwiches and coffee his mother made while he packed, but he ate them without company like he had on the way to Paradise.

A little more than a day later and he stood on the doorstep of Elizabeth's home waiting for someone to answer his knock and wishing he hadn't dropped his gloves on the bus. Indiana felt colder than Pennsylvania.

Elizabeth opened the door and he watched the mixture of emotions sweep over her face. "Saul? Is it really you? Pinch me, I must be dreaming. Ouch!" she cried and spun around. She shook her finger at a little boy. "What was that for?"

"You said 'pinch me' so I did!"

"It's an expression!"

He laughed and scampered away.

She turned back to Saul. "Come in. What are you doing here?"

"I've come to take you home."

"This is her home."

Saul looked over her shoulder. A big, burly-looking man stood behind Elizabeth and he didn't look friendly.

"Come in, Saul. *Daed*, this is Saul. He came from Paradise to see me."

Her father just stood there staring at him. "I believe he said he's here to take you home."

"I did," Saul spoke up.

"*Daed*, can we take the buggy for a ride?"

He regarded them, his arms folded across his chest. "As long as it's not back to Paradise."

Maybe the man had a sense of humor. Maybe. Saul gave him a wide berth as Elizabeth took his hand and led him through the kitchen where she introduced him to her mother. Then she grabbed her jacket and slipped it on as they went out the back door.

Together they hitched Agnes, one of the family's horses, to the buggy. Elizabeth pulled blankets from the back seat and they covered their laps with them.

"I was afraid you weren't coming back. *Are* you coming back, Elizabeth?"

"I told you I was."

"I came to make sure."

She searched his face. "Tell me why, Saul."

He pulled the buggy off the road and turned to her to touch her cheek. "Because I love you and I want you to marry me. I decided not to take any chance you'd be persuaded to stay here."

Tears sprang into her eyes. "You're sure? We haven't known each other very long."

"I don't need any more time. Do you?"

She shook her head and a smile bloomed on her lips.

He leaned forward and touched his lips to hers. Then he was drawing her closer and kissing her the way he'd wanted to for a long time.

"So when can we start home?" he asked her when they drew back.

She grinned. "What if I said I bought a ticket before I even left Paradise?"

"Really?"

"Really. And it's for the nine a.m. bus tomorrow."

"Not soon enough." He grinned at her. "Now all I have to do is figure where I'm spending the night."

"You can stay with us," she told him as he checked for traffic and got the buggy back onto the road. "You'll probably have to share a room with the boys."

"With the pincher?"

She laughed. "There's never a dull moment in this house." She sighed. "I'm glad I came back. I apologized to my parents for leaving the way I did. They didn't look happy when I said I was going back to Paradise, but I think they know they have to let go and allow me to find my own way."

"*Gut,*" he said. "So it was worth it coming here to talk to them."

"Family's always worth it, isn't it?"

"It is."

She slipped her arm in his and leaned against his shoulder. "Take me home, Saul. Take me back to Paradise."

RECIPES

Amish Pennsylvania Dutch Apple pie

1 (9-inch) pie crust, unbaked

Filling:

5 cups apples, cored and sliced (about 5 small, Granny Smith apples work well)
2 teaspoons lemon juice
½ cup sugar
½ teaspoon cinnamon
½ cup raisins (optional)

Topping:

¾ cup all-purpose flour
½ cup sugar
½ teaspoon cinnamon
⅓ cup butter (at room temperature)

Directions:

Preheat oven to 425 degrees.
Line a 9-inch pie pan with unbaked crust. Core and slice apples. Sprinkle the apples with the lemon juice. Stir in the sugar, cinnamon, and raisins, if desired. Mix well to evenly coat. Fill pie shell with apple mixture.

In a small bowl, mix the topping's flour, sugar, and cinnamon. Rub the topping ingredients and butter together with fingers until the mixture is crumbly. Sprinkle topping over pie.

Bake 10 minutes at 425 degrees then reduce oven temperature to 350 degrees and bake until crumb topping is browned and apples are soft, approximately 50 minutes.

Serves 6-8

Amish Chicken Casserole

8 ounces medium egg noodles, uncooked
½ cup butter
⅓ cup all-purpose flour
2 cups chicken broth
1 cup milk
2 teaspoons salt
½ teaspoon black pepper
2 cups chopped cooked chicken (to save time you can use a
  rotisserie chicken)
1 (4-ounce) can sliced mushrooms, drained
⅓ cup grated Parmesan cheese

Directions:

Preheat oven to 350 degrees. Cook noodles according to package directions; drain, and set aside.

Melt butter in medium saucepan over low heat; gradually add flour, stirring until smooth. Cook 1 minute, stirring constantly. Gradually add chicken broth and milk; cook over medium heat, stirring constantly, until mixture is slightly thickened and bubbly. Stir in salt and pepper, set aside.

Combine noodles, chicken, and mushrooms in large bowl; stir in sauce. Spoon mixture into a lightly greased 9 x 13-inch baking dish; sprinkle with cheese.

Bake uncovered, 20 minutes or until thoroughly heated.

Serves 6

Shoofly Pie

1 (9-inch) pie crust, unbaked

Crumb Mixture:

(reserving ½ cup for topping)
⅔ cup firmly packed brown sugar
1 tablespoon solid shortening
1 cup all-purpose flour

Filling:

1 teaspoon baking soda
¾ cup boiling water
1 egg, beaten
1 cup molasses

Directions:

Preheat oven to 375 degrees.

Mix brown sugar, shortening, and flour and set aside ½ cup for topping.

Combine soda with boiling water, then add egg and molasses. Stir well to create a syrup. Add crumb mixture, except for ½ cup reserved mixture. Pour into unbaked pie crust and cover with reserved crumb mixture.

Bake at 375 degrees F for 10 minutes, then reduce heat to 350 degrees and bake for an additional 35-45 minutes (until firm).

When cut into, the bottom may be "wet." This is okay because it is called a "wet bottom shoofly pie."

Serves 6-8

Amish Applesauce Cake

½ cup solid shortening or butter
1 cup sugar
1 egg
1 cup applesauce
½ teaspoon salt
½ teaspoon baking powder
1 teaspoon baking soda
½ to 1 teaspoon cloves
1 teaspoon cinnamon
½ teaspoon allspice
1 cup flour
1 cup raisins
½ cup chopped nuts

Directions:

Preheat oven to 350 degrees.

Cream the shortening or butter with the sugar. Add egg and beat until light. Add the applesauce and mix in. Stir in the salt, baking powder, baking soda, cloves, cinnamon, and allspice, mixing well. Stir in the flour, raisins, and nuts. Mix well.

Pour into a greased 8-inch pan (round or square) and bake for 45 minutes.

Serves 6-8

Amish Pork Chops

4-6 pork chops (about 3/4 -1 inch thick)
¾ cup ketchup
1 tablespoon Worcestershire sauce
1 can cream of mushroom soup
½ cup chopped onion

Directions:

Brown the pork chops in a skillet with a little cooking or olive oil, then transfer them to a baking dish. Mix the remaining ingredients and pour over chops.

Bake at 350 degrees for approximately 1 ½ hours.

Glossary

ab im kop—off in the head. Crazy.
Allrecht—all right
boppli—baby
bruder—brother
Daed—Dad
Danki—thank you
Dat—father
Der hochmut kummt vor dem fall. Pride goeth before the fall.
Englischer—what the Amish call us
grossdaadi—grandfather
grosseldere—grandparents
grossmudder—grandmother
guder mariye—good morning
Gut-n-Owed—good evening
haus—house
hochmut—pride
kaffe—coffee
kapp—prayer covering or cap worn by girls and women
kich—kitchen
kichli—cookies
kind, kinner—child, children

lieb—love

liebschen—dearest or dear one

maedels—young single women

mamm—mother

mann—husband

nee—no

Ordnung—The rules of the Amish, both written and unwritten. Certain behavior has been expected within the Amish community for many, many years. These rules vary from community to community, but the most common are to have no electricity in the home, not to own or drive an automobile, and to dress a certain way.

Pennsylvania *Deitsch*—Pennsylvania German

rumschpringe—time period when teenagers are allowed to experience the *Englisch* world while deciding if they should join the church.

schul—school

schur—sure

schweschder—sister

sohn—son

verdraue—trust

wilkumm—welcome

wunderbaar—wonderful

ya—yes

Discussion Questions

Spoiler alert! Please don't read before completing the book as the questions contain spoilers!

1. Elizabeth finds being the oldest in a large family to be too much. Where do you fall in your family's birth order? Oldest? Middle child? Youngest? How did this affect how you grew up and the choices you made?

2. Elizabeth decides she wants to change her life. She believes God has a plan for her life and acts on it believing everything will be all right. Have you ever done this? If so, what happened?

3. Amish young people get to experience *Englisch* life during a period called *rumschpringe*. While some youth use it as a chance to break out of the strict rules of the Amish community, most do not. Do you think teens of either culture need a period of unrestricted time to mature?

4. Many Amish believe God has set aside a marriage partner for them. Do you believe this? Do you believe in love at first sight?

5. Elizabeth goes to work at a store owned by Saul, a man she's attracted to. Do you think it's a good idea for a couple to work together?

6. Sometimes family is made up of our mother, father, and siblings. Sometimes it's made of friends who become family. Do you have friends who are family to you? How did this happen?

7. Elizabeth watches a CPR video with her roommate and later performs CPR on Saul's father. Have you ever had a situation where you felt you were put there to help a person?

8. In the Bible, Martha complains to Jesus she is doing all the work while her sister, Mary, does not help. What did Jesus tell her? What can women learn from this?

9. Elizabeth never dated back in Goshen and suddenly two men, one *Englisch* and one Amish, are interested in her. Do you think she would have ever dated the *Englisch* young man back in Goshen? What did Elizabeth learn from dating Bruce?

10. Elizabeth's mother says she has a servant's heart. What does this mean to you? Do you have a servant's heart?

11. Have you made a decision others disagreed with, but you felt was right for you?

12. Do you believe God has a plan for you? Do you know what it is?

AMISH ROADS

The age of sixteen to approximately the early twenties is a time of major changes in the lives of Amish teenagers. Freed from attending school and starting their vocations of choice, young people enter a time known as *rumschpringe*, a "running around" period. During this time, since the young adults have not yet chosen to become baptized into the church—the Amish believe in the individual choosing to be baptized rather than having adults choose for their infant children—many find the freedom of being allowed to make their own decisions is heady.

In the past, Amish elders saw this as a time when their young adults would court and choose a spouse. But in today's society, the differences between Amish and *Englisch* cultures continue to grow wider and the temptation for Amish teens to experience the *Englisch* world is great.

Amish teens are primarily rebelling against the *Ordnung*, the rules of the church, which—among other things—doesn't allow the use modern conveniences. When Amish teens are exposed to the *Englisch* world, especially *Englisch* teenagers, they struggle with maintaining their Amish identities.

For three young women, this time becomes one of resistance and contemplation of staying . . . or leaving the Amish community.

In the first book of the series, *The Road Unknown*, Elizabeth felt she had to run away from home and a life that grew unbearable there.

In *Crossroads*, the second book of the series, readers will meet Emma Mae, a young Amish woman who always thought she and her childhood sweetheart would get married. But when Isaac changes as he experiences his *rumschpringe,* she finds things changing very quickly.

Emma Mae longs for marriage, family, and community. She asks herself: Can a good girl reform a bad boy?

In *One True Path*, Book 3, Katie struggles with guilt. One day she slips away to take a joyride with some friends and leaves a younger sibling in charge. Four-year-old Sam, the baby of the family, gets injured. Up to that point, Katie had been an obedient daughter, avoiding the lures of the *Englisch* world. The one time she goes out to have some fun, tragedy strikes. Her parents try to reassure her that they don't blame her for Sam's accident, but Katie cannot forgive herself. She slides into a depression. Ben, the oldest son in a Mennonite family, says he knows what she needs. He offers to give her a ride in his car and suggests she have a beer to loosen up. Despite the fact that Katie feels a ride is what started all this mess, she must admit that the attention from Ben, and the thought of escaping this guilt, if even for a little while, lures her to agree.

But when she wakes later, feeling fuzzy, she's afraid that she's done more than have just one beer. Ben, meanwhile, is nowhere to be found. Paradise is a close-knit community where everyone knows everybody's business. Fortunately, Katie is relieved to find she suffers no consequence for that night she can't remember but she blames herself for poor choices and her depression reaches a new low. She moves in with Emma Mae and only after her friend's persuasion does she begin attending church again. With time and prayer, she starts the journey to forgive herself and Ben.

Love finds you when you least expect it. A few months later, at the meal after Sunday service, she meets John, a young man from a neighboring Amish community. He treats her with respect and courts her in the way her *daed* courted her *mamm*. But can she trust him with her heart?

And now, here's a glimpse of *Crossroads*, book 2 of the Amish Roads series . . .

1

"Pretty sweet sound, don't you think?" Isaac turned up the volume of the CD player in his buggy. Heavy metal music came pouring out.

Emma Mae gritted her teeth and wished she felt brave enough to plug her ears with her fingers. Isaac called it music. It sounded awful to her. She wanted to ask him to turn it down because it was giving her a headache but instead, she smiled and nodded. Maybe it was wishful thinking but she hoped his taste for such music was just him going through his *rumschpringe*.

Isaac's horse shook its head as he pulled the buggy down the road and Emma bit back a smile, wondering if horses got headaches.

Another buggy approached at a fast speed from the opposite direction. The driver leaned out and waved. It was Gideon B., one of Isaac's friends. As his buggy passed theirs, the sound from his own CD player blared even louder than Isaac's. A flock of chickens that had been grazing inside a fence near the road squawked and scurried away.

She sighed. Sometimes she wondered whether Amish boys enjoyed music or beer more during their *rumschpringe*.

Well, perhaps she couldn't call Isaac Amish anymore. She looked at him and wondered where the Isaac she'd loved since she was ten had gone. He wore jeans and a polo shirt.

And an *Englisch* haircut.

"Where are we going?" she asked him.

"It's a surprise."

"I don't know if I can stand another one," she murmured.

"What? I didn't hear you."

"Never mind," she said, raising her voice.

Now, as Emma sat beside Isaac in his tricked-out buggy, she remembered how she and her older sister, Lizzie, had argued the night before.

"I think Isaac's enjoying being a bad boy right now," Lizzie told her as they prepared for bed in the bedroom they shared.

"If he is, I can change him," Emma Mae said with a confidence she didn't entirely feel.

"You think a good girl can reform a bad boy? That doesn't work," she said with the wisdom of someone only two years older than Emma Mae's twenty-one. "You shouldn't try to change another person."

The buggy hit a bump in the road, bringing Emma Mae back to the present. Isaac was driving into town, away from their homes. She thought about their recent conversations and tried to guess what kind of surprise he'd planned.

The day was perfect for a drive. She sighed happily. A cool breeze drifted in the windows but the sun felt warm. Late spring weather could be iffy here in Paradise, Pennsylvania. A week ago Puxatawny Phil, funny little groundhog the *Englischers* watched for a prediction about winter ending had emerged from his burrow and seen no shadow so spring would come early.

They passed the Stoltzfus farm and she saw the FOR SALE sign in the front yard. She waited with bated breath. Were they going to turn into the drive? Isaac had always worked as a carpenter . . . maybe Isaac had decided he wanted to be a farmer after all. He hadn't seemed upset when his father told him one evening that he was selling the farm to Isaac's brother, not to him. But Isaac didn't share his feelings about things as much lately.

Well, she'd been raised on a farm and liked the idea of helping run one. They'd have *kinner*, lots of them if God willed it and they'd help as they grew older . . .

Lost in her daydream, it took her a moment to realize they were driving past the farm.

Okay, well maybe this farm wasn't where he was taking her. Maybe it was a different one. Maybe it wasn't a farm at all. Maybe it was a house he'd found and wanted to fix up. They didn't have a lot of money saved and property was so expensive in Lancaster County.

Isaac was so good with his hands, could build anything, fix anything. They could buy something that was run-down. A fixer-upper, she'd heard them called. They could buy one and make it theirs. Hopefully, they'd get it in good shape before a *boppli* came along to crawl in the sawdust.

She studied his profile, never tired of looking at him, being with him. As scholars, they'd passed notes in class and the minute their parents had allowed it, they'd attended singings and gone on buggy rides together. He'd been the cute little boy with blond hair and mischief in his big blue eyes who'd grown into a handsome man.

Lately, though, he seemed different. He spent hours working on his buggy after he got off work and this was the first time they'd been out in a week. When he picked her up he hadn't noticed she was wearing a new dress in the color he liked best on her—robin's egg blue—and he hadn't asked her about her new job.

"Can't stop looking, can you?" he asked, winking at her and giving her a mischievous smile. "Like it?"

"I—I don't know what to say," she told him honestly, staring at the short, razor-cut that had replaced his Amish haircut. "You look so different."

"That's the idea."

"You never said you were going to cut your hair like an *Englischer*."

He shrugged. "Decided to try it. If I don't like it, it'll grow back."

"Have your parents seen it yet?"

"*Nee*. I mean, no."

She winced as he corrected himself. It was a small thing but he seemed to be ridding his talk of Pennsylvania *Dietsch*. "When did you get it cut?"

"Two days ago."

"How could they not have seen it by now?" she wondered aloud. "Isaac? Isaac?"

"What?"

Emma reached over and turned the volume down. "How is it your parents haven't seen your haircut when you had it done two days ago?"

"I moved out."

Her eyes widened. "Moved out?"

"Yeah. I got my own place. I have a job. I can afford it."

"But I thought we were saving to get married in the fall."

He pulled the buggy into the drive of a run-down looking little cottage, stopped and turned to her. "We don't have to wait to be together. You can move in with me."

The minute Isaac saw Emma Mae's expression he knew he'd made a bad decision.

Shock mixed with horror on her face as she stared at him. "You're *ab im kop*," she said finally.

"I'm not crazy," he said, frowning. "You keep saying you want to be with me."

"I do. I want to be *married* to you!"

He bent his head and stared at his hands. "I know."

"You know but you bring me here and say this?"

There was no easy way to say it. Isaac looked up. "I'm not sure I'm ready to get married."

No, that wasn't the truth, he told himself. He owed her the truth.

"I'm not ready to get married," he said more firmly.

She pressed her fingers to her lips to stop their trembling. "But we've talked about it for . . . forever."

He sighed. "Maybe that was the trouble. We got too serious, too soon."

Emma Mae drew a handkerchief from her pocket and wiped at her eyes. "Are you saying you don't want to be engaged anymore? You want to date other women?"

"*Nee!*" he said quickly. "If I did, would I be asking you to move in with me here?"

She straightened, tucked her handkerchief away and straightened. "I think you do want to see another woman, Isaac. Because this woman isn't interested in living with you without being married."

He watched her look around her, at the fields just planted, and felt a stab of guilt when she took a shuddering breath.

"Would you take me home, please?"

"Emma—"

"Please." She twisted the handkerchief in her hands and avoided his gaze.

"*Allrecht.* I just need to put a box or two inside. Are you sure you don't want to look around?"

"That's the last thing I want to do," she said quietly.

He climbed out of the buggy, stacked the two boxes on top of each other and carried them into the cottage.

When he came back outside she was gone.

He had other boxes he wanted to put inside the cottage but that wasn't important now. After he ran back to lock up the place, he jumped into the buggy and retraced the route he'd taken. He looked up one side of the road and down the other but there was no sign of Emma.

How could she have just disappeared? He hadn't heard another buggy or car as he carried the boxes inside the cottage. Had someone picked her up? She wouldn't take a ride with a stranger, would she? Surely not. She was too smart, too sensible for that.

But she'd been so upset with him. More upset than he'd ever seen her about anything.

"C'mon, Homer, help me find Emma Mae. Where'd she go?"

The horse whinnied when he heard his name but of course he couldn't answer Isaac. The horse's hooves echoed rhythmically on the pavement but the sound was hardly soothing. Isaac called to Homer and shook the reins. Homer picked up the pace and the buggy rolled faster back toward Emma's home.

Isaac pulled into the drive and the wheels had barely stopped turning when he jumped out. He pounded on the front door.

Lizzie, Emma Mae's sister, opened the door and blinked when she saw him. "Isaac! I thought you just left."

"Emma Mae! Where's Emma Mae?"

She just stared at him. "She went with you."

"Did she come back?"

"Isaac, you're not making any sense."

Frustrated, he ran his hand through his hair. "Lizzie, could she have come home and you didn't see her?"

"I guess." She glanced around her. "I just got home. I'll check. Do you want to come in?"

"No. *Danki*," he added, aware that he sounded impatient.

She shut the door and was gone for a few minutes. When she returned she wore a frown as she opened the door. "She's not anywhere in the house."

"You're *schur*?"

"Of course I'm sure." She stared at him. "What did you do to your hair?"

"Cut it," he said curtly. "It's not important now."

"What did you argue about?"

Isaac met her gaze and he looked away. "I'd rather not say."

Lizzie crossed her arms over her chest. "I told her you were a bad boy and she shouldn't try to change you."

Shocked, he shook his head and opened his mouth to protest. But she was right. He wasn't a boy but he had been selfish in the way he'd treated Emma. How had he thought she'd just go along with moving in with him because he wanted it?

Well, maybe because Emma Mae had always gone along with what he wanted. She was sweet, smart, and above all, his best friend.

Had he ruined everything?

He turned and walked back to his buggy. Maybe she'd decided she wanted nothing to do with him and that was why she had left the buggy. He wouldn't blame her.

But he was going to find her and make sure she was safe if it was the last thing he did.

∼⤳

"Emma Mae!"

She turned and saw Elizabeth Miller waving to her from her buggy.

"Can I give you a ride?"

Emma Mae nodded quickly and fairly jumped into the buggy before Elizabeth brought it to a complete stop. "*Danki.*"

"Where were you going?"

"Just out for a walk."

"Long walk," Elizabeth commented.

She took a surreptitious glance back and didn't see Isaac coming out of the cottage. Still, she was relieved when Elizabeth got the buggy moving again.

"So how are you and Isaac doing?"

"Fine. You and Saul?" She turned and focused on Elizabeth. "I don't need to ask. You're glowing. Married life is *gut, ya*?"

Elizabeth laughed and nodded. "Very *gut*. But you'll find that out for yourself soon, I think."

The question hit Emma with a force that that was every bit as physical as a blow.

"I know, I'm being nosy," Elizabeth went on without waiting for an answer. "But it's so obvious that the two of you are a pair and have been for years. You're not going to surprise anyone when you two decide an announcement should be made."

Emma Mae felt grateful that who dated who wasn't discussed—or, at least, not encouraged. At least if it turned out that she and Isaac were not going to be married in the fall she might not get as many questions from others.

Fearing that Elizabeth might ask more questions, Emma Mae decided to ask some of her own. Though it pained her greatly after what had just happened to her dreams after what Isaac had said, there was one topic which would take her attention completely from Emma. Elizabeth's new life.

"Have you been able to do much to get your household settled since you work at the store with Saul?"

Elizabeth sighed. "Not as much as I'd like. But there's time. I—oh!" she stopped and pressed her fingers against her lips, then pulled the buggy off the road and stopped.

"Are you *allrecht*?"

After a long moment she took a deep breath and nodded. "*Ya*, I'm fine. I feel like I'm having heartburn. Must be something I ate. I'm sorry. I'll get back on the road in a minute."

"Don't rush, I'm in no hurry," Emma Mae told her quickly. "Why don't you take a drink of water and see if that helps?" she asked, indicating the bottle of water on the seat between them.

"Why didn't I think of that?" Elisabeth uncapped the bottle and took a drink, then recapped it and set it down on the seat.

Emma Mae thought about how much time had passed since Elizabeth's wedding the previous fall and tried to hide a smile. She doubted it was heartburn that was affecting her friend. By the time the next fall rolled around, she suspected Elizabeth might be a new *mamm*.

Next fall. That was when she'd hoped to be married. She sighed.

"What's the sigh for?"

"Oh, just thinking about something. Nothing important."

Elizabeth checked traffic, then shook the reins and her horse pulled the buggy back onto the road.

"You didn't have to work today?"

"I take one Saturday off a month to do bookkeeping at home. This afternoon I thought I might work in the kitchen garden." She sighed and looked rueful. "I'm still getting used to the differences in weather between here and Goshen, trying to figure out what I can plant this time of year."

"Talk to my *mamm*. Or Katie and Rosie, the twins at the store. They're wonderful gardeners."

"Tell me about it." Elizabeth pulled into the driveway of Emma's house. "I told Saul we're going to lose them one day. Their Two Peas in a Pod jams and jellies sell out constantly at the store."

She brought the buggy to a stop. "I'm so glad we had a chance to talk."

"Me too," Emma Mae said. Once she'd led Elizabeth down a different conversational path, she'd enjoyed it. "*Danki* for the ride," Emma said as she got out of the buggy.

"Be sure to tell Lizzie I'll see her day after tomorrow."

"I will."

Emma Mae felt depression weighing her down as she climbed up the front porch steps and went inside.

"There you are!" Lizzie cried as Emma walked into the kitchen.

"*Ya*, here I am," Emma Mae muttered as she filled the teakettle, set it on the stove then turned on the gas flame under it. She rubbed her hands for warmth. She'd felt so cold since Isaac had blurted out that they could live together.

"What happened?"

She turned. "What happened?"

"Isaac came looking for you."

"Oh." She turned back and stared at the teakettle, willing it to boil.

"Did you two have an argument?"

"I don't want to talk about it."

"Are you going to call him? He was really worried about you."

She shrugged.

"Emma Mae—"

"I don't want to talk about it."

An uncomfortable silence fell over the room.

"How did you get home?"

"I got a ride with Elizabeth Miller. She saw me walking home."

The front door opened, then closed. Their mother came in carrying several tote bags. "Will you put these things in the refrigerator? I'm going to go lie down. I don't feel so well."

"I told you it was too soon to be up and about," Lizzie scolded, acting like the *mamm* instead of the grown child. "That flu really took it out of you."

She helped her mother take off her sweater and hang it up. "You go change and get back into bed. I'll make you a nice hot cup of tea and bring it to you."

The teakettle began whistling as Emma Mae finished putting away the items her mother had bought that morning. Lizzie fixed a cup of tea for their mother, adding milk and sugar, and went to give it to her.

Emma Mae fixed a cup of tea for herself and sat at the big kitchen table to drink it. When Lizzie returned, she carried the cup of tea.

"She was already asleep when I got there." She sat at the table. "Guess I'll drink it."

"You don't like milk in your tea."

Lizzie shrugged. "No point in it going to waste." She stirred it then took a sip. "Now tell me what happened with Isaac."

"I said—"

"I know what you said. But it's obvious you need to do something."

Emma Mae rubbed her forehead and tried to fight back tears. "There's nothing I can do."

"Are you saying you're going to break off the engagement?" Lizzie asked, her eyes wide.

Restless, Emma got up, dumped her cold tea in the sink and poured more hot water into her mug. She sank down into her chair and dunked another tea bag in the water. "It's more like Isaac is breaking it off with me."

She told Lizzie what Isaac had said that afternoon. Lizzie went white and when Emma finished she listened to the clock ticking loudly.

"Well," Lizzie said at last. "Was that why you came home?"

Emma Mae nodded. "I saw a buggy approaching and got a ride."

"So what are you going to do?"

Emma Mae stirred her tea, studying the pattern the spoon made in the liquid. "I don't know," she said finally. "I'm not willing to live with him without us being married."

Lizzie stood. "I should say not!"

She reached out and grabbed her sister's arm. "You can't tell anyone."

"I wouldn't dream of it. Him asking you to do such a thing is too insulting for words." She paced the room. "Are you going to tell *Mamm* and *Daed*? I think they're expecting you and Isaac to get married after the harvest. When we were talking about the kitchen garden the other day she was saying she was thinking about planting extra celery."

Then Lizzie stopped. "Oh, Emma Mae, I'm sorry. The last thing I need to be talking about is *Mamm* planting celery in case there's a wedding dinner."

"I'm going upstairs."

Lizzie hugged her. "You'll feel better after you've had some rest."

Emma Mae doubted rest was going to make her feel better but she didn't have the energy to disagree. She just wanted to be alone.

As she started up the stairs, she heard a knock on the front door. She turned and looked at her sister. "If that's Isaac, I don't want to talk to him."

"You don't have to," Lizzie announced, a determined look on her face as she started for the door.

Emma Mae couldn't help herself—she stood on the stairs and waited to hear who the visitor was.

It felt like a hand squeezed her heart when she heard Isaac's low, deep voice. Her lips trembled but she stayed where she was until Lizzie sent him away. Then she climbed the stairs to her room, feeling decades older than her age, and threw herself on her bed.

She rolled over and punched her pillow to be more comfortable and her hand encountered her journal. Pulling it out, she flipped through the pages and began reading what she'd written a few days before: *"I'm worried about Isaac. I think he's still grieving over his brother but he says he's fine and he won't talk to me. We were friends before we decided we wanted to be married. I want my friend back."*

Tears slipped down her cheeks. She closed the book and held it to her chest. From the time she was ten she'd loved Isaac. She couldn't bear the thought of him not being in her life.

Want to learn more about author
Barbara Cameron and check out other great
fiction by Abingdon Press?

Sign up for our fiction newsletter at
www.AbingdonPress.com
to read interviews with your favorite authors, find tips
for starting a reading group, and stay posted on
what's new on the horizon. It's a place to connect
with other fiction readers or post a
comment about this book.

Be sure to visit Barbara Cameron online!

www.BarbaraCameron.com
www.AmishLiving.com
and on Facebook

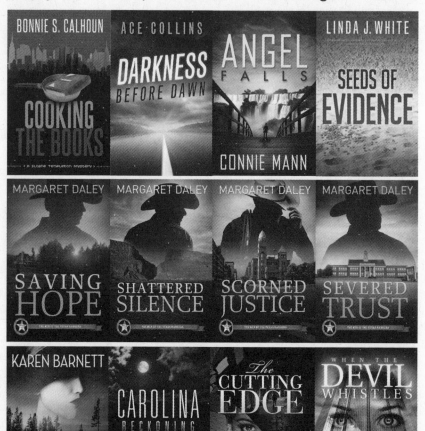